# Geek Abroad

Normally, calculating sums on command makes me feel like a circus seal balancing a ball on my nose while clapping my flippers and barking for a fish. But for the first time, I felt a rush of pride at my odd, geeky skill. It certainly seemed to impress Henry.

"Thanks," I said, quickly taking a gulp of my punch to hide my grin, as I contemplated just how attractive an English accent was.

As soon as the thought was loose and rattling around in my brain, guilt surged up within me. Dex had only been my almost-quasi-boyfriend for less than forty-eight hours . . . and already my head was being turned by some random English guy? Admittedly, a very cute random English guy, but still. What kind of an almost-quasi-girlfriend was I turning out to be?

**Also by Piper Banks**

*Geek High*

# Geek Abroad

## Piper Banks

nal
JAM
books

NAL Jam
Published by New American Library,
a division of Penguin Group (USA) Inc., 375 Hudson Street,
New York, New York 10014, USA
Penguin Group (Canada), 90 Eglinton Avenue East, Suite 700, Toronto,
Ontario M4P 2Y3, Canada (a division of Pearson Penguin Canada Inc.)
Penguin Books Ltd., 80 Strand, London WC2R 0RL, England
Penguin Ireland, 25 St. Stephen's Green, Dublin 2,
Ireland (a division of Penguin Books Ltd.)
Penguin Group (Australia), 250 Camberwell Road, Camberwell, Victoria 3124,
Australia (a division of Pearson Australia Group Pty. Ltd.)
Penguin Books India Pvt. Ltd., 11 Community Centre,
Panchsheel Park, New Delhi – 110 017, India
Penguin Group (NZ), 67 Apollo Drive, Rosedale, North Shore 0632,
New Zealand (a division of Pearson New Zealand Ltd.)
Penguin Books (South Africa) (Pty.) Ltd., 24 Sturdee Avenue,
Rosebank, Johannesburg 2196, South Africa

Penguin Books Ltd., Registered Offices:
80 Strand, London WC2R 0RL, England

First published by NAL Jam, an imprint of New American Library,
a division of Penguin Group (USA) Inc.

First Printing, May 2008
1  3  5  7  9  10  8  6  4  2

NAL JAM and logo are trademarks of Penguin Group (USA) Inc.

LIBRARY OF CONGRESS CATALOGING-IN-PUBLICATION DATA
Banks, Piper.
Geek abroad / Piper Banks.
p. cm.
Summary: While in London visiting her mother, fifteen-year-old Miranda guiltily enjoys the company of a British boy while wondering why Dex is out of touch, but she returns home to find her friendships, love life, family, and math team are all in turmoil.
ISBN: 978-0-451-22393-7
[1. Dating (Social customs)—Fiction. 2. High schools—Fiction. 3. Schools—Fiction. 4. Self-esteem—Fiction. 5. Stepfamilies—Fiction. 6. Genius—Fiction. 7. London (England)—Fiction. 8. England—Fiction. 9. Florida—Fiction.] I. Title.
PZ7.G2128Gee 2007
[Fic]—dc22        2007049716

Set in Bulmer MT    •    Designed by Elke Sigal
Printed in the United States of America

*For Sam*

# Geek Abroad

# Chapter 1

I was the only person on board the nonstop flight from Orlando to London who was happy.

True, the flight had been bumpy. And the dinner seriously sucked (cold salmon served on gelatinous potatoes, yuck). And, yes, we'd been circling around London's Heathrow Airport for more than an hour while we waited for our turn to land. And I was stuck in a center seat, squeezed in between a fat, farting businessman who had fallen asleep on my shoulder (and no amount of shrugging and shifting would dislodge him) and a tired mother with a fussy baby who had been screaming on and off the entire flight.

But I was happy. No, I was more than happy—I was completely and totally blissed out. In the past twenty-four hours, the Geek High Snowflake Gala dance that I had been in charge of planning was a huge hit. I landed a spot as a finalist in the prestigious Winston Creative Writing Contest. And—perhaps most astonishing of all—I found out that Dex McConnell actually liked me! Me, Miranda Bloom, who up until last night had been the dateless wonder of Geek High!

Actually, the *dateless* part isn't entirely true. I was supposed to go to the Snowflake with a freshman midget named Nicholas Pruitt, who had a disturbing tendency to stare at me dreamily during our

Mu Alpha Theta math competition practice sessions. When Nicholas worked up the courage to ask me to go to the Snowflake with him, I couldn't bring myself to hurt his feelings by saying no. It only occurred to me later that it might have been kinder in the long run to turn down his invitation. I'd thought we were going together just as friends. . . . Nicholas apparently believed our Snowflake date was the beginning of what was destined to be a great romance. And since he came down with chicken pox at the last minute, forcing him to cancel our date on the day of the dance, I hadn't yet had a chance to set things straight with Nicholas, to tell him that I don't like him *that* way.

But I couldn't worry about that now. . . . Not when my head was bursting with memories of Dex. My stepsister, Hannah, had told Dex about how my date with Nicholas had fallen through, and that I'd be attending the Snowflake stag. So Dex had shown up at the dance to be my surprise date.

Even better, Dex *kissed me*! And this was no ordinary kiss. It had to have been one of the all-time most romantic kisses in the history of the world. Top five, at least. But, then, Dex was no ordinary guy. He was the very cute and very funny lacrosse star of Orange Cove High. And—I had thought—totally out of my league. After all, I'm not just a geek, I'm a *math* geek. I can calculate complex sums in my head, which, let's face it, doesn't exactly scream *sexy*. Then there's my hair (frizzy), my nose (too big), and my fashion sense (nonexistent).

Despite these glaring defects, Dex actually *liked* me. In fact, he said he'd liked me for months. Which just goes to show: miracles do happen.

Now, twenty-four hours after kissing Dex, I was en route to London to spend the Christmas holidays with my mother, Sadie. Sadie's a romance novelist, and was temporarily living in London while she researched and wrote her next book, *Victorian Widow*. Which was all well and good for her, but it meant that I had been stuck living with my dad and evil stepmother, Peyton, aka the Demon, until Sadie decided to return home to rescue me. At first, I was furious at Sadie for deserting me, although I had to admit, my anger had been cooling as of late. Now . . . well, now I was too giddy to be angry with anyone.

I sighed happily and closed my eyes, recalling the memory of standing on the back deck of the Yacht Club that overlooked the moonlit water, while Dex leaned toward me, his lips moving closer and closer. . . .

"Waaaaaaaaaah!" screamed the baby, thrashing around in his mother's arms.

The noise startled me out of my reverie, and my eyes popped open. The mother made hushing noises at the baby, and rocked him as best she could in her cramped seat, and eventually the baby's wails tapered off to intermittent snorts of displeasure. The sudden quiet meant that when the fat businessman sitting to my left farted yet again, I could hear it loud and clear.

*Gross,* I thought, fanning the fart fumes away from me with the barf bag the airline had so thoughtfully provided.

I stretched my legs and arched my back, feeling stiff and suddenly eager to be off the plane, away from the farting businessman and the squalling baby. As if she'd been reading my thoughts, the FASTEN SEAT BELT sign suddenly lit up and the flight attendant's cool English-accented voice blared out from the intercom:

"We've received permission to land, and will shortly be making our final descent into London's Heathrow Airport. Please put your seats and tray tables in their full upright and locked positions. . . ."

A shiver of excitement ran down my back. Soon I'd be in London! The only question was, Where would Sadie and I go first? The Tower of London? Madame Tussauds Wax Museum? The London Eye? I clasped my hands together, so excited I could hardly sit still.

"Excuse me." I felt a tap on my right arm and turned. It was the frazzled mom. "Would you mind holding my baby for just a minute? I have to run to the bathroom before we land," she said pleadingly.

"Oh . . . um, sure," I said. Babies had never been my forte, but the mom looked so exhausted and strung out, I didn't have the heart to refuse her.

She gratefully handed over the baby, unbuckled her seat belt and dashed off toward the toilets. I held the baby gingerly out from me, my hands hooked under its armpits. We stared at one another for a long moment, until the baby finally grinned, exposing a toothless gummy mouth. Charmed, I grinned back. And just then, as I was smiling away, the baby—in what can only be described as a horror-movie-like moment—opened its mouth and ejected a stream of foul, neon green vomit right down the front of my T-shirt.

Speechless, I stared down at my now dripping shirt and then back up at the baby. He kicked his chubby legs and emitted a loud, satisfied burp. The farting businessman next to me actually had the nerve to pinch his nose and lean away. Granted, the baby vomit was pretty vile smelling—who knew someone so small and cute could produce something so revolting?—but considering the businessman had been befouling the cabin for the past seven hours, I didn't think he was in any position to complain.

The baby giggled suddenly and stuffed one round hand into his mouth. I sighed and smiled ruefully back. There was no point in holding a grudge. Besides, for once in my life everything was perfect. I wasn't going to let a little bit—okay, a *lot*—of baby vomit get me down now.

●

"Miranda! Yoo hoo! Over here!"

I craned my neck and looked from side to side. . . . And then I saw Sadie. Actually, she would have been hard to miss, considering that she was wearing a dramatic scarlet ankle-length wool cape that made her look like a matronly version of Little Red Riding Hood. Sadie was beaming and waving at me, standing just past Customs and ignoring the grumpy passengers who had to step around her. She'd changed her hair since I'd last seen her. The long blond curls were gone, replaced by a smart, sleek, dark brown bob. Actually, she looked fantastic, like the "after" picture in one of those make-over shows my stepsister and her friends are addicted to.

I rushed to Sadie, pulling my wheeled suitcase behind me, and she caught me up in her arms. She smelled so achingly familiar—a mixture of coffee, mint toothpaste, and Joy perfume—that I almost dissolved into tears. I hadn't realized until just that moment how much I'd missed her. Sadie pulled me close, and the wool of her cape felt scratchy against my cheek.

"Hi, Sadie," I said, my voice muffled.

"Hello, darling," Sadie crooned. "It's so wonderful to see you!"

"You too," I said. And then, because I couldn't help myself, I added, "Nice cape."

"Do you like it?" Sadie asked, delighted. She pulled back and spun around, so that the cape circled out for a moment. "I thought it was divine."

"It's very . . ." I searched for a neutral adjective. "Red," I finished lamely.

"Exactly!" Sadie beamed. "It's putting me in the mood for Christmas." Her expression suddenly shifted into a frown. She held me by my shoulders and looked down at my vomit-covered shirt, her nose wrinkling. "What's that? It smells like . . ."

"Baby vomit," I said. "I'm a casualty of modern air travel."

Sadie hustled me into the nearest bathroom, electing to wait for me outside and away from the smell. Once I'd changed and stuffed the vomit shirt in my suitcase, I rejoined Sadie. She linked her arm through mine, and I had to walk quickly to keep up with her, while dragging my suitcase behind me.

"Christmas in London is going to be magical! Just think of it, darling! It will be so Dickensian!" Sadie enthused.

"Dickensian?" I repeated. "You mean, like Scrooge and Tiny Tim and *bah humbug*?"

"Well, not the *bah humbug*," Sadie said. "I was thinking more along the lines of roast goose and mince pies and waking up to snow on Christmas morning! We've never had a white Christmas before."

That was true enough. We lived in Florida, where it was normally warm enough to wear shorts on Christmas Day. Every year, we wrapped twinkle lights around the palm trees in our front yard.

"Other than being vomited on, how was your flight?" Sadie asked, as we joined the throng of people filing out of the airport through large automatic doors.

I gasped as the frigid air hit me, as though I'd walked smack into an iceberg. It was *freezing* out. The wind was blowing so coldly, it felt like it was rattling through my bones. As we queued for a cab—even the taxis were cool here, all black and boxy and retro-looking—I unzipped my suitcase and pulled out my coat, and quickly slipped it on.

"Long," I said to answer Sadie's question. Suddenly I felt really, really tired. I checked my watch. No wonder: It was two in the morning at home, and I'd been too excited to sleep on the plane. Just thinking of it made me yawn—a long, cold, shaky yawn.

"You must be exhausted," Sadie said, patting my arm. "We'll get you home, and you can take a nice nap."

"But I don't want to nap," I said. "I'm only going to be in London for two and a half weeks! If I'm going to see everything I want to see, I have to start today. I just don't know where to begin."

But then I yawned again, and this time my eyes watered from the cold, causing my vision to go blurry for a moment. I rubbed my hands together and stamped my feet, trying to warm up, and wished I'd brought a heavier coat with me. Maybe Sadie's Little Red Riding Hood cape wasn't so crazy after all.

"There will be plenty of time to do everything," Sadie promised as we finally reached the front of the line and climbed into one of the big black taxicabs.

"Maybe I'll just power nap now," I said, leaning back against the gray leather seat. "Then I'll be rested up and ready to get started."

Sadie leaned over and squeezed my hand. "Good idea. I'm just so glad you're finally here," she said fondly.

"Me too," I mumbled, wondering what my first glimpse of London would be as we drove into the city. Would we pass by Big Ben? Or Tower Bridge? Or maybe even Buckingham Palace? But before I could ask Sadie, who was leaning forward to give the cabbie detailed instructions on where we were going, my eyelids drooped closed. I was asleep before the cab pulled away from the curb.

# Chapter 2

I woke up in the dark. I rubbed my eyes and tried to remember where I was. It came back quickly: My flight to London. Falling asleep in the cab. Sadie gently shaking me awake, and then guiding me upstairs to the guest room at the very top of a narrow three-story town house. Falling face-first on a chintz-covered bed, and passing out again almost immediately.

At this realization, I sat up so suddenly, I actually got a head rush. *Oh, no!* I thought wildly. *I fell asleep!* From what I could tell from how dark the room was, I'd been asleep all day. . . . Which meant I'd completely wasted my first day in London.

"Oh, no," I groaned out loud. I had so many things I wanted to do and see while I was in London; I didn't have time to waste an entire day sleeping.

*What time is it?* I wondered, instinctively glancing at my watch, before remembering that it was too dark to see anything.

I fumbled with the lamp on the bedside table. Dim light flooded over the room, which was truly astonishing in its ugliness. It looked like a flower shop had exploded all over the small space. There was hideous seventies-era brown and orange floral wallpaper, a faded chintz coverlet covered in pink cabbage roses draped over the bed, and a worn hooked rug featuring circles of daisy chains on the dark wood floor. Lace scarves covered the dresser and nightstand. The room smelled damp and vaguely catlike.

*That's it! It's a little-old-lady-with-too-many-cats room,* I thought. I wondered where the little old lady was now, and guessed that since the house had been available for Sadie to rent, the cat lady had probably moved on to the big floral-wallpapered house in the sky.

I got up out of bed and went out the bedroom door to stand on a narrow landing at the top of the stairs. I could hear muffled voices coming from downstairs. Did Sadie have a guest over? Or was that just the television I was hearing?

I padded down the scarily steep, creaking stairs, holding on to an old-fashioned wood banister for support. I had a hazy memory of Sadie telling me when we came in that the kitchen and dining room were on the first floor, the living room was on the second, and the bedrooms were on the third. The voices grew louder as I reached the second-floor landing. And now it didn't sound like the television at all. . . . There were definitely actual people over. More than one, from what I could hear.

The living room was down a short hallway, and the doorway was open. I craned my neck to see in. There was a small crowd of adults gathered inside—men in dark suits, women in cocktail dresses. Sadie, her dark eyes sparkling and her hair smoothed back from her face, stood in the middle of the crowd. She was wearing a crimson velvet pantsuit, and was gesticulating wildly as she spoke.

I groaned silently. This was *so* typical of Sadie. Back in Florida, she'd thrown so many impromptu parties—especially after she and my dad had divorced—that I'd gotten used to studying by the din of cocktail party chatter.

Even so, I couldn't help but feel a little resentful that she'd have people over tonight, my first night in London. I hadn't yet told her about Dex, or the writing contest, or how successful the Snowflake

Gala was. Besides, even after my daylong nap, I was still a bit groggy and not at all in the mood to make small talk with a bunch of people I didn't know. I hesitated for a moment, wondering if I could sneak back up to my room and wait it out until the guests left. I certainly wasn't dressed for a party—I was wearing the same rumpled jeans, not to mention the same *underwear* I'd worn on the plane. I was in serious need of a hot shower and clean clothes.

I heard Sadie's voice rising up over the others, saying, "Yes, Miranda just got in this morning. She's spending the holidays here with me! Isn't that fabulous?" Then, before I could sneak off, she spotted me. "Oh, wait, here she is now! Darling, come in here!"

*Gah,* I thought. I looked longingly back up the stairs, wishing I'd thought to shower and change before I ventured downstairs. But everyone had turned to look at me, as though I were an interesting zoo exhibit labeled DAUGHTER OF FAMOUS WRITER, so I had no choice but to smile gamely and make my way into the party, feeling horribly self-conscious the whole time.

"Come meet everyone, darling," Sadie said, holding out her arm, beckoning me to join her.

"Um, hi, Mom," I said, sidling over next to her. "You didn't tell me you were having a party," I hissed in her ear.

"Party? Don't be silly, darling. This isn't a party. It's a just a gathering of *bon vivants*," Sadie exclaimed loudly. "Come, let me introduce you around. I've been dying to show you off."

A flurry of introductions followed, although my brain was still so jet-lagged, I couldn't remember anyone's name. I just smiled and shook hands, and wished that everyone was wearing name tags. Among the group, there was a portly man with thick white hair who couldn't seem to hear a word I was saying, and kept asking, "But *whose* daughter is she supposed to be?" to the younger man standing next to him. Then there was a very thin woman with a long, hooked nose, giant ruby rings encircling every finger, and a thick Russian accent.

"How do you do?" the woman said gravely, inclining her head at me.

"Madame Aleksey was a famous ballerina," Sadie twittered excitedly in my ear. She turned toward Madame Aleksey. "Miranda used to love going to see *The Nutcracker* every Christmas. She dreamed of being a prima ballerina. Begged me for dance lessons."

I colored. "*Mom*. I was *five*."

"Is that so? *You* are a dancer?" Madame Aleksey asked, looking me up and down in disbelief.

"She took a year of tap lessons, and was devastated when she didn't get a solo in the school recital. Remember that, Miranda? Instead, she was in the chorus for the 'Good Ship Lollipop.' It was adorable. All of the little girls wore sailor suits," Sadie continued.

"*Mom*," I hissed again.

Sadie ignored me. "Miranda was so angry that the solo went to Kelli Simpson, she gave up dance after that," she continued.

"Hmph. Being a dancer requires a tremendous amount of commitment, as well as natural grace," Madame Aleksey said in a critical tone that made it clear she thought I lacked both.

I felt my face go hot with embarrassment. It was true, I was no dancer. But no natural grace? It wasn't like I'd tripped walking across the room.

"And this," Sadie said, pulling me over to a round-faced man with a snub nose and thick salt-and-pepper hair, "is Giles Wentworth, my British editor. Giles, this is my daughter, Miranda, the wunderkind."

"Ah, Miranda, it's delightful to finally meet you," Giles said. His voice was warm and rich. As he smiled benignly at me, it struck me that despite the graying hair, Giles had a very young face. He leaned forward, his blue eyes twinkling merrily. "Do tell me: What is the product of 426 times 9,567?"

"4,075,542," I said, smothering a sigh.

I was used to being quizzed by my parents' friends. For as long as I can remember, I've been able to calculate sums in my head. I even attend a special school for kids with high IQs, called the Notting Hill Independent School for Gifted Children. Everyone just calls it Geek High for obvious reasons.

But here's the thing: I don't really like math. Sure, it's easy for me. But just because something comes easily to you doesn't necessarily mean that you enjoy it.

"Amazing. Of course, I wouldn't know if that was the right answer or not!" Giles said, with a bark of laughter. "I'll have to take your word for it."

I smiled. Giles seemed like a nice man, so it was hard to hold the math quiz against him.

"My son is around here somewhere," Giles said, looking around from right to left. "Ah, there he is. Henry, my lad, come over here. There's someone I want you to meet."

A son. I had a sinking suspicion that Sadie and Giles had arranged this little meeting.... One that was confirmed as Sadie prodded me in the side with what was supposed to be a surreptitious elbow. When I glared back at her, she winked saucily.

"Giles and I thought that Henry could show you around London," Sadie said mischievously.

Oh, no. Oh, no no no no no *no*! It was a setup. How could Sadie do this to me?

For the first time in my life, I had a boyfriend. Okay, maybe Dex wasn't *technically* my boyfriend. Yet. But he had shown up at the Snowflake Gala to be my surprise date. And he'd kissed me, and told me how much he'd liked me. So if he wasn't my official boyfriend now, he probably would be as soon as I got back to Florida. The last thing I needed was to be set up with some British kid, who was apparently such a loser that he didn't have any friends of his own. He probably had bad teeth, horrible breath, and wore prissy coats and ties even when he wasn't in school.

"Ah, here he is," Giles said, nodding behind me. "Miranda, let me introduce you to my son, Henry."

I turned, expecting the worst . . . and found myself gaping up at the very tall, very cute Henry. He had the same round, pink-cheeked face as his father, but Henry's hair was dark and shaggy and his eyes were dark blue with green flecks. He was wearing faded Levi's and a blue cable-knit sweater that highlighted his broad shoulders.

"Hullo," Henry said. When he grinned at me, dimples appeared in his cheeks.

I was suddenly acutely aware of just how awful I looked, with my messy hair and rumpled clothes. There was a horrible taste in my mouth, sour and bitter at the same time. I tried to remember the last time I'd brushed my teeth, and realized with a sinking horror that it had been while I was back in Florida.

That was it. . . . As soon as I got Sadie alone, I was going to kill her.

"Hi," I said, trying to open my mouth as little as possible, so as not to blast him with my nasty jet-lag breath.

"Henry, we were just telling Miranda how we'd volunteered your services as a tour guide," Giles said.

"You don't have to," I said quickly, all too aware that babysitting me was probably the last thing Henry wanted to do.

"No, it'll be fun," Henry said.

"It will be perfect, darling," Sadie interjected. "I have to work, after all, and it will be nice for you to have someone your own age to hang out with." Then, spotting someone across the room, she said, "Giles, look, Alice Sands just arrived. I haven't seen her in ages. I have to say hello."

"I'll go with you," Giles said, and the two departed, leaving Henry and me alone together.

"Are you hungry?" Henry asked, gesturing toward the table, which was covered with food—dips, cheeses, sliced fruit, tiny pies, little sandwiches with the crusts cut off.

My stomach gave an embarrassingly loud rumble at the sight of all the food. I covered my stomach with one hand, willing Henry not to have heard, but I could tell by the way he grinned at me that he had.

"I take that as a yes," he said.

"I haven't eaten since dinner on the plane," I said sheepishly. I checked my watch. "Which was about fourteen hours ago."

He feigned horror. "Fourteen hours? You must be starving! Here." He handed me a cup of punch. "Drink this for strength." Then he seized one of the white buffet plates stacked up on the table, and began to pile it with crackers, cheese, and cookies, while I watched in amazement.

"Here you go," he said, handing me the plate. Then, noticing a platter of tartlets, he grabbed one to add to my plate. "And you have to have one of these mincemeat pies. They're brilliant."

"Thanks," I said, laughing a little as I stared down at the mountain of food he'd just gathered for me. I set the plate on a small table and picked the mincemeat pie off it. "Mmm," I said, once I took a bite. "That is really good."

"Told you," Henry said. "I never lie."

"Like the island of knights and knaves," I said without thinking, recalling a series of classic logic problems featuring an island where knights and knaves lived. The knights always had to tell the truth, and the knaves always lied. Then I blushed. Because bringing up logic problems at parties? Seriously not cool.

"You know about the island of knights and knaves?" Henry asked, his eyes widening with surprise.

I laughed at his shock. "We do have schools in America, you know," I said.

"And here I thought you were a country of Paris Hiltons," he joked.

"Oh, we totally are," I said, managing to keep a straight face.

"When I'm at home, I dye my hair platinum blond, and say, 'That's hot!' about everything."

"Yeah, I just bet," Henry said. "So, tell me, which one am I—a knight or a knave."

"I don't know," I said. "A knight could say he never lied, because it would be the truth. But a knave could also say it, because it would be a lie."

"Oh, that's right," Henry said, drawing out the word *right*. "I forgot. Aren't you supposed to be some kind of a mathematical genius?"

I couldn't help it: I blushed. "Not really," I said, shrugging.

"And modest, too," he said.

"No, it's just . . . well. I just don't like talking about it," I said.

"Fair enough. So you probably don't want me asking you what 732 times 569 is, huh?"

"416,508," I said, without thinking.

Henry's eyes went round with surprise. "Really?" he asked. "Is that right?"

I nodded. "Yeah. Great party trick, huh?"

"I'll say," he said, looking at me admiringly.

Normally, calculating sums on command makes me feel like a circus seal balancing a ball on my nose while clapping my flippers and barking for a fish. But for the first time, I felt a rush of pride at my odd, geeky skill. It certainly seemed to impress Henry.

"Thanks," I said, quickly taking a gulp of my punch to hide my grin, as I contemplated just how attractive an English accent was.

As soon as the thought was loose and rattling around in my brain, guilt surged within me. Dex had only been my almost-quasi-boyfriend for less than forty-eight hours . . . and already my head was being turned by some random English guy? Admittedly, a very cute random English guy, but still. What kind of an almost-quasi-girlfriend was I turning out to be?

# Chapter 3

"Mom, may I use your laptop to check my e-mail?" I asked Sadie over breakfast the next morning.

"Hmmm?" she asked, not looking up from her newspaper. Sadie has never been a morning person. There's no use trying to have a conversation with her before she's downed at least two cups of coffee. In fact, we still hadn't gotten a chance to catch up. When the cocktail party ended, Sadie went out to dinner with some of her guests. Despite having slept all day, I'd felt too jet-lagged to go with them, and instead went back to bed. But once in bed, I couldn't fall asleep. Which wasn't surprising, considering it was only two o'clock in the afternoon, Florida time. So I pulled out my journal and worked on the short story I'd been writing, about a teenage girl who wakes up from a coma and doesn't recognize her friends and family.

"Your computer," I repeated. "May I use it?"

"Help yourself, sweetie. It's upstairs in my office," Sadie said absentmindedly. She buttered a piece of cranberry-orange scone, popped it in her mouth, and then disappeared behind her newspaper again.

I dumped my plate and juice glass in the kitchen sink, and climbed up the stairs to the second floor. Sadie's office was in a little alcove off the living room, just big enough for a desk, chair, and printer stand. In typical Sadie style, the desk was a mess. It was covered with the debris of her life—pages edited in red pencil, bills, stray paper clips, receipts, empty coffee cups, invitations, fan letters. I pushed the mess off to the sides as best I could, and turned on the laptop. It hummed and then sprang to life with a computerized melody. I logged into my e-mail, and there was . . . nothing.

Well, not *nothing*. There was the usual spam, and a joke e-mail my friend Finn had forwarded:

To: mirandajbloom@gmail.com
From: finn@finnsgames.com
Subject: Best Titles Ever!

**Rejected Children's Book Titles**

1. Strangers Have the Best Candy
2. The Little Sissy Who Snitched
3. Some Kittens Can Fly!
4. Kathy Was So Bad Her Mom Stopped Loving Her
5. How to Become the Dominant Military Power in Your Elementary School
6. Controlling the Playground: Respect through Fear
7. The Kid's Guide to Hitchhiking
8. You Are Different and That's Bad
9. Things Rich Kids Have but You Never Will
10. POP! Goes the Hamster . . . and Other Great Microwave Games

But there wasn't anything from Dex. When we'd said good-bye to one another after the dance, he'd asked if he could call me the next day. And for one happy, stomach-fluttery moment, I was thrilled. . . . Before remembering that I'd be leaving for London, and that my cell phone wouldn't work over here. So knowing that his parents probably wouldn't be thrilled if Dex ran up their long-distance bill with overseas calls to Sadie's house, I gave him my e-mail address, and he'd said he'd write me.

*Well, it's only been a few days since I've seen him,* I reasoned. *Maybe he's busy with his friends or family or whatever.*

But even so . . . something suddenly occurred to me. I'd given my e-mail address to Dex. He hadn't given me his. It hadn't struck me as odd at the time. But now a little voice of doubt was starting to pipe up in my head. If Dex really was interested in me, why wouldn't he have given me his e-mail address, too? And even if he was busy, why couldn't he have dropped me an e-mail by now? Even if it was just a quick, hey-how-are-you-how-was-your-flight note? So did that mean . . . maybe he wasn't really that into me after all?

And just like that, my stomach soured.

*No,* I thought, shaking off the gloom. *Don't blow this out of proportion. So Dex didn't send an e-mail yet. Big deal. He's probably just waiting until he has something to say.*

I closed out my e-mail program and shut the laptop with a decisive click. I was not going to waste my first full day in London fretting about whether a guy was going to e-mail me. Even if that guy happened to possess the most gorgeous pale blue eyes and a smile that made my entire body quiver.

•

"So what are you planning to do today?" Sadie asked when I padded back into the kitchen. I'd showered and dressed, and my hair was still damp. In the time it took me to get ready, Sadie had evidently consumed enough coffee to be conversant. Which was a good thing. Except . . .

"Wait. What do you mean what am I going to do today? Aren't we going to do something together?" I asked.

"Oh! Didn't I tell you? I thought I did, but with the excitement of your getting here, and then the cocktail party, I must have forgotten," Sadie said, first smoothing down her royal blue robe and then shuffling the newspaper into a stack.

I narrowed my eyes suspiciously. Whenever Sadie gets twitchy like this, it usually means she's hiding something.

There was a long pause. "Well . . . as it turns out, I can't spend the day with you, honey," Sadie said apologetically.

"What?" I asked. This was unbelievable. I hadn't seen Sadie in four months, and I'd traveled all the way across the ocean to visit her. Now that I was finally here, she wasn't even going to spend my first full day in London with me? "Why?"

Sadie sighed heavily, as she downshifted into martyr mode.

"I wish I could. Believe me, I'd much rather spend the day with you than go to a boring old editorial meeting. But today's the only day this week Giles is free to get together and go over my research notes on *Victorian Widow*. You understand, don't you?" Sadie said pleadingly. Her eyes were so wide and mournful, she actually reminded me of my greyhound, Willow, when she's begging for food at the table.

"Well . . ." I said, hesitating. But then I felt like I was being bratty. She was going to a work meeting, after all. It wasn't like she was ditching me to get her nails done. "Of course I understand. It's just I haven't seen you in so long. I wanted to catch up. I have a lot to tell you."

"And I want to hear it *all*," Sadie said, brightening. "I thought tomorrow night we could go out for a nice dinner, and talk and talk and talk until we're all talked out."

"Tomorrow?" I repeated. "What about dinner tonight?"

"Oh, didn't I mention that? Madame Aleksey is having a dinner party tonight, and I can't get out of it, I'm sorry to say." Sadie made a face. "I'd invite you along, but you'd hate every minute of it."

I closed my eyes for a minute and counted to ten. This was *so* typical of Sadie. And she knew very well that she hadn't told me about the dinner party.

"Mom," I said, keeping my voice as level as possible. "Why did you invite me to spend Christmas with you if you were planning to spend the whole time going out and socializing with your friends?"

"Don't be silly, sweetheart. It's just this one day I'm booked up, and then I'll be as free as a bird for the next two weeks. Sure, there are a few holiday parties here and there, but I promise you, by the time you go home, you'll be sick to death of me," Sadie said brightly.

I opened my mouth, ready to argue, but then decided against it. What was the point? I knew she wouldn't change her mind. Sadie is genetically incapable of missing a party. And besides, she was right. We'd have loads of time to spend together. There was no point in getting into a stink over today's plans.

"Okay," I said.

Sadie looked surprised for a moment—she'd clearly expected a battle—but when she saw I wasn't going to pursue the argument, she smiled warmly and reached out to smooth a wayward lock of hair behind my ear.

"You're getting so grown up," she said wistfully.

The phone rang then, and Sadie turned to answer it.

"Why, hello there! Miranda and I were just talking about that," Sadie was saying into the phone. "Yes, that sounds perfect. . . . No, I'm sure. . . . Yes, she'll be thrilled . . . *thrilled* . . . No, I don't have to check with her. . . . Okay . . . right. Bye!"

Sadie hung up the phone. When she turned, I saw that she had a huge Cheshire Cat grin on her face.

"Who was that?" I asked, trying—and failing—not to sound suspicious.

"It was Henry. Remember? You met him last night," she said brightly.

Too brightly.

"I remember," I said cautiously.

"Guess what? I've arranged for him to take you sig' today."

"You arranged . . . but . . . but . . ." I spluttered.

"You don't have to thank me, darling," Sadie said happily.

"I wasn't going to thank you!"

Sadie's forehead puckered into a concerned frown. "I thought you wanted to go sightseeing," she said.

"I did. I mean, I do. It's just . . . why didn't you ask me first if I wanted to go with Henry? I'm not a child. I don't need you to set up play dates for me."

"What's wrong with Henry? I think he's adorable," Sadie said. "He's very smart. At the top of his class, from what Giles tells me." She smiled again. "I know you'll only be here for a few weeks, but you never know. . . . A little holiday romance could be fun."

"Mom," I said, aghast. "I don't want a romance. For your information, I happen to have a boyfriend back home."

This stopped Sadie cold. "You have a boyfriend?" she asked. *"Really?"*

The *really* was a little insulting. Although . . . it was true that Dex wasn't really my boyfriend. Not yet, anyway.

"Well. Sort of," I said, and I could hear the defensiveness creeping into my voice. "There's this guy, his name is Dex, and I think he likes me, and I really, really like him. It isn't official or anything yet, but I think once I get home . . ."

"That's so exciting! Why didn't you tell me all of this before?" Sadie asked.

I raised my eyebrows at her. "We haven't really had a chance to talk, remember?" I said pointedly.

"Oh. Right," Sadie said. She sat down at the kitchen table, looking thoughtful, and took a sip of her coffee. Then she hit her open palm against the table decisively, and said, "I'm going to call Madame Aleksey and tell her I can't come tonight," she said.

"You don't have to . . ." I began, but Sadie cut me off.

"I want to," she said firmly. "You and I are going to have dinner. Alone. Together. Tonight. And I want to hear all about this—what did you say his name was?"

"Dex," I said.

"Hmmm. Dex. That's an interesting name," Sadie said. "It's strong, but quirky. I like it."

"Mom, look, you don't have to cancel your plans on my account," I said.

She looked torn. "Your first boyfriend is big news, and I want to hear all about him," she said.

"He's not my boyfriend. Not yet," I said. "More of a . . . quasi-almost-boyfriend. So go ahead and go to your dinner. I'll tell you about him tomorrow."

"If you're sure . . ."

"I'm sure," I said firmly. "But what should I do about Henry?"

"What do you mean?" Sadie asked.

"What should I tell him when I call to cancel our sightseeing trip?" I asked.

"Oh! Well . . . the thing is, you can't, darling. He's going to meet you at the Tube stop in twenty minutes," Sadie said. "In fact, you'll have to hurry if you're going to make it on time. Do you have any blush? You're looking a little pale. You can use some of mine. It's in the upstairs bathroom."

"But . . . but . . ." I stuttered.

"But nothing. You want to see London, and Henry's offered to show you around. There's no reason not to. It's not like it's a date. And even if it was, you said yourself, this Dex isn't officially your boyfriend. Not yet," Sadie rationalized.

"No . . . but I wouldn't be too happy if Dex was showing some English girl around Orange Cove while I was away," I said.

Just the thought of that, of Dex walking along the beach with some cute girl with a shiny mane of hair and pink cheeks, while pointing out the best spots for para-surfing made my stomach feel queasy. Was that why he hadn't e-mailed me? Because he was too busy hanging out with some British chick?

"This is different," Sadie said breezily.

"How so?" I asked.

"It just is. Anyway, you can't cancel on Henry now, so you might as well have a good time," Sadie said.

I opened and closed my mouth a few times, wanting to protest, wanting to tell Sadie that since *she* was the one who'd agreed to this plan, than *she* should have to meet Henry at the Tube stop to tell him I wasn't going sightseeing with him. That I had an almost-quasi-boyfriend, and was therefore not available to go on almost-quasi-dates with other guys.

But I couldn't do that, of course. Henry seemed like a nice guy, and it wasn't his fault that Sadie had shanghaied him into spending the day with me. So finally I just drew in a deep breath and said resignedly, "Okay, *fine*. But I'm *not* putting on blush."

# Chapter 4

As it turned out, walking to the Tube stop was actually pretty exciting. The South Kensington neighborhood where Sadie lived was lined with gorgeous white town houses fronted with black wrought-iron fences. Little cars so small they almost seemed like toys were parked bumper to bumper at the curb. And there were so many pedestrians out. Most of them looked straight ahead, their eyes fixed on some distant point, or jabbered into their cell phones, but I passed by one pleasant white-haired man, walking a jaunty Westie on a leather lead, who doffed his tweed hat to me.

"Hi!" I said with enthusiasm. Because it had finally hit me . . . I was actually in London! Walking briskly down the sidewalk, just like a real urban warrior! Speaking to actual British people!

It was nippy out, and the wind stung as it blew against my face, but the sun shone surprisingly brightly. I'd expected the weather to be dark and gloomy and the sky to be thick with clouds. I tucked my hands in my coat pockets, and resolved to buy gloves and a hat at the first Gap store I came across.

*Do they have the Gap in London?* I wondered.

"Miranda! Over here!" a familiar voice called out.

I looked up and saw Henry standing at the Tube entrance. He was wearing a dark blazer, a striped oxford shirt, untucked, and faded jeans. A gray-and-black striped scarf was wrapped around his neck. His dark hair shone in the sun, and his cheeks and the tip of his nose had flushed pink in the cold. When he waved and grinned, I felt a whoosh of excitement fizz up inside of me. . . . Followed by a wave of guilt-laced confusion. I liked Dex, really liked him. So why was I getting stomach flutters over Henry?

*It's just because he's so good-looking,* I reasoned. *That's all. If Prince William suddenly appeared, I'm sure I'd get butterflies, too.*

"Hey, Henry," I said when I reached him.

"Hi," Henry said, grinning at me.

"Thanks for offering to show me around," I said. And then, feeling the familiar need to apologize for Sadie, I added, "I hope my mom didn't bully you into doing this."

Henry shook his head. "No, no worries. This'll be fun. Is there anywhere in particular you wanted to go?"

"Well . . . I have always wanted to see Buckingham Palace," I said, feeling a little silly as I said it. Going to gape at the queen's residence was tourism at its cheesiest. But how could I possibly come to London and not see the palace with its famous guards in their bright red coats and tall fur hats?

"Buckingham Palace it is," he said. "I think that's the Green Park tube stop. Do you have a Tube pass?"

I did not. So Henry ushered me into the tube station and showed me to the machines that dispensed Oyster cards, and then once I had my card in hand, where to scan it to get through the turnstiles. We headed downstairs, following the blue signs for the Piccadilly Line until we reached the platform. Trains were arriving and departing with loud whooshes, and a clipped voice rang constantly from the loudspeakers, notifying passengers of delays.

I felt a thrill of excitement as our train arrived.

"Mind the gap," the disembodied voice said coolly, and then suddenly people were pushing forward and I was on the train. The seats were all taken, so Henry and I held on to poles by the door, bracing ourselves as the train started to roll forward.

"This is so cool. I'm actually riding on the London Tube," I said, not able to contain my excitement. I glanced at Henry, half-expecting to see him roll his eyes. But he just smiled at me.

"We could just forget sightseeing, and spend the day down here instead," he said.

"I know, I sound like a total small-town hick," I said, blushing.

"Not at all. I take it you don't have trains in Florida," Henry said.

I shook my head. "Not like this. At least, not in Orange Cove," I said. "It must be great. You can get around on your own, without waiting for your parents to drive you. Until I'm old enough to drive, the only independent transport I have is a bike."

"Actually, I usually bicycle to school," Henry said.

"You go to school here in London, then?" I asked. My sole insight into the British educational system was the Harry Potter books, which had given me the impression that most kids in England went away to school.

"Yeah. A formidable institute known as Pembrooke Hall," Henry said. "But only for another year. Then I'll be off to university."

I had to force myself not to repeat everything he said, imitating his accent. He'd think I was making fun of him, when really I just loved the way words sounded in his round, plummy English accent. And I was more than a little jealous. Why couldn't I have been English and grown up in London? Why was I stuck in Orange Cove, Florida, being raised by dysfunctional parents? Don't get me wrong, I loved my mom and dad. But you'd need the patience of a saint not to get irritated with them from time to time. And I'm no saint.

For the rest of the ride, Henry told me how he was studying to take something called his A-levels, which were basically a series of exams on various subjects, the results of which would determine where he went to college. He wanted to go to Cambridge, but it was really competitive, and he wasn't sure he'd get in. And then suddenly we were pulling into Green Park Station, where we exited the train and followed the crowd of people pushing toward the escalators that led out.

As thrilling as I'd found traveling by Tube, I was a bit relieved to be back outside, breathing in the fresh air, and no longer being crowded and jostled.

"How about you?" Henry said, as we walked from the Tube stop to the edge of St. James's Park.

"What about me?" I asked.

"Where do maths geniuses go to university?" Henry asked.

"I don't know," I said honestly. Because, the truth was, I didn't. I knew that if I wanted to pursue math, I could pretty much go anywhere I wanted. MIT, maybe, or the University of Chicago. But that was just it. . . . I didn't want a career in mathematics. In fact, I was pretty sure I wanted to go to a college with a strong creative writing program.

An awkward silence fell between us.

"I don't know why I asked you that," Henry finally said. "I'm tired of everyone asking me where I plan to go."

"Yeah, I know," I said. "I mean, I haven't gotten that question a lot, since I won't be applying for colleges until my senior year. But I can imagine it would get irritating to hear the same thing over and over. It's like people asking me to calculate sums in my head."

"No, that's far better," Henry argued. "Because at least you have a skill you're showing off. In my case, everyone knows that I haven't got in anywhere yet. So if I admit that I want to go to Cambridge and don't get in, everyone will know I failed."

"You could just lie," I said. "Tell everyone you want to go somewhere you know you'll get in, and then they'll all be amazed at your brilliance when you get into Cambridge."

Henry grinned. "That's an idea," he said. "Subterfuge. So give me your top three."

"My top three what?" I asked, as we walked through an arched gate into St. James's Park. It was gorgeous, full of trees and flowers. There was a paved path that wound down in front of us, and a river over to the right, where geese and swans paddled around. Despite the chill, the park was busy, full of people walking dogs and mothers pushing baby carriages.

"Your top three least favorite questions that adults ask you," Henry said.

"Hmmm." I thought about this. "Do I have to rank them? From one to three, or three to one?"

"No. You can list them in any order you choose," Henry said.

"The first one is easy: I hate it when people ask me to calculate sums for them," I said. "The second would have to be when I'm asked what it feels like to have such a talented, famous woman for my mother. Gag."

Henry laughed.

"The third would be . . ." I paused. Because while I knew very well what it was, it also wasn't the sort of thing I normally shared with other people. But Henry was looking at me, his expression curious.

"The third would be when people ask me if it's hard to have a sister who's prettier than I am," I said, speaking quickly, as though that would dull the embarrassment. I didn't even know why I was admitting this to him. Maybe it was that I already felt comfortable with Henry, like I could tell him anything and he wouldn't judge me for it.

He whistled and raised his eyebrows. "People have actually said that to you? About your sister being prettier?"

I nodded. "Yeah, all the time. You see, Hannah—she's my stepsister—is gorgeous. People are always curious what that's like to live with. Most of them assume that I resent her for being so beautiful."

"Do you?" Henry asked.

I liked that he asked me that, that he didn't rush in to tell me that I was beautiful. Okay, to be perfectly honest, I wouldn't have minded if Henry had told me he thought I was pretty. But I didn't want him to do it now, when he would have just been saying it because he thought he had to.

I considered his question. "Sure, sometimes," I said. "But not as much as people think. Because I see other sides to her."

"So she's an evil beauty? Like one of those Bond girls who's always ready to sell out humanity for a cool billion?" Henry said.

"No, that's just it. I mean, yes, she can be pretty unpleasant at times. But just at the moment when I'm prepared to think that she really is evil, she always manages to redeem herself," I said. "Now, my stepmother, on the other hand, is truly evil. Think: Snow White's stepmother trying to kill her off."

"Does she feed you poisoned apples?" Henry asked, looking amused.

"She would if she thought she could get away with it," I said darkly. "I call her the Demon."

I didn't add that I used to call Hannah Demon Spawn, back before I realized that she wasn't as bad as I had once thought she was.

We went through a second arched gate, and I could see a huge gated building to my left.

"Is that it?" I asked eagerly.

"Yep. That's the palace," Henry confirmed.

"Wow! Come on, let's get closer," I said. "I want you to take my picture standing next to the palace guard."

And in my excitement, I almost—*almost*—reached for his hand. Thankfully, I caught myself in time, and quickly balled up my hands and stuck them in my coat pockets.

*That was a close call,* I thought.

# Chapter 5

Henry and I had a busy day. After we watched the changing of the guard at Buckingham Palace, we walked all over the City of Westminster—which was, Henry explained, what the central bit of London was called—where we saw Big Ben, the Houses of Parliament, and Westminster Abbey. We also took a ride on the London Eye, a huge Ferris wheel with amazing views of the city.

I learned quite a bit about Henry, mostly by playing his Top Three game. I found out, for example, that his top three favorite bands were Coldplay, the Raconteurs, and the Killers. His top three foods were gingerbread, potato chips—or crisps, as he called them—and an Indian dish called lamb vindaloo. His top three favorite things to do in his free time: listen to music, hang out with his friends, and play soccer. Henry was an only child, like me, and his favorite things about being an only were that no one messed about with his things, his parents had taken him on a bunch of trips to really exotic locales, and there was no one around to tattle on him. And his top three least favorite conversations to overhear: anything involving childbirth, anything involving a woman's menstrual cycle, and anything that involved adulation of the Beatles, who were, in his opinion, a good band, but highly overrated.

"Sadie would have a coronary if she heard you say that," I said, as we emerged from the High Street Kensington Tube stop, where I'd met Henry that morning.

"Why do you call your mum that?" he asked.

"What, Sadie? That's her name," I said. But I knew what he meant, so I shrugged. "She prefers it to Mom, which she says makes her feel old."

"She is old," Henry said, so bluntly, I laughed. "You know what I mean. Old enough to be a mum."

"Will you do me a favor and tell her that the next time you're over? When I'm around? I'd love to see the expression on her face when she hears it," I said.

"So you're inviting me over, then?" Henry said.

Suddenly, I had the weirdest feeling that he was going to kiss me. I don't know what it was. He hadn't moved at all; he was still just standing there while people bustled past us, doing their last-minute Christmas shopping on the high street. But there was something about his eyes, which a moment ago had been filled with laughter, and now seemed to be looking at me more intently. Or maybe it was his mouth, which wasn't quirking up in a smile anymore.

Then again, maybe I was just imagining it. Because I am not—and never have been—the sort of girl that inspires cute guys to kiss her. Except for Dex, of course, and it had taken him ages to work up to kissing me.

*Dex.* The thought was like a virtual slap across the face, waking me out of my Henry trance. I couldn't kiss Henry, because of Dex. And as amazing as Henry was, and as much as I liked him, and, yes, as much as I would probably enjoy kissing him, I couldn't do that to Dex. I just couldn't.

I don't know if it was guilt or panic that was motivating me, but I suddenly took a giant step backward, away from Henry.... And right into the path of a woman pushing a little metal shopping trolley in front of her. The woman managed to stop short, but the trolley rolled forward and slammed into my ankle.

"Ouch!" I said.

"*Real*-ly," the woman said, pulling herself upright and infusing as much disapproval as she could into the two syllables. "You should watch where you're going."

"Yes, I will. I'm sorry," I said, hopping on one foot, as though this would lessen the pain shooting up through my ankle.

The woman stalked off, and I thought I heard her muttering something about drugs under her breath.

"I'm not on drugs," I said, offended. "I'm just clumsy! Really!"

Henry, meanwhile, was obviously trying very hard not to laugh.

"Is your ankle okay?" he asked, reaching forward and touching my arm.

"Yes, fine. I'm fine," I said. And then, worried that he might still try to kiss me after all, I blurted out, "Home."

Henry looked at me blankly. "What?" he asked.

"Home," I repeated. "I have to get home. Sadie will be wondering where I am. She's probably worried."

This was an outright lie. Sadie had probably already left for her dinner party. But Henry didn't know that.

"I thought you said your mum—Sadie, I mean—was going out to dinner," Henry said.

Okay, maybe he did. When had I told him that? Of course, we'd been talking about everything and anything all day, that way you do when you meet someone new whom you don't really know, yet have a weird instant bond with.

"Oh, right." I glanced at my watch. It was only five, although it was already so dark out, I'd thought it was later. "I'm sure she hasn't left yet. She's probably waiting for me to get home before she does."

"Right," Henry said. "Do you know the way home, or shall I walk you?"

I actually wasn't sure I did remember the way back to Sadie's town house. On my way to the Tube stop that morning, I'd been so excited at finally being out and about in London, that I hadn't been paying close attention to landmarks or street names.

Then again, if I had been right, and Henry really had been on the verge of kissing me, then letting him walk me home would only give him another opportunity to try.

"No, thanks. I know the way," I said, with more bravado than I felt. "Thanks for taking me around today. You were an excellent guide."

"I enjoyed it. I haven't been to Westminster Abbey since I was a kid," Henry said. "We had a field trip there with school. One of my mates tried to dare me into opening one of the tombs to see if there was a skeleton inside."

"Did you?" I asked.

"Nah. You couldn't get close enough, and even if you could, those things are heavy. I wouldn't have had the arm strength." Henry grinned. "At least not back then. I'm a bit bigger now. Perhaps I should have tried again today."

"You would have gotten us both arrested."

"And you would have had a great story to tell your mates back home," Henry said.

I laughed. "That's true. I love how you call them my 'mates.' It's just so . . ."

"So what?"

"So English," I said sheepishly, realizing how stupid this sounded.

"Well, I have to confess something," he said, and he leaned toward me, so close his mouth was only inches away from my ear. "I happen to be English."

Goose bumps erupted up and down my arms. I was glad I was wearing a coat and that Henry couldn't see the effect he had on me.

"Thanks for clearing that up," I said, struggling to keep my voice light.

*Dex,* I told myself sternly. *Remember Dex.*

Henry leaned back. "We should do this again. You're here for two weeks, right?"

"Yes . . ." *Dex.* "I mean, yes, I'm here for two weeks. But I should probably check with Sadie before I make plans. I'm sure she's going to want to spend a lot of time with me while I'm here," I said.

"Sure, check with her, and let me know," Henry said easily. "I'll call you in a few days. Bye, Miranda."

"Bye," I said. And I turned, and started to walk down the street.

"Miranda!" I heard Henry calling my name, and—my heart thumping in my chest—I turned back around. Why was he stopping me? Was he going to kiss me after all?

"Miranda, you're going the wrong way," he called out. Really much more loudly than necessary, even considering the noise from the traffic. Several people passing by turned to smirk at me, the lost girl, and I felt my cheeks burn with humiliation.

I retraced my steps back to where Henry stood.

"Your mum lives in that direction," Henry said, pointing in the opposite direction from which I'd walked. "Take a right just past the pub, walk up to the next road, take a left, and it's three streets up on your right."

"Right. I knew that," I said.

"Clearly," Henry said.

I punched him lightly on the arm, and then, smiling to myself, headed off again, this time in the right direction.

•

Despite Henry's directions, I still got lost. I took the right past the pub, and then took a left, and a right, but that didn't look familiar, so I turned back and went up to the next street, but that looked just as strange, so then I tried to get back to my original route so I could start over, and somehow got turned around and couldn't find it.

Here's the thing about South Kensington: Every street looks the same. They're all lined with white town houses and fronted with the black iron fences I'd found so charming at first. It makes it really confusing and difficult to find your way around.

"Like it'd kill these people to paint a few of these blue or red, so you'd know what street you were on," I muttered resentfully.

It had gotten colder out now that the sun had set, and my feet felt like they were encased in ice. I never had gotten around to buying gloves and a hat—oh, no, I'd been too busy playing Top Three with Henry to do something sensible like track down gloves—and my hands and ears were so cold, it felt like they'd never be warm again.

*I know what this is,* I thought, as I turned down yet another strange street and looked around helplessly. *This is the universe punishing me for spending the day with Henry and thinking about kissing him. I finally have a nice boyfriend at home—okay, fine, an almost-quasi-boyfriend, anyway—and at the very first opportunity, I let my head be turned by a cute accent and a pair of dimples.*

I spotted a bench on the sidewalk, and slumped gratefully down on it. My feet were killing me. My shoe had rubbed a blister on the back of one of my heels. I hadn't noticed it until about an hour ago, although now that I had, the pain was so intolerable, I had to limp. And the ankle on my other foot was still throbbing from where the mean woman had nailed me with her shopping trolley. But despite the pain, walking had at least kept me warm. Now that I was sitting, my earlier belief that I couldn't possibly be any colder was quickly proven to be a mistake. The bitingly cold wind hurt even more as it whistled against my cold cheeks and exposed ears. I shuddered and hunkered down, wrapping my arms around myself for warmth.

I was cold and lost and generally as miserable as I could ever remember being. This was worse than listening to my parents yell at one another in those terrible months before they separated for good. Worse than being taunted by Kimmy Shelton on the school bus back when I was in fifth grade. Worse than falling flat on my face in front of Emmett Dutch back when I had a crush on him. I could feel hot tears burning in my eyes, and a strangled sob catching in my throat.

*That's just great,* I thought bitterly. *On top of everything else, I'm going to cry.* I hate crying. It always gives me a sore throat, and makes my face red and puffy. And when you have a nose as large as I do, you don't want to do anything that makes it look even larger.

But I couldn't help it. The tears were coming, and my breath was ragged and noisy. My nose started to run, and the only tissue I had was an old tattered one I found at the bottom of my coat pocket. Miserably, I blew into it. And it had been such a good day, too. Right up until Henry and I said good-bye, and I'd gone and gotten lost.

"Is everything alright, miss?"

I turned, and saw a policeman standing there. He was wearing a rounded hat and a long dark coat.

*A bobby,* I thought, recalling a picture book I'd had as a kid. That's what they called the policemen here.

"I'm lost," I managed to croak. And then because I thought more explanation was probably necessary, I said, "My mom lives around here somewhere. On Tulip Street. But I've been walking up and down and I can't find it anywhere."

"Tulip Street? I know where that is," the bobby said kindly. "Come with me, miss. I'll show you the way."

•

Amazingly, Sadie was home when I returned. She was too busy pulling me into her arms and saying things like "scared to death" and "Henry said he'd left you hours ago" to remember to flirt with the bobby who'd delivered me to the doorstep. But then once she saw that I was all in one piece and hadn't been mugged or taken hostage, she turned one of her beaming smiles on the policeman and tried to bully him into coming inside for a cup of coffee.

"No, really, ma'am, thank you, but I must be off," the bobby said for the fourteenth time, before Sadie finally gave up trying to coax him inside.

"Thank you again!" she called out as he fled, looking relieved. "Good night!"

She closed the door and then turned to look at me. "How on earth did you get lost?" she asked. "And why didn't you call me?"

"My cell phone doesn't work here," I said. "So I didn't bother bringing it with me."

"You could have used a pay phone," she said.

"I couldn't remember your phone number," I mumbled. I hated to admit this. People always assume that because I'm good at math, that I should be able to automatically memorize all phone numbers. Which, okay, that was actually true. I usually could memorize number sequences pretty easily. But the phone numbers here had one more digit than American numbers, and the different dialing rhythm threw me off.

"I'm just glad you're back safe," Sadie said, hugging me again. "I was worried sick. Oh, you'd better call Henry and let him know you got in safely."

"*What?* Why?"

"Well, you were so late, I called Henry's house to see if the two of you had gone back there. Henry said that he'd left you at the Tube stop ages ago. I think he's feeling badly that he didn't walk you home. He even called a half hour ago to see if you'd gotten home yet," Sadie said.

"Oh," I said, while conflicting emotions lapped over me. Partly, I was dismayed that I would now have to call Henry back tonight to let him know I'd gotten home, especially since I'd already decided it would be best if I didn't see or talk to him again. Partly, I was pleased that Henry had cared enough to call back. And partly, I was really annoyed at Sadie for telling Henry I'd gotten lost. It made me sound like a complete idiot.

The phone rang then.

"That's probably Henry now," Sadie said brightly. Before I could stop her, she plucked the portable phone up off of a sideboard. "Hello," she said. "Oh, hello, Henry. Miranda was just about to call you. Yes, she's finally back. Can you believe she got lost walking home from the Tube stop?"

Sadie stopped twittering on for a moment to laugh gaily. My heart gave a great lurch. It felt like it was trying to tunnel its way out of my chest cavity via my throat. *What? What were they laughing about? Me?*

"Yes. Yes! I know," Sadie chortled.

"Mom," I hissed, and made a grab for the phone.

"Wait a minute, Miranda's right here, and she's *dying* to talk to you," Sadie said. "Hold on, here she is."

I grabbed the proffered phone from Sadie's hand, while simultaneously fixing her with the evilest evil look I could muster. I may have zero dating experience, but even I know you never tell a guy you're dying to talk to him. It makes you look desperate and sad. I wasn't interested in Henry—at least, that's what I kept telling myself—but I still didn't want him to think I was swooning around over him like a lovesick moron.

Sadie just looked amused at my annoyance.

"Teenagers," she said, shaking her head and rolling her eyes heavenward, as she turned and strolled back to the kitchen.

I kept my hand over the phone until she was safely out of earshot, and then took a deep breath, and said, "Hi. It's me." Then, as though he could possibly have me confused for someone else, I added, "Miranda."

I braced myself for his response. I knew he'd probably tease me for getting lost. It's what I would have done, had our positions been reversed. And I also knew that if he did, it would bother me immensely. I was cold and tired, and up until a few minutes ago, had been very, very scared. Irrationally scared. I wasn't just worried that I wouldn't find my way back to Sadie's tonight, I was worried that I would be lost *forever*. That no one would ever find me. That I'd spend the rest of my life wandering the streets of London.

My fears sounded silly and overblown now that I was in Sadie's safe, snug house and my body was slowly defrosting. But the after-effects left me feeling prickly and on edge, and not at all ready to be teased about my ordeal.

But Henry surprised me. He didn't tease me about getting lost, and he didn't tell me I should have let him walk me home. Instead he said, "So what's 9,528 times 1?"

And I couldn't help it: I laughed.

# Chapter 6

Dex didn't e-mail me the next day, nor the day after that. I tried not to let it bother me. In fact, I tried not to think about him period. After all, I had plenty to keep me busy. True to her word, Sadie cleared her schedule to spend the days leading up to Christmas with me. We went to the National Gallery to look at priceless works of art, took high tea at Brown's Hotel, and drove way out into the countryside to see the standing stones of Stonehenge, which were really very cool in person. We decorated the short, fat Christmas tree Sadie had ordered with tinsel and round metallic-hued balls, and even baked little mincemeat tartlets topped with pastry stars.

But the truth was, the more I tried not to think about Dex . . . the more I thought about him. I found excuses to check my e-mail ten times a day, and every time I saw that he hadn't written, a thud of sour disappointment would settle in my stomach. And then I brooded over his silence.

Had I somehow misinterpreted it when he kissed me? I didn't think I had, but, then again, guys weren't exactly predictable. Who knew what they were ever really thinking, or why they acted as they did? I'd heard the stories: girls who were left bitterly confused after the guy who had swept them off their feet suddenly stopped calling without a word of explanation.

It's just, Dex didn't seem like the sort of guy who would do something like that. He'd always seemed so nice and so thoughtful. Or was that exactly what every girl who'd been abruptly stood up also thought?

I was fretting over this possibility late Saturday morning, after checking my e-mail and yet again finding my in-box empty, when the phone rang. I picked up the extension Sadie kept on her desk.

"Hello," I said.

"Miranda? Hi, it's Henry."

"Hey, Henry," I said. Despite the pledge I'd made to keep my distance from Henry, I was pleased to hear from him.

He'd called two days earlier to invite me to get together with him and a few of his friends. I truthfully told him that I couldn't— that was the afternoon that Sadie and I went to Brown's for high tea—and he'd been nice enough about it, although I could tell he was disappointed. Which was, of course, hugely flattering. And made me seriously consider relocating to London. Less than one week here, and I already had a cute guy calling me. I'd spent almost sixteen years living in Orange Cove, and—other than my one kiss with Dex—I'd gone completely unnoticed by the local male populace.

"What are you up to today? Have you wrangled an invite from the queen yet?" Henry asked.

I laughed. "No. Her Majesty hasn't returned my calls," I said.

"In that case, a few of us are getting together to go see the new Bond movie this afternoon. Care to join us?" Henry asked.

I hesitated only for a moment. I was on my own that afternoon. Sadie had an editorial meeting and some last-minute shopping to do. She'd told me not to wait on her for dinner. And it wasn't like Henry was asking me on a date. It was a group thing.

"Sure, that sounds like fun," I said.

"Brilliant," Henry said.

We made plans to meet in front of the movie theater, which was in walking distance of Sadie's house. I knew where it was—Sadie and I had passed by it a few days earlier on the high street—but Henry gave me very specific directions.

"Don't worry, I won't get lost this time," I said.

"I'm not worried," he said. "But why don't you take down my mobile number just in case?"

•

When I got to the movie theater, Henry was waiting outside for me. He was wearing faded Levi's and a navy peacoat that made his eyes look even bluer than usual, and his cheeks and the tip of his nose were pink from the cold. Henry grinned when he saw me.

"You made it," he said.

"I'm not *always* lost," I said.

"Good to know. Shall we head in?"

I looked around, surprised. "Aren't we meeting your friends? Or are they already inside?"

"Actually . . . neither. Joseph said he wasn't feeling well, and Oliver's mum made him go to his granny's for dinner," Henry said. His voice was casual, but he glanced away as he spoke.

"Oh, that's too bad," I said. "I wanted to meet your friends."

"We can get together another day. You're here for a bit longer, right?"

"Until January third," I said.

"So you'll be around for New Years'," Henry said.

I nodded.

"Excellent. Then you'll be able to come to the party at my house," Henry said. "My parents have one every year."

"Sounds like fun," I said. I noticed that there was a line queuing in front of the ticket booth. "We should probably buy our tickets."

"I already got them. I bought them online," Henry said.

"Let me pay you back," I said, pulling my wallet out of my coat pocket.

But Henry waved me off. "Don't worry about it."

I hesitated. "Are you sure?"

He nodded. "You can get the popcorn," he said.

We went inside, and I purchased an extra large tub of popcorn and two sodas, and then Henry and I made our way to the theater where our movie was showing. The movie theaters in London worked differently than they did back home; instead of picking which seat you wanted when you went inside, you were assigned a seat when you bought your tickets.

"But what happens if you don't like your seat? Or if someone really tall sits in front of you?" I asked. "Can you move?"

"Sure. It's not like the seat assignments are enforced by a police presence," he said.

"There isn't a Movie Special Ops?"

"Not that I know of. If they exist, they must be top secret," Henry said. "One of those government agencies that you need clearance to even know about."

It wasn't until we were sitting down and companionably digging into the tub of popcorn that it occurred to me: Henry and I were on a *date*. At least, I thought we were. After all, he'd asked me to go to the movies with him, and he'd bought my ticket. Maybe his friends really did back out at the last minute. . . . But maybe they were never really planning on coming in the first place.

I wished for the ten zillionth time that I had more experience in guy-related matters. My stepsister, Hannah, might not be able to calculate the square root of the number one, but she'd certainly know whether or not she was in the middle of a date with a cute guy. And right about now, her brand of genius would really come in handy.

•

After the movie, Henry and I went to Pizza Express for dinner. We each ordered our own pizza—I had the Quattro Formaggi and

Henry ordered something called Il Padrino, which turned out to be a pizza covered in chicken, tomatoes, and vegetables. Henry didn't seem horrified that I ate as much, if not more, than he did, which was another point in his favor. I'm not one of those girls who can eat a few lettuce leaves and pretend I'm stuffed.

"Did you like the movie?" Henry asked as we ate.

"It was great," I enthused. "I especially liked the chase scene with the helicopter, the high-speed train, and the motorcycle. How about you?"

"Yeah. I thought it was brilliant," Henry said. "I really want one of those pens that double as a grappling hook."

"Because you have a pressing need for grappling hooks here in London," I teased him.

"Hey, you never know when you're going to have to scale the side of a building." Henry folded his slice of pizza and took a big bite. He swallowed before speaking again. "Look at James. He got a lot of use out of that thing."

"Yes. Although, to be fair, he was chasing down an evil oil tycoon's henchmen after they tried to kill him with a high-tech laser gun," I said.

"Well, yes, if you're going to argue semantics," Henry said. "So, give me your top three bad guys."

"In real life or fiction?"

"Fiction. It's less depressing."

I thought about it for a few minutes. "Well. The White Witch from *The Lion, the Witch and the Wardrobe* would be on my list," I said, thinking of Peyton, who bore more than a passing resemblance to that cold-blooded witch. "And the Queen from *Snow White*. Actually, all of the evil stepmothers. Cinderella had a nasty one, too."

"I'm sensing a theme," Henry deadpanned.

I grinned at him, and then inspiration struck. "Number three is Hannibal Lecter from *Silence of the Lambs*," I finished triumphantly.

"Not bad, not bad," Henry said. "I would put Hannibal on my list, too."

"Who else?"

Henry pondered this. He took his top-three lists very seriously, and wasn't one to rush in with a slapdash answer.

"The possessed girl from *The Exorcist*. She was seriously creepy. And Voldemort from the Harry Potter books. Although the book version of Voldemort, not the movie version," he said.

I shrugged and nodded. That was a given. "I think your list is better. Maybe I should rethink mine. Top three heroes?"

This time Henry didn't hesitate. "That's easy: Indiana Jones, Han Solo, and Bond, James Bond," he said.

"Han Solo? Really? I thought Luke was supposed to be the hero in *Star Wars*," I said.

"Luke was a prat," Henry said firmly. "Although to be honest, the best character in that movie was Boba Fett. Boba Fett was the ultimate in cool."

"Cooler than James Bond?"

Henry had to think about that. "I don't know. It would be a close call. On the one hand, Boba has the Wookie-pelt cape and the wrist-mounted flamethrower."

"I'm not even going to ask how it is you know that," I said.

Henry ignored me. "But Bond gets all the cool MI gadgets and the hot girls," he said.

"So you're torn between a hot girl and a Wookie-pelt cape?" I asked.

Henry shook his head definitively. "No, you're right. I'd totally go for the Wookie-pelt cape," he said.

"What is it with guys and Boba Fett?" I asked. "My friend Finn is a total Boba Fett freak. I even gave him a Boba Fett T-shirt for his birthday."

"They have Boba Fett T-shirts in America?" Henry exclaimed. When I nodded, he whistled. "It truly is the land of opportunity."

He hesitated, looking down at his pizza for a minute. "So . . . this Finn bloke. Is he your boyfriend?"

"God, no," I exclaimed, and shuddered at the very idea of being romantically involved with Finn. It's not that Finn is unattractive—I suppose he has his charms—but he was *Finn*. We'd been friends for so long that it was impossible—and frankly a bit creepy—to think of him as anything else. Besides, while brilliant and extremely funny, Finn has no moral center. "We're just friends," I said firmly.

Henry coughed and looked embarrassed. "Do you have a, um, boyfriend?" he asked.

I thought about Dex and our kiss and how he hadn't sent me a single e-mail in the week since I'd gotten to London.

"No," I said truthfully. "I don't."

Henry looked up and grinned at me. The smile reached his eyes, which were the exact color of the river that runs through Orange Cove at its deepest point.

"Good," he said.

And I couldn't help but feel a thrill of excitement at knowing that Henry liked me.

After that, Henry and I started to spend more and more time together. Partly it was because Sadie was restless to get back to work, so my afternoons were freed up while she wrote. And partly I just had fun with Henry. I felt like I could be myself around him. When I was with Henry, I wasn't the brainy girl who goes to that geek school. . . . I was just me. Miranda.

Another thing I really liked about Henry was how happy he seemed to accompany me on my various sightseeing expeditions. He didn't roll his eyes and act like it was all beneath him. He even seemed enthusiastic about going. Together we went to the Tower of London, which was amazingly cool. And we took a water taxi down the Thames River to Greenwich, where we hiked up a huge hill to the Royal Observatory to stand on the prime meridian, each foot planted on a different hemisphere. Even though it was touristy and more than a little cheesy, we even went to Madame Tussaud's Wax Museum, with its gory Chamber of Horrors.

I was learning a lot about Henry. He was smart. (His top three university choices: Oxford, Cambridge, and the University of London.) He wanted to be a barrister. (His top three alternative careers: pro soccer player, movie critic, hypnotist.) He and his friends were accomplished practical jokers. (Top three practical jokes of all time: Henry switching around the keys on his friend Simon's laptop, so that Simon grew increasingly frustrated as he kept misspelling everything he typed; Joseph slipping an antitheft security strip in Henry's pocket, so that he set off the alarm at a Virgin Megastore, and was subsequently tackled by a security guard; and Oliver stashing a handful of frozen prawns in the glove box of Joseph's car.)

"That's just gross," I said, appalled.

Henry had started to laugh as he told me about it, and by now, he was chortling so hard, his eyes teared up. "Joseph kept saying, 'Do you smell that? It's all pongy in here.' Pongy, I tell you!"

"But what happened? Didn't it ruin the car?" I asked.

"Well, I won't say it ever smelled good after that," Henry said, wiping his eyes.

"Remind me never to get on your bad side," I said.

"Girls never appreciate practical jokes," Henry said philosophically. "Must be a genetic thing."

But despite all of the time we spent together, Henry never once tried to kiss me or even hold my hand. As clueless as I was about guys, even I couldn't have misinterpreted his interest. . . . Or could I have? Maybe he'd finally noticed that I have a horrible, too-big nose and the sort of frizzy hair that turns bushy in the humidity. But, even so, he seemed perfectly happy hanging out with me most afternoons. It was very confusing.

I checked my e-mail every day, but Dex never wrote. Finn sent me the occasional note, and Charlie wrote frequently. She'd started dating a guy named Mitch, a junior at Orange Cove High who worked at Grounded, our favorite coffee shop. When I'd last seen Charlie and Mitch together, they hadn't seemed all that serious. But in the two weeks since I'd been gone, they'd apparently gotten really close. In fact, it was all Charlie wrote about—how good Mitch smelled, how she loved the shape of his ears, how his brown eyes were the exact color of a slab of dark chocolate. It was actually pretty revolting, and very un-Charlie-like, so much so that I wondered if she'd sustained a blow to the head in my absence. The Charlie I knew and loved was deeply unromantic.

On Christmas Eve, while I waited for the quiche Sadie had baked to be ready, I checked my e-mail and was soon rolling my eyes over Charlie's latest gushing letter about the bracelet Mitch had given her and how much he'd like the portrait she'd painted of him. Trying to stay positive and supportive—no one wants to hear that they're acting like an idiot over a guy—I wrote back and told her that all sounded great and I was happy for her. Then, my duties as best friend discharged, I launched into my current dilemma. I outlined the Henry situation and the lack of communication from Dex, and then begged Charlie for some advice.

*So what should I do? Do you think Dex has forgotten me? Is Henry really interested in me? If so, why hasn't he made a move? Do you think it's because I'm leaving in eight days, and he doesn't want to get attached?* I wrote, and then hit the send button. Charlie's response came back five minutes later.

To: mirandajbloom@gmail.com
From: blankcanvas@artmail.com
Subject: Re:[Re:] Love is in the Air
    You're overthinking this, Miranda. When love is right . . . it's just right. I can't explain it, but if Henry's the one you're meant to be with,

you'll just know. Trust me. I knew with Mitch, on a deep—so deep it
was almost cellular—level.

As for the Dex situation, well . . . I wasn't going to tell you this, but
since you asked . . . I actually ran into Dex a few days ago. Mitch and
I went to see that new Joaquin Phoenix movie—Mitch was so sweet,
he insisted on paying for everything, and while we were watching
the movie, he had his arm around me and was drawing circles on my
shoulder with his fingers, and I just about melted. . . .

Where was I? Oh, right: Dex. He was there. At the movies. And
he wasn't alone. He was with a girl. I don't know if it was a date—I
didn't see them kissing or anything—but they were laughing a lot.
I'm so sorry. I hate being the one to tell you about it, but I also
don't want you to waste your time in London worrying that you're
cheating on Dex.


I stopped reading Charlie's e-mail, and then started again from
the beginning. But the content didn't change. Dex had been out on
a date. With some other girl.

I began blinking very fast, trying to keep back the tears that were
welling up in my eyes and clinging wetly to my lashes. My stomach
felt pinched and sour, and my throat was oddly dry and prickly at
the same time, as though I'd swallowed a fistful of feathers.

So that was why Dex hadn't written to me . . . he'd found someone else. A girl who made him laugh. Charlie hadn't said whether
the girl was pretty, but I had to assume she was. Dex's last girlfriend
was a model. In fact, maybe that was why he'd lost interest in me;
maybe I wasn't pretty enough for him.

I could actually feel a throbbing pain in my heart. I had liked
Dex. Really, really liked him. And I'd thought he liked me, when
clearly . . . he hadn't. Or, at least, he hadn't liked me enough. Which
was almost worse.

I wondered what would have happened if I hadn't come to
London. What if I'd canceled my trip at the last minute and stayed

home? Would Dex and I be together then? Would he be at the movies with me, laughing at my jokes?

"Miranda." It was Sadie, calling from the bottom of the stairs. The house was so tall and narrow that her voice echoed in the stairwell. "Dinner's ready! And I put the *Mame* DVD on!"

I inhaled a deep, ragged breath, and tried not to sniffle.

"Okay, I'm coming," I said, shutting down my e-mail, without responding to Charlie's note.

*Merry Christmas to me,* I thought, and sadly wiped the tears off my cheeks with the back of my hand before heading downstairs.

# Chapter 7

Sadie and I had plans to spend a quiet Christmas lounging around in our pajamas, drinking cocoa and watching a movie marathon of all our old favorites: *Jerry Maguire, Moonstruck, Gone with the Wind*. We ate leftover quiche for breakfast, and Sadie planned to roast a duck for dinner. I felt too depressed over Dex to really get into the Christmas spirit, but I tried to fake it for my mom's sake. And I was—temporarily, at least—cheered when I opened Sadie's gift to me: the new laptop I'd been pining away for.

"Mom!" I cried, pulling the laptop out of its box and cradling it against my chest. "It's perfect, perfect, perfect!"

Sadie beamed at me. "I thought you'd like it," she said. "And I adore my new bookends."

Sadie loves all things Art Deco, and I'd been lucky enough to score a pair of vintage bronze greyhound bookends on eBay. She'd already set them out on her desk, where they stood guard over a row of her best-selling novels, which she wrote under her pen name, Della De La Courte.

My dad had sent me a pretty gold bracelet, Peyton gave me a gift certificate for a pedicure (which I knew was her way of criticizing the state of my feet), and Hannah gave me a cute T-shirt with a picture of the Union Jack on it, which just goes to show she can be oddly thoughtful at times. Finn gave me a computer game he'd designed, and Charlie had painted a tiny portrait of my dog, Willow.

All in all, it was a great Christmas. . . . Except for the part where I was completely heartbroken over Dex.

"Forget about him," Sadie declared once she'd finally dragged out of me the truth about why I was so mopey. "Have I taught you nothing? You don't need a man, Miranda."

"I know," I said sadly. "I just really thought he liked me."

"Well, if he doesn't, there must be something wrong with him," Sadie said.

"Of course you'd say that. You're my mother."

At this, Sadie looked surprised. "Yes, but that doesn't mean I'm blind to your faults." To prove her point, she began to tick them off on her fingers. "You can be obstinate, a bit of a smart-ass, grouchy when you first wake up. . . ."

"Talk about the pot and the kettle," I grumbled.

". . . And you suffer from low self-esteem," Sadie finished.

"I do?" This truly surprised me. I'd never thought of myself as having a poor self-image.

"You do. Of course, it's not your fault. It's practically pathological how low self-esteem is at your age. You young girls spend all your time worrying about boys and whether or not you look fat in your jeans. . . ."

"I never worry about whether I look fat in my jeans!" I exclaimed.

"That's because you don't have a spare ounce of fat anywhere on your body," Sadie said, looking me up and down. "It's your metabolism. I was the same way when I was your age. I could eat anything I wanted and never gained a pound. Just wait until you turn thirty. . . ."

"I know, I know, then it will all catch up with me," I said, rolling my eyes.

"Well, it will. Anyway, where was I?"

"You were talking about my low self esteem. Right before you told me how fat I'm going to suddenly get when I turn thirty."

"Oh, right. No, darling, your only problem is that you don't appreciate all of the wonderful and unique characteristics that make you you," Sadie said. "You don't see yourself for the lovely, personable, intelligent young woman you are."

I thought about this. Could it be true? Was it possible that I was really drop-dead gorgeous and just couldn't see it through the veil of my low self-esteem? I turned to look in the large ornate mirror that hung on one wall of the living room, the glass of which was smoky with age, and studied my reflection.

The large nose was still there. Ditto for the frizzy hair, today in extra-bushy condition since I hadn't bothered to brush it. So, okay, my eyes were a nice enough shade of brown. My chin wasn't so bad, and my skin was relatively clear. Overall, I was . . . presentable. Maybe even cute on a good-hair day. But gorgeous? No way. Not a chance.

"A late bloomer," I muttered aloud, remembering something my father had said.

"What, darling?" Sadie asked.

I turned away from the mirror, back toward her. "Oh, nothing. It's just something I overheard Dad and Peyton talking about one night this fall. They said I was a late bloomer. Actually, Dad said I was a late bloomer. . . . I think the word Peyton used to describe me was *odd.*"

Sadie doesn't get mad very often, but I could tell that this revelation had truly angered her. The color drained away from her face, her eyes narrowed and flashed, and her lips pursed so tightly they were white at the edges.

"That woman called you *odd?*" she asked slowly, carefully enunciating every word.

I nodded, and wished I hadn't said anything. I hadn't meant to upset Sadie; I just wanted her opinion on whether or not she thought it was true.

"Sorry, forget it," I said quickly.

"I will not forget it," Sadie thundered. She stood and paced around the living room. "Where's the phone? I'm going to call your father."

"You can't call him now. It's four in the morning in Florida," I protested. "You'll wake everyone up."

"Your father will be lucky if that's all I do to him," Sadie muttered ominously. "How dare he let that woman talk about you that way?"

"You don't think I'm odd?" I asked hesitantly.

"No! Absolutely not!"

Her absolute tone relieved me more than her answer. I knew Sadie would disagree with Peyton on principle, but surely if I really *was* an oddball, Sadie wouldn't be so vehement in her denial.

"How about the part about me being a late bloomer?" I asked.

Sadie stopped her frantic and as of yet fruitless search for the phone, and turned to look at me. She sighed. "Would that be such a bad thing?" she asked.

"So you do think I am a late bloomer!" I exclaimed, my voice getting shrill with despair.

So that was why Dex had dumped me. Laughing Girl probably wasn't a late bloomer. If anything, she was probably an *early* bloomer. The type of girl who started wearing a bra at the age of eight, and by sixteen was drinking martinis and getting Brazilian bikini waxes.

"I think you're you," Sadie said enigmatically. She crossed the room toward me and enveloped me in her arms. "And that's the most wonderful thing in the world."

•

Now that I was no longer looking forward to returning home to Orange Cove and Dex, the last nine days of my London vacation flew by, the way time always does when you least want it to. Sadie and I spent time together, visiting museums, eating out at sleekly modern restaurants furnished with lots of stainless steel and dark wood, and going to the West End to see live productions of *The Lion King* and *Mary Poppins*. I came up with a great idea for a short story about a teenage actress starring in a big-budget musical, who's also trying to have a normal life outside of her job. The story flowed so easily, I had to write like crazy, scribbling away in one of my journals, as I tried to get it all out before I forgot something.

On the days when Sadie worked, Henry and I spent time together. Sometimes we went sightseeing; other days we'd catch a movie or hang out at his house, watching bad but oddly addictive British television. Despite how often I was seeing Henry, I was pretty sure we'd downshifted into friend status. It was probably sensible, considering I was going home in a week, but I couldn't help feeling a twinge of discomfort. It was just further proof that I was actively repulsing boys. Every guy who had ever shown the slightest bit of interest in me was suddenly backpedaling away as fast as his legs would carry him.

Now when I opened up my e-mail program, I did so with the heavy certainty that my in-box would be a Dex-free zone. I did get other e-mails. My stepsister, Hannah, wrote once. She was visiting her dad and stepmother in New York City. It sounded like she was having the time of her life, between the nonstop shopping and attending a series of glitteringly sophisticated parties.

*My stepmother said there's no reason why I couldn't be the next Hilton sister. You know: famous for being famous,* Hannah gushed. I got the feeling that this was meant—and taken—as a compliment, not an insult.

Charlie wrote, too, although not as often as she normally did when one of us was away. When she did write, her e-mails were always the same: Mitch, Mitch, and more Mitch.

I wasn't the only one to notice the drastic change in my friend. When Finn wrote, it was to complain bitterly about how annoying he found this new, smitten Charlie.

To: mirandajbloom@gmail.com
From: finn@finnsgames.com
Subject: annoying much?

It's not just that Charlie talks incessantly about her stupid
boyfriend. It's the *way* she talks about him. She calls him *Mitchy*. Blech.
I almost hurled right then and there when I heard her. It's like the
real Charlie has been taken over by the Pod People.

It has given me an idea for a new computer game: an updated
*Invasion of the Body Snatchers*. Extra points if you can blow up the Pod
Girl's putz boyfriend.

Finn sounded unusually ruffled; normally nothing gets to him.
Seriously, he's the only guy I know who relishes the idea of being
expelled from school. (Finn is a genius at creating computer games.
He made his first million when he was twelve, so it's not exactly
like he has to worry about getting into a good college as a route to
securing a future job.)

But I've always had the feeling that Finn and Charlie have
stronger feelings for one another than they've ever let on, not that
either one of them would ever admit to it. Now that Charlie had
fallen head over heels in love with Mitch, a romance blossoming
between her and Finn seemed even more unlikely. I just hoped that
it didn't ruin their friendship.

•

"Happy New Year!" Sadie crowed, as Henry's mom opened the
black lacquered door to the Wentworth home. It was a tall, graceful
white town house that stretched four stories high.

"Sadie! It's so wonderful to see you!" Henry's mom said. She
beamed at us. Beatrice Wentworth was plump with brown curly
hair, a warm smile, and the dark blue eyes that Henry had inherited
from her. "Hello, Miranda, how are you? You look lovely."

"Thanks," I said shyly. Since I hadn't brought any dress-up

clothes with me to London, Sadie had dragged me out the day before on a shopping expedition. Normally, I hate to shop, but I had to admit, it was fun trying on all the exquisite dresses for sale in the little jewel box of a shop Sadie had taken me to. As soon as I'd tried on the silk beaded slip dress I was now wearing, Sadie clapped her hands decisively and announced that I had to have it. The dress was a soft rose color, and shimmered in the candlelight as I slipped off my coat. "And thanks for inviting me," I added.

"We're delighted to have you," Beatrice said. She turned and called out, "Henry! Miranda's here!"

Henry must have heard her somehow, even though the party was already in full swing and the house was alive with the din of talk and laughter. He materialized out of the crowd, grinning down at me, his dimples appearing.

"Henry, you look divine!" Sadie declared, causing the tip of Henry's nose to turn pink.

She was right: Henry looked very handsome in his blue blazer, white button-down shirt, and gray wool trousers.

"I'm glad you're here. My parents' daft friends keep cornering me. If one more person asks me where I'm set on going to university, I'll go mental," Henry told me.

Beatrice rolled her eyes. "I hope that's not what you told them," she said, attempting to sound stern, although a smile was twitching at her lips.

"Nah. I told them I was skipping college to embark on a career of petty crime. A few burglaries, maybe a bank job or two," Henry teased.

"Oh, you," Beatrice said, playfully whacking her son in the arm. "Go on and get Miranda a Coke. Ah, here's Giles. Giles, dear, will you get Sadie a drink?"

As our parents headed off into the crowd of partygoers, Henry and I retreated to the big, cheerful kitchen at the back of the house. The caterers, all wearing long, starched white aprons, were gathered there, assembling trays of bite-sized food and goblets of champagne. Henry grabbed two Cokes and a handful of canapés from the fridge.

"Come on, let's go to my room," he said, grimacing. "Before someone finds us and starts asking how school's going. Or makes you calculate sums."

"Good idea," I said, following him up the back staircase.

Henry's bedroom was on the top floor of the house, in a room with sloped ceilings and a round window on one wall. He had a plaid comforter on his oak bed, posters of soccer teams tacked up, and a big desk and bookshelf unit along one wall. The shelves were crammed with books and magazines, and a small television hooked up to play video games. It was a very masculine room, and I suddenly felt awkward being there, all dressed up in my pink sparkly gown. Henry looked a little uncomfortable, too. He stuffed his hands in the pockets of his trousers and averted his gaze. For the first time since we'd met, neither one of us could think of anything to say.

Then I spotted a familiar-looking box on the shelf.

"Is that *Grunge Aliens*?" I exclaimed, recognizing the ugly mustard yellow extraterrestrial cartoon on the video game box.

Henry brightened and nodded enthusiastically. "Yeah, it is."

"My friend Finn designed that game," I said.

Henry's expression turned to awe. "Are you serious?"

"Yep! That's his best-seller, too."

"It's a brilliant game," Henry said reverentially. "I can't believe you know the bloke who invented it. And he's our age?"

"Uh-huh. He goes to school with me. We've been friends for ages," I said.

"Wow. He must be a genius," Henry said. "What's he like?"

I paused to consider this question. "He's brilliant, yes, but in a twisted evil genius sort of way. Actually, you'd probably get on great. He's big on practical jokes, too."

"You think?" Henry said, his eyes shining with hero worship. Which was seriously deranged, because who would worship Finn? He's a total goofball.

"Do you want to play?" I asked, nodding toward the game.

"Yeah!" Henry said. "Are you any good?"

"I can hold my own," I said modestly.

I wasn't much of a gamer, but Finn had sweet-talked me into being a tester for *Grunge Aliens*, so I'd logged some considerable hours on the game. It was a fantasy-action game that put the players in the role of space explorers and pitted them against a series of increasingly ugly and hard-to-kill extraterrestrials. In vintage Finn style, when shot each monster exploded with a dazzlingly gory display of blood and guts.

Henry popped in the game and handed me one of the controllers. We sat side by side, cross-legged on the bedroom floor—me in my dress, Henry in his jacket and trousers—and began blowing up aliens.

I impressed Henry by knowing the location of several Easter eggs—secret treasures that Finn had hidden in the game and that you could only get if you knew where they were. Henry was especially pleased when I showed him the nuclear bomb blaster hidden in the stomach of a certain monster. You had to kill him and slice open his corpse to get it.

"Brilliant!" Henry kept exclaiming.

Henry was a lot better than I was, but I held my own, especially when it came to the Toxic Waste Ogres—monsters who developed evil powers after being raised in swamps of industrial intergalactic waste. I seemed to have a special talent for slashing the ogres' throats with my laser sword, sending their glowing, decapitated green heads bouncing off the screen, while their headless bodies writhed about at my feet.

"I worry about Finn. How does he come up with this stuff? It's seriously twisted," I said as I rapidly punched the buttons on my controller to escape the meteor spray Henry's space ranger had just thrown at me. "Ha! Missed me!"

"I think it's brilliant. And I think the excessive violence is meant to be a postmodern comment on the current state of international unrest," Henry said with relish.

I let out a snort of laughter. "Um . . . no. I know Finn. Trust me, this isn't a political statement. He just likes to up the gore factor. Oh! You killed me!" I exclaimed.

"Ha!" Henry said. "Take that!"

I dropped my console in disgust. "You play dirty," I announced.

"How do you figure that?"

"You distracted me with your commentary," I complained bitterly.

"It's not my fault you're so easily distracted," Henry said. "Shall we play again?"

"You're on," I said, taking a sip of my Coke before retrieving my gaming console. "This time, I'm taking you down."

"Big talk from the little lady," Henry said. "Game on."

•

We were so intent on blowing up space aliens and each other that Henry and I lost track of time. We took a break once to run down and retrieve dinner, and then again to get another round of Cokes. But we quickly reconvened to the floor of Henry's bedroom to do battle. Over the course of the evening, Henry shed his jacket and rolled up his sleeves. I envied him for this. My dress wasn't a comfortable lounging outfit. Maybe that's why Henry was able to beat me in game after game.

"Argh," I said, tossing aside my controller after Henry had killed me yet again, this time with a nuclear grenade. "I give up. This is a stupid, stupid game."

Henry did a little seated victory dance. "Say it," he said.

"No," I said.

"That was our deal. . . . You have to say it," he crowed happily.

I sighed, puffing out my cheeks in exasperation. "Fine. You are the golden god of *Grunge Aliens*," I said in a disgusted monotone. "Happy?"

"Ecstatic," Henry replied. He cocked his head to one side. "Do you hear that?"

I listened. From three floors below, I could just barely make out the sound of a crowd chanting. They were counting down.

"Thirty, twenty-nine, twenty-eight, twenty-seven . . ."

Henry glanced at the clock. "It's almost midnight," he said.

"How did it get so late?" I asked, bewildered.

"It's easy to lose track of time when you're fighting space aliens," Henry said with a grin.

"Twenty, nineteen, eighteen, seventeen . . ."

"We should probably go downstairs," I said. "Sadie will want to leave soon."

"Let's wait until the countdown's over," Henry suggested.

"Good idea," I said.

"Twelve, eleven, ten, nine . . ."

I felt Henry's eyes on me, and when I turned to look at him, he didn't look away. Instead he smiled at me in a way that made my toes tingle.

"Six, five, four . . ."

Henry leaned forward toward me. He reached out and took my right hand in his. His skin felt cool and dry against mine. I fervently hoped he didn't realize how sweaty my palms were.

"Three, two, one . . . HAPPY NEW YEAR!"

Henry kissed me. His lips pressed gently against mine, and I could feel the soft warmth of his breath. I opened my eyes, but then saw that his were closed—and very, very near—so I quickly closed mine. The thing was . . . the kiss was really nice. Really, really nice. But it was hard not to compare it with the amazing kiss Dex and

I had shared right before I left for London. Which just reminded me yet again of Dex, and how he was probably now—maybe even right this minute—kissing the Laughing Girl Charlie had seen him at the movies with. Or, if not now, he would be later on, when the New Year rolled around in that time zone. This realization was like a gut punch that sickened and saddened me at the same time. . . . And made it really hard to focus on how nice it was to be kissing Henry.

I opened my eyes and saw that he'd leaned back a bit, his expression unfathomable. For a moment, I worried that he'd known I'd been faking the kiss. But when he smiled, I knew he hadn't guessed.

"Happy New Year, Miranda," Henry said.

"Happy New Year," I said.

# Chapter 8

I flew home three days later. I saw Henry twice more before I left. On New Year's Day, we went to Henry's favorite curry house. The restaurant had dark red carpeting and flocked wall paper, and the tables and chairs were rickety, but the food was fabulous. Since I didn't have much experience with Indian cuisine, I let Henry do all the ordering. Everything was delicious, from the spicy lamb to the cream-sauced chicken to the huge, soft, doughy rounds of flat bread called *naan*.

The next day I was packing, and Sadie surprised me with tickets for the West End production of *Phantom of the Opera*, which I'd always wanted to see. We were going to go out for dinner before the theater to a restaurant called the Ivy. Sadie gleefully informed me that it's where all the movie stars went when they were in town, and so maybe we'd end up eating dinner next to George Clooney.

Henry stopped by in the afternoon. I took a break from my packing, and Henry and I went for a walk through Hyde Park. It was cold and the wind was biting, but we didn't really notice. We talked easily, as we had from the beginning, about everything and nothing. We played Henry's Top Three game, and complained good-naturedly about our parents, and as we passed by the Peter

Pan statue, Henry took my hand in his. Our hands fit well together, I noticed.

"You'll come visit again," Henry said.

"I think so. I guess it depends on how long Sadie stays here," I said. "Maybe you could come visit me, too."

"I've always wanted to go to Florida," Henry said.

"I'll take you to Disney World," I said. "It's only a few hours away from where I live."

Henry looked amused. "Aren't we too old for Disney World?"

"You're *never* too old for Disney World."

"Okay. It's a deal, then."

He squeezed my hand in his, and I felt a thrill of happiness. True, Henry didn't have the same breathless effect on me that Dex had. . . . But I truly liked Henry. And I had a feeling that the more time I spent with him, the more I'd like him. Besides, he was nice to me, which was more than I could say for Dex, who'd gone off with another girl as soon as I'd left town.

"What's wrong?" Henry asked, breaking in on these dark thoughts.

"Nothing. Why?"

"You were frowning," he said. He grinned and swung our arms between us. "When you frown, you get two little lines right here over the bridge of your nose." Henry pointed to the space on his own face to demonstrate.

"I just wish I wasn't leaving so soon," I said, which was half-true. I really didn't want to go back to my life in Orange Cove, constantly hoping I wouldn't run into Dex out and about with his new girlfriend.

And then there was my forced cohabitation with my dad, Peyton, and Hannah. Peyton and I hadn't ever really gotten along, and I guessed it was going to be even worse now. Even though I'd begged her not to, Sadie had called my dad on

Christmas Day. She was angry that Peyton had called me odd, and that Dad had let her do it, and that I'd overheard the whole thing. The fact that I'd been eavesdropping at the time hadn't mattered to my mom.

"Children eavesdrop," Sadie had said definitively. "As your father and that woman are well aware of. Or, at least, they should be."

Sadie had shut me out of her office while she called the States. I tried to listen at the door—clearly, I hadn't learned my lesson on eavesdropping—but I couldn't hear anything. Sadie's voice was a low, angry hum, and I could only make out every few words of what she was saying: ". . . Should not have happened . . . difficult age . . . low self-esteem . . . not helping."

Later, Sadie told me that my dad was concerned and that he planned to talk to Peyton about it, and then they'd both work harder to make me feel welcomed in their home. Which meant that Peyton would probably just hate me that much more and continue to shoot icy glares at me. I shivered at the thought.

"Cold?" Henry asked, jolting me into the present.

"No, I'm okay. I'm just bummed that I'm leaving."

"Me too," Henry said. "We'll keep in touch, though. I have your e-mail address."

This, too, reminded me of Dex, and his broken promise to e-mail me. But this time I stopped myself before I frowned.

"Yes. I'll write you, too," I said.

"Promise?" Henry asked. He stopped then, and I turned to face him. We were standing next to a pond, where cold-looking ducks were paddling around, trolling for crumbs.

"I promise," I said.

This time, when Henry leaned over to kiss me, all other thoughts flew from my mind.

"You have your passport?" Sadie asked for the ten millionth time, as she walked me through the airport toward the security check-in.

Even though I knew I had it—I'd just given it to the Virgin Airlines employee when I checked in for my flight, and distinctly remembered zipping it back in the pocket of my backpack—I patted my bag to make sure it was there.

"Yep," I said.

"How about money? Do you have enough pocket money?" Sadie continued.

"I think so. I won't need much, right? Dad's going to meet my plane in Orlando," I said.

"Even so, you may want to buy some chocolate or a magazine or something while you're waiting. Here, take twenty pounds. No, that's not enough. Take forty," Sadie said, pressing crumpled pound notes at me.

"This is too much," I said, trying to give her back one of the twenties, but Sadie waved me off.

"Take it. Just in case," she said.

"Okay. Thanks," I said, pocketing colorful bills. British money was so much prettier than American bills.

"What else? Do you have anything to read? Did you remember to pack your new laptop? And all of your other presents?"

"For the last time, yes, yes, and *yes*," I said, sounding more grumpy than I felt to hide my sadness at saying good-bye. We'd reached the security checkpoint, where people were lined up to go through metal detectors and have their bags searched. I felt guilty for snapping, so I put my free arm around Sadie to give her a quick hug. "I had a really good time."

Sadie hugged me back, squeezing me against her. "I did, too, darling. I wish you didn't have to leave," she said. She leaned back to look at me, and I noticed that she, too, had parallel lines appear between her eyebrows when she frowned. I guess I inherited that from her. "Maybe we should have looked into having you stay here for the semester."

"What about school?" I asked.

"Well, there's that. Maybe . . . I don't know. It's probably too late," she said.

"I guess," I said, wishing that it wasn't, wishing that I could stay. "School starts the day after tomorrow, though. And there's Willow."

Dad was taking care of my greyhound, Willow, while I was gone. I knew Dad liked Willow and would take good care of her. But my stepmother, Peyton, hated all dogs, and Willow in particular. I just hoped she hadn't "accidentally" let Willow out in my absence. Willow was sweet and gentle, but she had no sense of direction, and would easily get lost.

"Give Willow a kiss for me," Sadie said. She hugged me again, as though she didn't want to let me go. "Why don't you think about spending the summer here?"

"Are you going to still be here then?" I asked.

"I might be. The book's going slower than I thought, what with all of the publicity I've been doing for the British release of *The Gentleman Pirate.*" Sadie's expression suddenly turned sly. "Just think: If you come for the summer, you'll be able to see Henry again."

I blushed. I hadn't told Sadie about Henry kissing me, obviously, but she'd guessed that our friendship had deepened into a budding romance.

"I should go. They're going to be boarding my flight soon," I said.

"Okay. Come give me one last hug. I'm going to miss you so much."

My mom enfolded me into her arms one last time. I could feel my throat closing, and tears stinging my eyes.

"I'll miss you, too," I croaked.

"Don't worry about a thing, darling. You're going to be just fine," Sadie said.

I wasn't sure if she was talking about the flight or about life in the larger sense. I had a feeling it was the latter.

I hoped she was right.

# Chapter 9

My dad was waiting for me just outside of the international gateway at the Orlando airport. He was very tall, with thinning, dark straight hair, the too-big nose I'd unfortunately inherited from him, and brown eyes that squinted when he smiled. He waved cheerily to me, and I lurched toward him, staggering under the weight of my carry-on. The flight home had seemed longer than the flight over, and my legs were stiff from sitting.

"Hi, Dad," I said. I'd been a little worried about seeing my dad after Sadie had bawled him out. But he didn't seem angry. . . . Just happy to see me. Which made me feel a little guilty for tattling on him.

I couldn't seem to find my footing with my dad. He'd all but disappeared from my life for three years after he and Sadie got divorced. During that time, he met and married Peyton, a mouthwash heiress, and they'd moved into a big modern mansion on the beach. I'd seen him for the occasional Saturday-night dinner, but it was always awkward.

But then Sadie had moved to London while she wrote her new book, and I'd had no choice but to move into the beach house with Dad, Peyton, and Peyton's daughter, Hannah, who was my age. I had to give my dad credit; he'd been working hard trying to rebuild his relationship with me. I appreciated the effort.... Although sometimes it felt like it was all coming a little too late.

"Hi, honey," Dad now said, taking the bag off my shoulder. He leaned down and kissed me on the cheek. "How was your flight?"

"Very, very long," I said. My stomach rumbled so loudly, my dad could hear it over the airport din.

"Hungry?" he asked.

"Yeah, I'm starving. The food on board was awful. They actually served fish for dinner. Who wants to eat fish on an airplane?"

"I certainly wouldn't." My dad glanced around. "Do you want to run into the newsstand and get a candy bar or something?"

"I was sort of hoping we could get an early dinner," I said. It was only four in the afternoon, but Orange Cove was more than an hour away. I glanced around and spotted a little restaurant just past the newsstand. Airport food wasn't much better than airplane food, but I was too hungry to be picky. "Do you mind if I grab a burger?"

"Well . . . the thing is, your sister and stepmother are waiting in the car," Dad said.

"Stepsister," I corrected him automatically. "They drove down with you?"

"No. Hannah flew in today, too. She was in New York visiting her dad."

"Yeah, I know." I didn't tell my dad that Hannah and I had exchanged e-mails over the break. He had this whole fantasy that Hannah and I would become as close as sisters. I didn't need to add the weight of his unrealistic expectations onto our fragile, not-yet-gelled friendship. "When did she get in?"

"About two hours ago," my dad said nonchalantly.

I had a bad feeling about this. "So you've been waiting for me all this time?" I asked.

Here's the thing: Not only does Peyton hate me, she also hates to wait. For anything. Ever. So having to wait for two hours in an airport for me to arrive back home? That was probably Peyton's idea of hell. And she isn't exactly sweet-natured normally. I could only imagine how pissy she was going to be.

My dad hesitated just long enough to confirm my worries. Peyton's also not big on the silent-suffering thing. If she was mad, she would make the fact well known to all.

"So I guess no burger," I said, resigning myself to another hour of hunger.

"Sorry, kiddo," my dad said. And he really did look sorry. "Come on. Let's grab some snacks for the ride home."

My dad shouldered my bag, and we headed into the newsstand. I picked out a package of peanut butter crackers, a Kit-Kat, a bag of cashews, and a bottle of water. Once my dad paid for the snacks, we made our way to the baggage carousel, which was slowly spitting out the suitcases from my flight.

"Don't you have to take your bag through customs?" Dad asked.

"I already did. We got our baggage down by the international arrival gate, then walked them through customs, and then they took them back from us so that we could collect them down here," I said.

"No wonder it took you so long to get out of there," Dad said.

"Yeah, it was pretty much an exercise in bureaucratic time wasting," I said. "Although they did take down one woman who had a banana in her purse. The sniffer dog nabbed her."

"The nefarious international banana plot," Dad said.

I was glad my dad was in a jokey mood. It meant that he really wasn't angry at me. I relaxed, the knots in my stomach unraveling.

We finally were able to claim my suitcase, seemingly the last one to be tossed onto the conveyer belt, and headed for the walkway that bridged over to the parking garage.

"Peyton and Hannah are parked over there," Dad said, nodding to our right when we finally reached the garage. Peyton's enormous white Cadillac SUV was parked in a handicapped spot.

I felt a dropping sense of dread in my stomach, but followed my dad over to the SUV. He opened the back to put my bag in, and almost instantly, the cacophony of shrieking could be heard.

"Richard! What on *earth* took you so *long*?" Peyton screeched.

"This is *ridiculous*! I have a date tonight! I'm not going to have any time to get ready!" Hannah fumed.

"I've never had to wait so *long* in my *life*!" Peyton continued.

"Why did we all have to drive in the same car?" Hannah asked.

Wordlessly, Dad heaved the suitcase inside and then shut the back door. He turned to look at me.

"I think they're a little upset," he said.

"A little?" I asked. I glanced around, looking for an escape. "Maybe I should find a nice serial killer who will let me hitchhike back home with him."

"Come on. They'll calm down," Dad said.

He opened the driver's-side rear door for me, and I climbed up onto the smooth caramel leather seat next to Hannah. She had her arms crossed, and was puffing with indignation.

"Hi," I said, trying to sound cheery.

"Hey," Hannah said irritably.

"Miranda. What. Took. You. So. Long?" Peyton hissed, turning around in the passenger seat to glare at me through her tinted sunglasses. Peyton was very thin, very pale, and had very short, white blond hair.

"Believe it or not, I wasn't actually flying the plane. I didn't exactly have a lot of control over our arrival time," I said.

Peyton opened her mouth again, presumably to start screaming some more, but Dad cut her off. He swung into the driver's seat and said mildly, "Peyton, honey, don't yell at Miranda. It's not her fault that her flight got in late."

"We've been waiting here for hours!" Peyton said.

"I have to pee," Hannah announced.

"Why didn't you go before?" Dad asked her.

"Don't you take that tone with her," Peyton snapped.

"I wasn't using a tone. I just don't understand why she didn't use the facilities while you were waiting," Dad said, reasonably enough.

"I didn't have to go then," Hannah said, opening her door. "Don't worry, I'll be quick."

But since Hannah has never made a quick trip to the bathroom in her life—she can't help gazing at her lovely reflection in the mirror while reapplying her lip gloss or smoothing back her long, shiny golden blond hair—we ended up waiting for what did seem a ridiculously long time. It was made even longer by my Dad and Peyton's increasing irritability with one another.

"If I had known this was going to take all afternoon, I would have hired a limo service to pick Hannah up," Peyton said accusingly.

"You're the one who insisted we drive down together," Dad replied.

"It's not my fault I don't like driving on the highway," Peyton replied, her voice growing increasingly shrill.

Dad shrugged. "I told you that Miranda's flight was getting in later than Hannah's. That there was a good chance she'd get delayed going through customs."

"Why's that? Did they stop her?" Peyton swiveled around and fixed me with a beady look. "Did you try to smuggle something in?"

"No!" I said. "What do you think I'd be smuggling, anyway?"

"There was that story on *Dateline* a few months ago about how drug dealers use plain-looking girls to act as mules. They're not stopped as often going through customs," Peyton said. Her eyes narrowed as she stared suspiciously at me.

"Peyton!" Dad exploded.

"You think I'm a drug smuggler?" I asked mildly. I was more surprised than angry. The idea was so ludicrous.

"Who's a drug smuggler?" Hannah asked, climbing back into the SUV.

"No one," Dad said emphatically.

"Your mom thinks I am," I said.

Hannah snorted. "Yeah, right. Like someone like *you* would ever do something like *that*."

"Exactly," I said. "Wait . . . what do you mean, *someone like me*?"

"Well, no offense, Miranda, but you're kind of a Goody Two-shoes," Hannah said.

I have a theory that whenever someone starts off a sentence by saying *No offense*, whatever follows after is pretty much guaranteed to be offensive.

"I am not," I said indignantly, even though I really am, sort of. I mean, it's not that I try to be a Goody Two-shoes. . . . More that I'm just not very good at getting into trouble. None of my friends are into drugs, I don't like the taste of beer, and smoking cigarettes just seems like a really dumb habit to take up. But *Goody Two-shoes* seemed unnecessarily pejorative. Besides, who even said that anymore?

"Besides," I said, "it's not like you're exactly the town's Bad Girl."

Hannah could be selfish and was maybe the most narcissistic person I'd ever met. But she didn't drink or take drugs, either. I wasn't sure if her disdain for such substances was for moral or aesthetic reasons. I'd once overheard her disparaging some girls in her class at Orange Cove High for being partiers, finishing by tossing her hair and saying, "Don't they know that drinking makes your skin all gross and puffy and stuff?"

Of course, she did throw a party a few months earlier, when my dad and her mom were off on a romantic weekend in Miami.

That was certainly wilder than anything I'd done. But I don't think Hannah enjoyed the party much. She mostly just seemed annoyed at the mess her friends had left for her to clean up.

But now Hannah smiled enigmatically. "Like I'd waste my time making a splash in this Podunk town," she said.

That was a sentiment I hadn't heard my stepsister express before. Hannah was one of the reigning princesses of Orange Cove High. She'd always seemed to revel in her local popularity.

"As soon as I'm old enough, I'm going to move to Manhattan," Hannah continued.

At this, Peyton stopped sniping at my dad and fell silent. I could see her face in profile, and it seemed to grow even more pinched and twitchy than usual. Clearly, Hannah's trip to Manhattan had made an impression on her. . . . And Peyton didn't seem too happy about it.

"Are you going to go to college there?" I asked.

Hannah shrugged. "Maybe. I don't know. I don't really see the point of college. I just want to be one of those women who goes to parties and gallery openings and things like that."

"A socialite?" I asked.

"Exactly," Hannah said, favoring me with her prettiest smile.

The fact that someone so vapid and shallow could be so beautiful had often made me seriously doubt in the existence of a fair and just God.

"That's your life's ambition? To be a regular on the Manhattan party circuit?" I asked, shocked that anyone—even Hannah—could aspire to such a goal. "Don't you want a career?"

"A career?" Hannah wrinkled her nose, as though I'd just suggested she volunteer her free time giving pedicures at a homeless shelter. "No way. It would totally get in the way of all of the events I'd want to attend. Once I'm really old, like thirty or so, I'll probably decide to settle down and marry someone. As long as he has his own jet and a house in the Hamptons."

"It's good to have standards," I said.

Hannah nodded seriously, not realizing I was being sarcastic.

"And will you and this jet-owning man have kids?" I asked.

Hannah looked horrified at the idea. "No way! Do you have any idea what having a baby does to your body? It makes it all stretched out and saggy." She shuddered in horror at the idea. "No, we'll adopt. Like Angelina Jolie did. She has all of those kids she got from third world countries. I'd totally do that. . . . If I could pick out the kid, of course. I'd want to make sure I got a cute one."

This left me speechless. I gaped at my stepsister.

"Don't be ridiculous, Hannah," Peyton said, jumping into the conversation. "You're going to college. And that's the end of it."

"Why? Jackie didn't go to college," Hannah said.

"Who's Jackie?" I asked.

"My stepmom," Hannah said proudly. "And she's had an amazing life. She used to go to Studio 54, and she knew Mick Jagger and . . . and . . . well, a bunch of other celebrities who I can't remember. They're all really old now, anyway. But it was all very glamorous and exciting. Jackie said she'd have died if she'd had to miss out on all of it just to go to some boring college."

"Jackie," Peyton said, "has never worked a day in her life."

I thought this was a bit ironic coming from Peyton, who had inherited millions from her family in mouthwash money. But I decided it wouldn't be prudent to point this out at the moment, not while Peyton was still fuming about waiting so long for my arrival.

"She did too work," Hannah protested. "She was a model."

Peyton snorted. "Participating in a charity fashion show is not a modeling career."

"She was in a hair commercial, too," Hannah said.

Peyton glanced back at Hannah. "There'll be plenty of time for you to move to New York *after* you get your education. I don't want to hear any more nonsense about not going to college. And if I have to make that a condition of your trust fund, believe me, I will."

Her sharp tone startled me. I'd never heard Peyton be so strict with Hannah. And Hannah was obviously surprised, too, because for once she didn't argue back. Instead she crossed her arms again and slumped back in her seat.

"Miranda," Peyton said, turning to stare coldly at me. I had just unwrapped my Kit Kat bar and had it halfway to my mouth when she spoke. I froze under her icy gaze. "I don't want you eating in my car."

"Honey, Miranda's starving," Dad protested mildly. "She needs a snack."

Peyton pursed her lips so tightly together, they were lined in white.

"I'd better not find any chocolate smears on the leather," she finally said, her tone menacing.

"Okay," I mumbled through a mouthful of Kit Kat.

We rode the rest of the way home in total silence.

◆

Back at the beach house, I greeted my brindle greyhound, Willow, who was overjoyed at our reunion. She romped around me, slurping at my hands with her long pink tongue and grinning up at me. Her long, skinny tail wagged happily.

"Hi, girl. I missed you, too," I said, dropping to my knees and hugging her.

Once Willow had settled down, I ate a few slices of leftover pizza I found in the fridge, managed to stand up long enough to take a shower, and finally dropped into bed, exhausted. I pulled the sheets up to my nose, closed my eyes, and immediately fell into a heavy, dreamless sleep.

I awoke to the sound of a voice. More specifically, Hannah's voice.

"Miranda?" she was saying. "Mi-*ran*-da . . . wake up!"

She appeared to be sitting on the edge of my bed. I decided to ignore her, hoping she'd go away.

"Are you asleep?" she asked. This time she bounced up and down on the edge of the bed, jostling me.

"Yes. Go away," I said.

"You can't be asleep if you're talking to me," Hannah said triumphantly.

"I'm talking in my sleep," I grumbled.

"Really?"

"Yes. Go. Away."

"Come on. This is important," Hannah said. She bounced again.

I opened my eyes and gave her what I thought was my evilest of evil looks.

"Why are you squinting like that?" she asked. "Does your nose itch?"

"Hannah, what do you want?" I asked groggily.

"How was your trip?" she asked.

I stared at her and then turned to look at my alarm clock. A red 9:52 was glowing at me. I groaned and fell back against my pillow.

"You woke me up to ask me how my trip was?"

"We didn't get a chance to talk earlier," Hannah said.

"We were sitting side by side in the car for over an hour."

"I didn't feel like talking then." Hannah reached over and switched on my bedside lamp. The light was so bright, it felt like it was piercing my eyeballs. I groaned and pulled the covers up over my head.

"Have you talked to Dex yet?" Hannah asked.

"No," I said through the soft weight of the down comforter.

"Why not?"

She sounded genuinely concerned, so I threw back the comforter and looked at her.

"He's dating someone else," I said.

"No!" Hannah said, looking shocked. "But he was so into you!"

I shrugged, trying to disguise my pain by feigning indifference. "He never got in touch with me when I was in London. Then my best friend said she saw him out at the movies on a date."

"How did she know he was on a date? Did she ask him?"

"Of course not!"

"Well, why not?"

"Because that would have been weird. She's only met him once. She couldn't exactly march up to a guy she barely knows and demand to know if the girl he was with was his date," I said.

"She could have done it in a subtle way. Besides, that's not the point," Hannah said.

"It's not?"

"No. The point is that before you jump to, like, *conclusions* about this other girl, you should find out if it was even really a date," Hannah said. She crossed her legs and tossed her golden blond hair over her shoulder.

"First of all, he couldn't have been cheating on me, because we weren't officially going out. We only had one date. And it wasn't even a real date. I mean, he didn't ask me out or anything. And second, I told you, he hasn't gotten in touch with me since that night. I think it's pretty obvious that he doesn't like me," I said.

"But I *know* he likes you."

My heart gave a little skitter of hope. "Did he tell you that?"

"Well . . . no," Hannah conceded. My heart stopped skittering. "But I could totally tell from the way he was looking at you at the Snowflake," Hannah said. "And when I asked Dex to meet you at the dance, he was really into the idea."

"Yeah, well." I shrugged, wishing Hannah would go away and let me get back to sleep. This conversation was too depressing to stay awake for. "I guess we were both wrong."

"I still think you should find out what happened. I'll talk to him for you."

"No!" I practically shouted. Having my stepsister interrogate Dex about why he'd dumped me for the Laughing Girl was pretty much the one thing that could make this situation even more mortifying than it already was. "Please don't say anything to him, Hannah. *Please*."

"Okay, okay, I won't say anything," Hannah said, a bit too airily for my comfort.

"Promise," I insisted.

Hannah inhaled deeply and then sighed. "Fine. I promise I won't say anything to him. But for someone who's supposed to be a genius, you're being really dumb."

"Gee, thanks," I said.

"I mean it. If I saw Emmett out with another girl, I wouldn't automatically assume that they were on a date, or that he didn't like me anymore. I'd wait and make him explain," Hannah continued.

I just looked at her. Only someone as gorgeous as Hannah would have the self-confidence to assume that her boyfriend wasn't cheating on her if she caught him out with another girl. But, then, who would cheat on Hannah? Emmett certainly wouldn't. He adored her.

Emmett was a junior at Geek High, and absolutely beautiful. He had chiseled cheekbones, wide shoulders, and sun-bleached blond hair. I used to have a major crush on him, but then he and Hannah started dating. At first I'd been traumatized by their romance, but eventually, I got over it and Emmett. I had to admit, he and Hannah made an adorable couple. They both looked like they'd walked hand in hand off the pages of a J.Crew catalogue.

"So, guess what?" Hannah said, tiring of a conversation that didn't revolve around her. "Mom's throwing me a sweet-sixteen birthday party next weekend."

I had a sudden vision of all of Hannah's friends sitting around the living room, wearing birthday hats and looking bored, while Peyton tried to talk them into hitting a piñata with a broomstick.

"At first I was like, no way. Birthday parties are *soooooo* juvenile. But then Mom told me it's going to be at the Canyon," Hannah continued.

"The canyon?" I repeated, confused. We didn't have canyons in Florida. Was it possible Hannah was throwing her party somewhere out West? Like in California or Nevada?

"Yeah. That new restaurant downtown. Mom planned the whole thing while I was away as a welcome-home surprise for me," Hannah said. "We're going to have the restaurant all to ourselves, and there's going to be a band and everything."

I couldn't help but wonder if Peyton had planned the party in order to compete with Hannah's stepmom, Jackie, who always spoiled Hannah rotten whenever she visited. Then again, as evil as Peyton was, she did seem to genuinely love Hannah. Sure, she expressed that love by showering her daughter with material goods, but even so. There was real affection there. It's pretty much the only thing that's convinced me so far that Peyton isn't directly employed by the devil to wreak chaos and misery on the world. Unless the minions of Satan are capable of love . . . I wasn't sure about that. It might require some Internet research.

"Anyway, you have to come," Hannah continued.

"Really? You want me there?" I asked, surprised. Hannah and I had reached a détente in our previously hostile relationship. . . . But that didn't necessarily mean she was going to start being nice to me in front of her friends.

"Uh-huh. It'll be fun. And you should bring a date," Hannah continued.

"Can I bring my friend Charlie?" I asked.

Even though Hannah had met Charlie at the Snowflake Gala— which Hannah attended as Emmett's date—she looked at me blankly.

"Boy or girl?" she asked.

"Girl. You met her. Remember? My best friend? The artist?" I reminded her.

Hannah still looked blank.

"She has pink hair?" I tried again.

"Oh . . . right. I remember. No, you can't bring her," Hannah said.

"Why not?" I asked, stung.

"Because you have to bring a real date. A guy. Like Dex," Hannah said.

I sighed heavily. "I'm not bringing Dex," I said.

"So who are you going to bring?" she asked.

I could always bring Finn, I thought. But, then again, probably not the best idea. Finn is incapable of missing the opportunity to pull a prank. He'd end up doing something that he alone would find funny—like switching out the Diet Coke with the full-sugar, full-calorie Coke to screw with the girls who had eating disorders—but that would tick off almost everyone else. And I'd end up in trouble by association.

"I'm not. I'll just come on my own," I said.

Hannah pouted. "But you can't. Everyone's going to have a date," she said.

It was the story of my life: dateless among the dated. I wondered briefly if Henry would consider flying out for the event, before dismissing that idea as crazy.

"I'm going back to sleep," I said.

I shut my eyes. Hannah sighed heavily. I felt the bed shift as she stood, and then a moment later my door squeaked open and closed with a soft thud. I was finally, blessedly, alone.

# Chapter 10

Still on London time, I was up and dressed by five the next morning. As a result, I was the first one to arrive at geology class, a subject I was just starting that semester. While I waited for the rest of the class to arrive, I opened my new laptop and checked my e-mail.

To: mirandajbloom@gmail.com
From: hewent@britmail.net
Subject: Greetings from London
Hi Miranda,

Hope you had a nice flight back. Think of me here in cold, gloomy London while you're basking in the Florida sunshine.

**Top Three Reasons I want to visit America, in reverse order:**
3. Not having to wait for all of the top movies to be released.
2. Getting to hear people refer to their trousers as "pants."
1. To see you.

Yours,
Henry

I felt a little squirm of pleasure in my stomach. Henry wanted to see me! Maybe it hadn't just been a holiday fling after all! Okay, it was crazy to think that we could have a proper relationship living so far away from one another, and on different continents at that. But even so . . . he was thinking about me. And that was a very, very nice feeling. Especially after the sting of being so summarily rejected by Dex.

> To: hewent@britmail.net
> From: mirandajbloom@gmail.com
> Subject: Greetings from Florida
> Hi Henry,
>     It may be sunny here, but trust me, I'd much rather be walking through St. James's Park playing Top Three with you than sitting here in boring old Geek High.
>
> **Top Three Reasons You <u>Should</u> Visit America, in reverse order:**
> 3. Hamburgers and onion rings at the Orange Cove Grill.
> 2. Going to the beach (have you ever surfed?).
> 1. I'm here.

I read my e-mail over a few times before sending it, hoping it didn't sound too dorky, and even then I felt a nervous flutter in my stomach as I hit the send button. We were flirting via e-mail! I'd never done that before. Then again, I'd hardly ever flirted before, even in person.

"Hey, world traveler," a familiar voice said.

I looked up and saw Finn loping into class. He had his knapsack slung over one shoulder, his laptop tucked under his arm, and he was grinning at me. Finn was very tall, very thin, and very pale. He had shaggy brown hair that fell into his blue-gray eyes and a scar over his mouth from the surgery he had as a baby to correct a cleft lip.

"Hey!" I said. "I thought you were taking Environmental Science?"

"And miss out on Rocks for Jocks? Not a chance," Finn said, swinging into the chair next to mine.

"Rocks for Jocks?" I asked, amused. Geek High isn't exactly known for its jock population. In fact, the only sports teams the school fronted were golf and tennis. "You do know Mr. Douglass is teaching this class, don't you?"

Finn paled. "Douglass? I thought Keegan was teaching it," he said.

Mr. Douglass was the only teacher at Geek High that Finn feared. Well, maybe *feared* wasn't the right word. . . . I don't think Finn was actually afraid of Douglass. But the two of them had certainly never gotten along. Most of the Geek High faculty found Finn's easy humor and good-natured antics charming, but not Douglass. He was an old grouch who lectured in a monotone and was always happy to hand out detentions to anyone not paying attention in his class. And Douglass detentions were the worst. Usually, getting a detention at Geek High just involved sitting in the teacher's room after school, working quietly. And let's face it—in a high school full of geeks, the opportunity for some quiet study time wasn't that onerous of a punishment.

But Douglass made unruly students in his class spend their detention time cleaning out the cages of the snakes he kept as pets in his room. And Finn *hated* snakes.

"Nope. Keegan's teaching Enviro Sci," I said. "Didn't you notice what classroom we're in?"

"I wasn't really paying attention. I wonder if it's too late for me to transfer," Finn muttered. He glanced nervously back at the long reptiles slithering around in their glass aquariums.

"It is," Charlie said, walking in with a group of our classmates, and tossing her bag on the open desk next to me. "I checked, and the class is closed. Keegan's only taking five students this semester, because of all of the field trips they're going to be going on."

"Charlie!" I said, grinning at her. "Hey!"

The last time I'd seen her, Charlie's hair had been pink and spiky. In my absence, she'd colored it a rich, dark burgundy and had cut it in a short, choppy style that accentuated her large brown eyes and pale skin. She was wearing a Sex Pistols T-shirt with an artfully torn denim miniskirt and her clunky black Doc Martens. It was an outfit that would look ridiculous on me, but Charlie was able to carry it off with great panache.

"Hey, you," Charlie said. She leaned forward and gave me a quick hug. "When did you get back?"

"Last night. Sorry I didn't call. I was exhausted and went straight to bed," I said.

"It's okay. I wasn't home anyway. I was out with Mitch," Charlie said. Suddenly her expression became dreamy and unfocused. She hugged her arms around herself and smiled goofily. "We went for a walk on the beach as the sun was setting. It was so romantic."

Finn let out a disgusted snort. I turned to glance at him, but he was glowering down at his laptop. I could tell he wanted nothing to do with this conversation.

Charlie didn't seem to have heard Finn. "And then later we were looking up at the stars, and I was pointing out some of the constellations to Mitch, and do you know what he said?" she continued in a nauseatingly gushy voice.

Charlie paused, waiting for me to respond.

"Um. No. What?" I asked.

"He pointed up to this really bright star and said that it would be *our* star. Can you believe that? All couples have a song, but how many have their own star?" she exclaimed.

I stared at her for a long moment. "Who are you, and what have you done with my best friend?" I finally said.

Finn sniggered, and Charlie shot him a dirty look. For the first time since I'd set eyes on her, she looked like her old self. The Charlie I knew and loved was sarcastic and cynical and amazing. That Charlie, the old Charlie, would have been disgusted by the way this current Charlie was mooning over some guy's idiotic line. I mean, *come on*. A couples star? It was appallingly sappy.

"Sorry. I just thought you might be interested in what's new with me," Charlie snapped, not sounding at all sorry.

"I am," I said, attempting a conciliatory tone. "So things are going well with Mitch?"

Charlie beamed. "Amazing," she said, with a deep, self-satisfied sigh.

"How about everything else?" I asked.

"Like what?" Charlie asked.

"You know. Anything. Everything. How about your painting? Are you working on your new show?" I asked.

Charlie's an incredibly talented artist and has had several shows at local art galleries. The last one was so successful, a big-name gallery in Miami offered to host her next show there, and I knew Charlie had been really excited about it. She was just waiting until she had enough new paintings to exhibit. I knew it was only a matter of time before she was ready. Plus, she's bipolar, and when she's on one of her manic swings, it's not unusual for her to stay up all night painting.

"Oh. You know. Nothing much lately," Charlie said vaguely.

I stole another look at Finn. This time he looked back at me. I could tell from his raised eyebrows that he was thinking the same thing I was: It was one thing for Charlie to go all mushy over Mitch, but quite another thing altogether for her to stop painting. Art had always been her life.

"But what about your exhibit?" I asked, turning back to face Charlie. She hadn't noticed Finn and me exchanging dark looks.

"What exhibit?" she asked.

"The one down in Miami!" I exclaimed.

"Oh, that." Charlie shrugged dismissively. "We didn't set a date or anything. The guy at the gallery just said to contact him when I was ready. So it's not like there's a rush."

"But I thought you were really excited about the show," I said.

"I was. I mean, I am. Wait . . . why are you so obsessed with this?" Charlie asked.

"I'm not. I just . . . I just don't want you to miss out on such a great opportunity," I explained.

"Well, don't worry about it," Charlie said. She glanced at the clock. "I'm going to see if Mitch is online."

She opened up her laptop, clicked on her instant-messaging program, and a minute later was tip-tapping away, the goofy smile back on her face.

"Hey, Miranda," Sanjiv said, appearing in front of my desk. Sanjiv Gupta was a gangly, serious boy who wore thick glasses and had a prominent Adam's apple. He was the captain of the Mu Alpha Theta math competition team, and he took his position very seriously. But, then, Sanjiv took everything seriously. I don't think he actually possessed a sense of humor.

"Hi, Sanjiv. How was your holiday?" I asked.

"Fine," he said. "Don't forget we have our first team practice tomorrow."

"Oh, right. Okay," I said.

Once Sanjiv had returned to his seat, Finn said, "You're not going to stay on the MATh team, are you?"

I shrugged. "Yeah. I sort of have to."

Mr. Hughes, the headmaster of Geek High, had blackmailed me into rejoining the MATh team the previous semester. In return, he'd let me make the necessary changes to turn the Snowflake Gala into a fun dance (up until this year, it had been a horribly dull dinner featuring a dry academic lecturer). Which sounds like a fair bargain . . . except for the part where I hadn't wanted to plan the stupid Snowflake in the first place, and did so only under duress from the headmaster. To make matters even worse, being on the MATh team had meant I couldn't join the staff of the *Ampersand*, Geek High's award-winning literary journal. For a brief time, I'd thought

I might be able to juggle both extracurricular activities, but then Sanjiv had scheduled a practice at the same time that a mandatory informational meeting for the *Ampersand* was being held, and so I had to miss the *Ampersand* meeting. . . . Which meant that I wasn't able to join the journal this year. It was hugely disappointing.

"But the Snowflake is over," Finn said. "Hughes can't make you stay on the team now."

I'd be lying if I said I wasn't tempted to quit. I may be gifted in math, but it wasn't something I enjoyed. Not like the other members of the MATh team, anyway. They actually thought it was fun to spend their afternoons sitting around working on math drills. But Sanjiv and the rest of my MATh teammates would be royally ticked off at me if I quit now. They were counting on me.

"I have to," I said, yawning. "I said I would."

Finn shrugged. "If you say so," he said, unconvinced. Finn never does anything that he doesn't want to do. Except go to school, and even then, he treats it all like it's one big laugh.

Which reminded me—I hadn't checked out Finn's blog, geekhigh.com, in a while. He wrote the blog anonymously, updating his readership on all of the school gossip. I clicked over to the Web site, but saw that it hadn't been updated since the last time I'd checked it while I was in London. Instead there was a note at the top of the Web page that read: ON HIATUS.

"On hiatus?" I read aloud, and raised my eyebrows at Finn.

He shrugged moodily. "I haven't felt much like blogging lately," he said. I could have sworn I saw him cast a hurt glance at Charlie, who was still too immersed in her IM conversation with Mitch to notice.

Just then, Mr. Douglass came in. He was, as usual, wearing a three-piece suit. He was the only teacher at Geek High who wore a suit to work—the rest of the male teachers wore chinos and polo shirts—but it was hard to imagine stiff, fussy old Mr. Douglass dressed casually. His hair and mustache were white, and his fleshy face and hands were covered with liver spots. He looked up at the class, jowls quivering. The few students still standing quickly took their seats.

"Quiet down, quiet down," Mr. Douglass said grumpily. "Or I'll start taking down names for cage-cleaning duty."

Finn slouched down in his seat, looking disgusted.

"This semester we're covering the subject of geology. This is not, as some students have derisively called it"—Mr. Douglass's eyes raked over the class, and he had a very sour expression on his wrinkled face—" 'Rocks for Jocks.' So if you're here thinking that this course will earn you an easy A, you can just leave now."

Mr. Douglass paused, as though waiting for one of his students to stand up and march out of the room. I glanced over at Finn again, thinking that if anyone was going to leave, it would be him. But Finn didn't move. Instead, he had his fingers primed on the keyboard of his laptop, ready to take notes. Which was really rather shocking for Finn, considering he normally spent class time playing around on the Internet or working on one of the computer games he was developing.

*He must be even more afraid of snakes than I thought,* I decided.

Mr. Douglass looked a bit disappointed that we'd all stayed rooted in our seats. He cleared his throat and continued. "Geology is, of course, the study of the solid matter of the earth, and thus is considered part of the earth sciences." He coughed. "Eh-eh-eh." It was a disgusting, wet, phlegmy sound. "Do any of you know how old the planet Earth is?"

A half-dozen hands immediately shot up into the air. The propeller-hand phenomenon was common at Geek High. In a school full of geniuses, everyone was a know-it-all. Well. Everyone but me. I had no idea how old the Earth was. I glanced at Charlie. She didn't have her hand up, either, and from the speed with which she was typing—as well as the dreamy, drippy expression on her face—I got the distinct feeling she was still instant messaging with Mitch.

*If Douglass catches her doing that, she'll get stuck cleaning up snake droppings for sure,* I thought.

"Yes, Mr. Frost," Mr. Douglass said.

"The earth is four-point-six billion years old. The outermost shell of the earth is called the lithosphere, which is fragmented into tectonic plates," Christopher Frost began, speaking in the flat monotone he always used. Christopher had sandy-colored hair and rarely blinked behind his thick glasses. I was familiar enough with Christopher's idiosyncrasies to know that he would keep talking until he was stopped. If Mr. Douglass didn't cut him off, Christopher would cover the entire syllabus.

Douglass seemed to have figured this out. "That's enough," he said curtly.

"The tectonic plates move independently of each other. . . ." Christopher continued, blissfully unaware.

"I said, *that's enough.* Do you not understand what those words mean, Mr. Frost? Shall I look them up in the dictionary for you?" Mr. Douglass asked, his voice rising and his face coloring.

Christopher fell silent and blinked a few times. I frowned. Sure, Christopher could be annoying, there was no doubt about that. But that was just what he was like; he didn't know any better.

"Jerk," Finn muttered under his breath.

"Now. Where were we?" Mr. Douglass asked. "Eh-eh-eh." He plucked a cotton handkerchief out of his pocket and hocked up into it. "Right. Tectonic plates."

*Revolting,* I thought, with a shudder. It was going to be a long semester.

•

"Doesn't Douglass know that Christopher is autistic?" Finn asked later that day, after school.

"Is he?" I asked.

Finn stared at me. "Did you seriously not know that?"

"No. I just thought he lacked some social graces. That's not so unusual," I said, shrugging. "There are lots of kids at Geek High who don't really fit in anywhere else."

It was true. In fact, when I was a kid and my parents first became aware of my ability to calculate sums in my head, they'd had me tested to see if I was on the autistic spectrum. I think it was because of the movie *Rain Man*, which featured a severely autistic man, played by Dustin Hoffman, who was also able to solve complex math problems in his head. Insert an eye roll here, considering that (a) it wasn't the most flattering comparison for them to make, and (b) I didn't have any of the other symptoms that Dustin Hoffman's character had. I was a pretty normal kid in all, except for the calculator that came hard-wired to my brain.

"Seriously, I'm just amazed that they're not lined up outside the school ready to study us," Finn said darkly.

"Who?"

"You know. Doctors. Psychiatrists. Sociologists." Finn shrugged. "You have to admit, the Geek High student body would make an interesting case study."

Finn, Charlie, and I were at Grounded, a coffee shop and our favorite after-school hangout. Actually, Finn and I were there together, sitting at one of the small round tables and drinking lattes. Charlie had come with us, but she was perched on one of the tall stools lined up near the counter, sipping an iced coffee through a straw and giggling at something Mitch said.

Mitch had a square face, large vacant eyes, and a snub nose. He gelled his dark hair up into spikes that stood straight up on top of his head, making him look like a porcupine. Mitch worked at the coffee shop, and so he was standing behind the counter and wearing a navy blue apron over a maroon GROUNDED T-shirt. But there weren't any other customers in the shop, so he was able to stare at

Charlie with a sappy, lovestruck expression that was the mirror of the one Charlie wore.

Finn followed my gaze.

"I know. They're revolting," he said.

"Well. She seems happy," I said loyally, not wanting to run Charlie down behind her back. Unfortunately, at that very moment, the two lovebirds began to kiss noisily.

Finn snorted. "Happy? She seems possessed," he said. "And in the worst way possible."

"I'm sure it's just a stage. Once they've been going out for a while . . ." My voice trailed off. I had no idea what they'd be like after they'd been going out for a while. Maybe this was the sort of affliction that got worse over time. Maybe in a few weeks, they'd be surgically attached at the lips.

A curly-haired woman wearing workout clothes walked into the coffee shop, sending the bell on the front door jingling. She strode up to the counter and waited patiently to place her order. A minute passed. And then another. And another. The whole time, Mitch and Charlie were so busy kissing, they hadn't noticed she was standing there.

"Excuse me," the woman said.

Still no response from the kissing couple. The woman looked over at Finn and me.

"I just want a cup of coffee," she said helplessly. "Is there anyone else working here?"

Finn sighed. "Hold on," he said. He stood and walked around the counter, passing by the oblivious Mitch, and poured a cup of coffee for the woman from the large thermos by the cash register. She started to hand him money, but Finn waved her off.

"This one is on the house," he said.

"Thanks," the woman said, smiling at him. "I'm glad someone's doing their job around here."

When she left, the door jingling closed behind her, Mitch and

Charlie finally broke apart. Mitch looked around, his brow wrinkling in confusion when he saw Finn behind the counter.

"What are you doing? Did I just hear the door?" Mitch asked.

"Nope. You didn't hear a thing," Finn said, now helping himself to coffee before coming back around the counter and over to our table. He held up his paper cup in a mock toast to me, and said, "M, I'm out of here."

"What . . . now?" I asked. I opened my eyes wide and tilted my head meaningfully at Charlie and Mitch, who had gone back to smooching.

I knew Finn understood that I didn't want to be left alone with the couple. But he just shrugged, winked at me, shot one last disgusted look at Charlie, and then headed out of the coffee shop.

Mitch looked up again as the bell jingled on the closing door. His mouth was red and chapped, and his eyes looked a little dazed. "Did someone just leave?" he asked. Charlie giggled and leaned in for another kiss.

I sighed, slumped back in my chair, and tried to avert my eyes.

# Chapter 11

Modern Literature class was a yearlong course, so we were continuing where we'd left off before Christmas. On our first day back, Mrs. Gordon—my favorite teacher—had assigned us *Tender Is the Night* by F. Scott Fitzgerald. I'd started reading it, and been immediately enchanted with the idea of moving to the French Riviera and living the life of the ultraglamorous American expatriate. Minus the insanity and alcoholism, of course.

As usual, the desks in Mrs. Gordon's small, messy classroom were set up in a circle. Posters from Shakespeare plays were tacked to the wall, and a tall narrow bookshelf behind Mrs. Gordon's desk was crammed full of books. Padma Paswan, wearing an inadvisable amount of turquoise eye shadow, was already there, deep in conversation with horsey-faced Tabitha Stone, when Finn, Charlie, and I walked in to class. Tate Metcalf, Christopher Frost, and Sanjiv were also in their seats. Tate brightened when he saw Finn.

"Dude, I played *Mutant Monkeys* last night. You were right, it's a great game," Tate enthused. Tate had skin the color of dark coffee, a wild frizz of hair, and loved video games almost as much as Finn did.

"*Mutant Monkeys?* That's not one of yours, is it?" I asked Finn.

"No, it's an online RPG," Finn said. As though I had any idea what an RPG was. "Tate, did you get as far as Death Wish Island?"

Finn sat down in the desk next to Tate's so that they could discuss the mutant monkey game. Charlie and I took the two empty desks next to Finn.

"Do you want to go to Grounded after school?" Charlie asked.

"I can't. I have Mu Alpha Theta practice. Sorry," I said, although I wasn't at all sorry. The last thing I wanted to do was spend yet another afternoon sitting by myself, feeling increasingly uncomfortable while Charlie canoodled with her boyfriend. Besides, she only wanted me there so she'd have someone to talk to if Grounded got busy and Mitch had to work. I didn't like being her backup plan.

"That's too bad. You and I haven't had a chance to catch up since you've gotten back," Charlie continued.

I looked at her. *Is she serious?* I wondered.

"What?" Charlie asked, wrinkling her forehead in confusion.

"Um . . . I've been around," I said.

"I know. It just feels like we haven't really had a chance to talk," Charlie continued.

I decided to just let it go. After all, what was the point? Finn muttered mutinously every time Charlie brought up Mitch's name—in other words, every time the three of us were together—and Charlie just ignored him. She didn't seem to care that her two best friends weren't at all thrilled by how drastically she'd changed in such a short period of time. Or maybe she was so caught up in her new relationship, she hadn't noticed.

*This is temporary,* I told myself. *The newness of it will wear off, and eventually she'll go back to being the same old Charlie. And I've never had a boyfriend. Maybe this is just what it's like.*

So instead, I just said, "Yeah, I know. It does feel like that."

Felicity Glen and Morgan Simpson came in, their heads bent

together, as they whispered intently about something. Felicity was thin with green eyes, petite features, full, pouty lips, and dark brown hair that fell in sleek waves around her pretty face. Morgan, on the other hand, was a short, squat girl with piggish features and an unflattering bob of limp dirty-blond hair.

I watched them warily. Felicity and I had never gotten along—she'd pretty much hated me from the moment she set eyes on me on my first day at Geek Middle—and she rarely passed up the opportunity to say something nasty to me. My nickname for her was the Felimonster, and it was well deserved. But last semester, she and I had been on the Snowflake Gala committee together, along with Morgan, Finn, and Charlie. We'd all pulled together to make the dance a success. I'd wondered if this shared experience would permanently defrost relations between us. Felicity glanced over at me. There was a familiar malicious gleam in her moss-green eyes.

I braced myself. Apparently, the hostilities were back on.

"Miranda," she said, tossing back her shiny hair. "I forgot to ask you yesterday—how was your trip to London?"

"It was fine," I said warily.

"Real-ly," Felicity said, drawing out the two syllables. "Because I heard that your boyfriend dumped you, like, five minutes after you left."

I instantly flushed, my cheeks going hot with embarrassment. How had Felicity found out about Dex? The only person at Geek High who knew he'd blown me off was . . .

I glanced at Charlie. Surely, she hadn't told Felicity. . . . Had she? I wouldn't even have had to wonder about the old Charlie, but with this new Charlie, I wasn't so sure.

"I have no idea what you're talking about," I said to Felicity, trying to keep my voice cool and calm and above her petty nastiness.

"You know. That guy you were at the Snowflake with. I thought he was your boyfriend," she continued with an evil grin. "No? My mistake. I guess it was just a pity date for him."

Morgan giggled in sycophantic glee. "A pity date," she repeated rapturously.

As angry as I was, this remark cut way, way too close to the truth. Furious, I opened my mouth, ready to blast Felicity, but before I could say anything, Mrs. Gordon came in calling out, "Good morning, class. I hope everyone read the first two chapters of *Tender Is the Night* and came prepared to discuss them. I'd like to begin with some of the themes that Fitzgerald focused on in these early chapters."

Felicity and Morgan, still smirking, took their seats. Charlie whispered, "Ignore her. She's such a troll."

Tabitha Stone immediately raised her hand. I gave a mental eye roll. Tabitha was the resident literary wunderkind at Geek High, and had been ever since her book of poetry had been published the previous year. But there was something about Tabitha that had always rubbed me the wrong way. Maybe it was that she always took herself way too seriously.

Mrs. Gordon beamed at her. "Yes, Tabitha," she said.

Tabitha cleared her throat importantly. "Fitzgerald's main theme is youth. It's especially noticeable in his descriptions of Rosemary. For example, he writes that 'the dew was still on her.' And he describes her cheeks as being flushed like a child's after a bath. Not to mention that the motion picture she starred in was called *Daddy's Girl.*"

"Excellent," Mrs. Gordon said. She turned to the white dry-erase board, uncapped a black magic marker, and wrote down the word YOUTH. "Anyone else?"

I stared down at my laptop, trying to keep my face stony as I began taking notes. I don't know what bothered me more—Felicity having discovered that Dex had unceremoniously dumped me before we even really started dating, a piece of knowledge she would doubtless torment me with into the indefinite future.... Or the possibility that Charlie was the one who had told Felicity about it.

I glanced at Charlie, thinking I'd send her a quick IM to ask her what she'd said to Felicity. But then I noticed that Charlie was already IM'ing someone. And from the goofy, love-dazed expression on her face, it didn't take a genius to figure out just who that was.

•

The period seemed to last forever. When the bell finally rang, Mrs. Gordon said, "All right, everyone, your homework assignment is to read the next two chapters of *Tender Is the Night*. Miranda, stay after class for a moment, please."

I packed up my bag, and as the rest of the class filed out of the room, I heard Felicity say "pity date" to Morgan, who snickered. Once everyone had left, I walked up to Mrs. Gordon's desk. She had her back to me as she wiped down the blackboard.

"You wanted to talk to me, Mrs. Gordon?" I said.

She turned around and smiled. She was short and plump, with intelligent eyes and a ready smile. As usual, she looked a bit unkempt. Today, her hair was falling out of a loose bun, and there was a stain on the front of her cardigan.

"Yes, Miranda. I forgot to give this to you yesterday." She handed me two pieces of paper, stapled together. The top was a letter, congratulating me on being chosen as a finalist in the Alfred Q. Winston Creative Writing Contest, and included a brief history of the contest, naming some of the past winners who'd gone on to become famous writers. It was an impressive list, and as I read it, my stomach felt wriggly with nerves.

I was pretty sure I wanted to be a writer, but I seriously doubted if I had the talent. Even if I didn't particularly enjoy math, I figured it was my destiny. Why would I have this extraordinary gift if I wasn't meant to use it? But then Mrs. Gordon had talked me into submitting one of my short stories to the Winston Creative Writing

Contest. . . . And somehow, I'd actually made the finals. It was the first real sign I'd had that maybe I could be—would be—a writer.

"Great, thanks," I said.

"Make sure you fill out that second sheet and send it in to the address listed there," Mrs. Gordon said. "It's to notify the Winston people that you're planning to attend the finals."

"I will."

"Congratulations again," Mrs. Gordon said, smiling brightly at me.

"Thanks!" I returned her smile as I slung my knapsack up on my shoulder and left the classroom. Outside, Finn and Charlie were waiting for me to walk to Latin with them. From the dreamy look on Charlie's face, and the pained expression on Finn's, I instantly knew what—or, rather, *who*—they were discussing.

"You should really talk to Mitch. The two of you have a lot in common," Charlie was saying as I joined them.

Finn looked like he'd smelled something particularly nasty. "I truly doubt that," he said.

"No, you do. Mitch is into computer games, too," Charlie said.

"What sort of games?" Finn asked suspiciously.

I should have warned Charlie then not to say whatever it was she was about to say. Finn had strong views on gaming. More precisely, he had strong views on which computer games were worthwhile and which were garbage, and the sort of losers—his word, not mine—who wasted their time playing the latter. I had a feeling that Mitch would not pass this test.

"He likes that game where you create houses and jobs and things for people," Charlie said vaguely. "I can't remember the name."

"*Sims?*" Finn asked, his voice dripping with disdain. "He plays *Sims?*"

"I think that's the one," Charlie said, nodding.

"Only middle-aged women play *Sims*," Finn said acidly. "The kind who have, like, five cats whom they've named after the T. S. Eliot poems. Only worse, they don't even know the names were originally from a poem, since they got them from the musical *Cats*. *Those* are the sort of people who play *Sims*."

The smile slid off Charlie's face as though Finn had slapped her. She even took a step back from him.

"That's a little judgmental," she said coldly. "Especially coming from a guy who spends every spare moment shut up in his room playing on his computer. You're the walking, breathing stereotype of a nerd. I think that's a whole hell of a lot more pathetic than having a few cats."

Finn's face—already pale to begin with—went white with rage. His scar from the cleft-lip surgery he'd had as an infant stood out prominently against his blanched skin. "You really want to know what's pathetic? Acting like a fool over your idiotic boyfriend." Finn's voice rose into a mocking falsetto. "Oh, *Mitchy*, you're so *big* and *strong* and you brew coffee so well. Kiss, kiss, giggle, giggle."

I glanced around nervously. Finn's and Charlie's raised voices were starting to attract curious glances from students passing by. Padma Paswan, who had been standing nearby, getting a book out of her locker, was staring at them, her mouth slightly open.

"Jealous much?" Charlie spat back. Her entire body was rigid with fury, and her hands were balled into fists at her sides.

"You think I'm jealous of that idiot?"

"Mitch is not an idiot!"

"In my game *Nuclear Knights*, there was a troll who was so stupid that if you talked to him long enough, he'd hit himself over the head with his club and knock himself out. That's how dumb *Mitchy* is," Finn sneered. He slung his knapsack onto his shoulder. "I am so out of here."

With that, Finn turned on his heel and stalked off down the hall.

"Jerk!" Charlie called after him.

I had been just standing there, stunned into silence during this exchange. The last thing I wanted to do was to get in the middle of their fight. I agreed with Finn—the way Charlie behaved around Mitch was irritating—but I didn't think yelling at her in the middle of the school corridor was the best way to broach the subject.

"I can't believe him," Charlie seethed, as we turned to walk toward our Latin classroom. "I had no idea he was such a snob!"

"Snob?" I repeated, surprised. Finn may be many things—devious, crafty, lacking a moral center—but he wasn't at all snobbish.

"Yes! He's a snob! You heard him. The only reason he doesn't like Mitch is because he thinks Mitch isn't as smart as he is. Which is just ridiculous," Charlie snapped.

I stayed quiet. I didn't know Mitch very well, and had no idea how smart he was. But Finn was insanely smart, probably in the top one-tenth of one percentile of all people who had ever lived. So the off chance that Mitch was as smart as Finn wasn't great. But that wasn't really the point, anyway. I'd long harbored the suspicion that Finn and Charlie had feelings for one another. . . . Feelings that went deeper than just friendship. I doubted if either of them would ever admit it—even to themselves—and especially not now that Charlie was dating Mitch. I wondered if that was what was really at the heart of this argument.

Luckily, Charlie was so incensed at Finn, she didn't notice my silence.

"And why does it matter what computer games Mitch plays, anyway?" she continued angrily.

I shrugged. "Finn's always had strong feelings on gaming," I said. "You know that."

"Yeah, but to decide he doesn't like someone just because of the games they play. That's ridiculous. It's prejudiced," she said.

"I don't know," I said doubtfully. "Doesn't everyone do that? Judge people based on what they like and don't like, I mean?"

"I don't," Charlie snapped.

"So you'd be friends with someone who had posters of kittens or Anne Geddes babies up in their room?" I teased her.

Charlie hated schmaltzy posters with a purple passion. Last year, she'd waged a war against the Geek High librarian, Mrs. Krandall, for hanging a sickly sweet poster featuring a pair of puppies reading a book together. Mrs. Krandall finally just took the poster down, worn out by Charlie's tireless arguments that "bad art is visual pollution!"

"Yes, I would. If they were kind and worthwhile, I would be their friend no matter what sort of art they liked," Charlie said loftily.

I snorted my disbelief. Charlie grinned, despite herself.

"Okay, so maybe I would judge them on their posters. But that's different. Art is an expression of a person's soul. Video games are just a way to pass the time. It's like with TV shows . . . sometimes you'll watch a bad one just for the sheer entertainment value of it," Charlie argued.

"Maybe for you," I said, shrugging. "But for Finn, computer games are his life. That is how he expresses his soul."

"And that's supposed to be a good thing?" Charlie asked darkly.

"It is what it is. Finn is who he is," I said.

"Finn is an idiot," Charlie said. "Come on, we're going to be late for Latin."

•

Charlie and Finn's fight had made me temporarily forget Felicity's taunts about my breakup with Dex. I didn't remember to bring it up with Charlie until lunch. Normally, she, Finn, and I ate lunch together in the school dining room, sitting at our favorite table in the corner. At Geek High, lunch isn't served in the normal cafeteria style. Instead, platters of sandwiches, fruit, and

cookies are put out on each table, and the students help themselves, family style.

But at lunch Finn was nowhere to be seen. I looked around for
him, hoping he hadn't cut school—Finn's fondness for practical
jokes kept him perilously close to being expelled, and so he really
couldn't risk skipping—but Charlie seemed unconcerned. In any
event, Finn's absence gave me a chance to finally question Charlie
about whether she'd said anything to Felicity about the abrupt end
of my romance with Dex.

"Have you talked to Felicity lately?" I asked casually as I selected a chicken salad sandwich from the platter.

"Ugh. Not if I can help it," Charlie said, grabbing a ham and
cheese, along with a handful of chips. "Why?"

"Because of what she said in class. About Dex, well, dump-
ing me," I said, trying to ignore the stab of pain I felt whenever I
thought about Dex.

"I wouldn't talk about that with her," Charlie said, frowning at
me. Then suddenly her face lit with understanding. "She was at the
movies that night! The night I saw Dex out with, well, you know."

"Laughing Girl," I said darkly.

"Right. Anyway, Felicity was there, too, with Morgan. I saw
them in the popcorn line. They were going to see whatever the
chick flick of the week was. She must have seen Dex there on his
date," Charlie said.

I felt guilty for doubting Charlie, and was glad that I'd been
wrong. The image of Dex out with his new girlfriend was depressing enough. I wondered if he kissed her the same way he kissed
me—resting one hand on her cheek, the other cupping the back of
her neck, his warm lips somehow feeling both soft and hard as they
pressed against hers. . . .

*No,* I thought, giving myself a mental shake. *This is not a good
thought path to wander down.*

Because not only had Dex failed to e-mail me while I was

in London, he also hadn't called me in the two days since I'd gotten home. So even if there was some teeny-tiny chance that it had all been some huge mistake—like, maybe he'd lost my e-mail address, or maybe Laughing Girl had been the daughter of one of his mother's friends, and she'd forced him to take her out—well, now there was no excuse. The phone number at the beach house was listed, and he went to school with my stepsister, who could have given him my cell phone number. So there was absolutely no reason why he couldn't have gotten a hold of me. If he'd wanted to.

Which clearly meant he didn't.

"Pass me the cookies," Charlie said, interrupting my negative thought bog. As I handed her the plate of peanut butter cookies, her face took on the dreamy expression I'd already started to dread. "Did I tell you what Mitch said about my hair yesterday?"

"Yeah, I think you did," I said. She hadn't, but I didn't want to encourage her.

But Charlie continued as if I hadn't spoken. "He said that it smelled like roses. Can you believe that?"

"Sure," I said, shrugging.

"Do you think it does?"

"I've never really noticed," I said.

Charlie leaned forward, pointing the top of her head at me. "Smell it," she insisted.

"I'm not going to smell your hair," I said. "I'm *eating*."

"Anyway," Charlie said, leaning back in her seat. "Mitch also told me that he'd always fantasized about dating a redhead."

Unfortunately, this just reminded me yet again of Dex, who had red hair with copper highlights that shimmered when he was standing out in the sun. I remembered how he'd looked when I saw him a few months ago on the beach, dressed in the wet suit he wore while parasurfing, looking so beautiful. . . .

*Go away,* I told the vision, and tried to think of something else.

*London. Henry. Yes. Think of Henry, the guy who likes me enough to actually e-mail me.*

"But you're not a redhead," I said. Charlie's burgundy-colored hair had come straight from the bottle. In fact, she'd been coloring her hair for so long, I no longer remembered what her original color was. "What color is your hair? Really, I mean. Aren't you a blond naturally?"

Charlie scowled at me. "That's not the point, Miranda," she said huffily. "The point is, I'm Mitch's fantasy girl." Cue the annoying dreamy look again. "Isn't that just amazing? I never thought I'd ever be someone's fantasy girl."

As irritating as this new lovestruck Charlie was, I knew what she meant. She and I had both gone through life as brains, the sort of oddballs who didn't fit in with normal kids. We were used to it, used to being seen as geeks. I was the math geek; Charlie was the art geek. It was an image that was hard to shake. So the idea of being seen as something other than as a geek girl—as the pretty girl, the fantasy girl—that was heady stuff.

"I was thinking of dyeing it more of a true red," Charlie continued. "You know, like a natural redhead red."

"What . . . you mean, because Mitch wants you to?" I asked.

"No! I mean, he didn't ask me to. But if he really likes redheads, maybe I should become a redhead," Charlie said, her voice getting a defensive edge to it.

"Wow," I said flatly.

"What?"

"I just never thought you were the type to change your appearance for a guy," I said.

"I don't know what you're talking about. I dye my hair all the time," Charlie said, and now she was starting to sound angry.

I stared at her. She may color her hair all the time, but when she did, she dyed it pink or purple or green. She never colored it a shade that occurs in nature.

But still. I didn't want to argue with Charlie. It was bad enough that she and Finn were fighting. So I just shrugged and said, "I guess." I tried to steer the conversation to safer ground, like the U.S. policy on the Mideast, or whether people who didn't recycle their newspapers should face criminal sanctions.

# Chapter 12

After my last class of the day—Art of the Renaissance—I walked down to Mr. Gordon's room, where all of our Mu Alpha Theta practices were held.

The Geek High Mu Alpha Theta team participated in math competitions all around the state. Our school's team would compete against another school's team, each player taking a turn to answer a series of increasingly complex math problems. I'd been on the Geek High MATh team for three straight years, and in that time we'd never lost a competition. . . . However, we'd also never won a state championship.

The problem was that you had to have a team of five to compete, so if you were even one team member short, you had to forfeit the competition. Whenever Geek High had fielded a team of five, we won. But for the past three years, circumstances had conspired against the Geek High team to keep us out of the state finals.

Three years ago, Duncan Murray, team captain at the time, had to have an emergency appendectomy the night before the championship. Two years ago, Grace Dillonhoffer had her wisdom teeth out. She'd actually had the extraction scheduled for two weeks before finals, assuming she'd recover in time, but there was some sort of complication that resulted in her jaw clamping shut so she couldn't speak and had to drink milkshakes out of a straw. Then last year Barry Sonnegard had an interview at MIT that conflicted with state finals, and he couldn't reschedule.

This history was weighing heavily on my teammates.... Although not on me. I didn't care if we made state finals or not. In fact, I didn't care if we won any of our competitions. I hadn't wanted to be on the MATh team in the first place, and now I was just biding my time until the season was over.

I was the first one to arrive at Mr. Gordon's room for practice. Only Mr. Gordon himself was there, wiping the dry-erase board clean with a paper towel. Mr. Gordon was our MATh coach, and, along with his wife—my Mod Lit teacher, Mrs. Gordon—he was one of my favorite teachers at Geek High. Mr. Gordon was very tall and very thin, and his head was bald on top with a Friar Tuck fringe around his ears. He was, as usual, wearing his round tortoiseshell glasses, and one of his many argyle sweater vests.

"Hi, Mr. Gordon," I said. I plunked my book bag down on a desk, and sat.

Mr. Gordon turned and smiled when he saw me. "Hello, Miranda. Ready to get cracking on some algebra problems?"

"Sure," I said without enthusiasm. Algebra—that meant it would be an easy day. I could solve algebraic equations in my sleep. Which wasn't a good thing. If I was going to be stuck solving math problems all afternoon, what I really needed were the sort of complicated equations that would take my mind off of Dex, and the fight Charlie and Finn were having.

Sanjiv came in then, accompanied by Kyle Carpenter, who was shaped like a block and had such a low hairline that he looked like Teen Wolf. Leila Chang—who had a round, pretty face and who wore funky cat's-eye glasses—came in a moment later, and just behind her was Nicholas Pruitt, the fading remains of his chicken pox scars still visible on his thin, pale face. Nicholas looked at me, grinned, blushed, looked down at his feet, and then hopefully back up at me.

*Uh-oh*, I thought.

With everything that had happened since the Snowflake, I hadn't thought about Nicholas in weeks, or about our cancelled Snowflake date, or about his unrequited crush on me, except to hope that the time apart would cause his feelings for me to fade.

Clearly, that hadn't happened.

"Hi, Miranda," Nicholas said, still blushing furiously. He hurried over and quickly sat down at the desk next to mine, before Leila could drop her bag there, as she'd just been about to do.

Leila stopped, bag still in hand, and looked confusedly down at the suddenly occupied desk.

"O-kay," Leila said, sounding amused. She looked from Nicholas to me and smiled. "I guess I'll just sit here." She plopped down in the desk behind Nicholas's.

"How was your trip, Miranda?" Nicholas asked eagerly. He was sitting on the edge of his chair, and his entire body was leaning toward me.

"Um, it was fine, thanks," I said, feeling a bit disconcerted.

"I got you something," Nicholas said. He dug into his knapsack and pulled out a small package wrapped in Christmas paper. He handed it to me. "It's a belated Christmas gift."

"You got me a Christmas present?" I asked faintly, the heat rising on my cheeks. Although I didn't dare look back at her, I could almost feel Leila's eyes on us. I really hoped she didn't think there was anything going on between Nicholas and me, and I made a mental note to set her straight after the practice ended.

I stared down at the red-wrapped present. I didn't want to accept it. In fact, what I wanted to do was to thrust the package back in Nicholas's hands and tell him in no uncertain terms that I didn't have any romantic interest in him whatsoever. But that seemed mean, and I didn't want to be unkind. Nicholas didn't deserve that.

"Yes! Unless . . . wait. Are you Jewish? Because if so, then it's a

Hanukkah gift," Nicholas said quickly. His forehead wrinkled with concern that he had offended me.

"I celebrate Christmas," I said. I drew in a deep breath before I continued. "But, Nicholas . . . I can't accept this."

Nicholas's face fell, as I handed him back the present. "Why not?" he asked.

"B-because . . ." I began, stammering, and then stopped. I could still feel the weight of Leila's curious gaze on us, as well as the added pressure of Nicholas's disappointment.

*Gah.* I should have seen this coming, and wished desperately that I'd thought through what I should say to him. It would be mean to tell Nicholas the truth: that I would never be able to return the feelings he had for me. So instead I tried to think up a convincing lie, one that would spare his feelings while making it perfectly clear that I wasn't ever going to be his girlfriend.

There was only one solution I could think of—I'd have to tell him I had a boyfriend. The only problem was that it was a bald-faced lie. I didn't have a boyfriend. Nor was there any chance I'd get one any time soon. And if I told him I was dating someone, and it became really obvious I wasn't, well, that would hurt Nicholas's feelings, too. . . . Maybe even more so than if I told him straight out that I didn't like him.

Unless . . . unless there was a reason why my fictitious boyfriend was never around. Inspiration struck as I suddenly remembered Henry's laughing blue eyes and his cheeks flushed pink from the cold.

"Because I have a boyfriend. I, um, started seeing someone while I was in London," I said quickly.

Yes, it was a lie. But it wasn't a total lie. I mean, Henry did exist. And there had been something between us. Sure, we weren't *technically* going out . . . but so what? It's not like Nicholas would ever find that out.

Although Nicholas's disappointment was still evident, he straightened up a bit in his chair.

"You did?" he asked. "Who?"

"His name is Henry. He's the son of my mom's UK editor," I said.

"Oh," Nicholas said. "Oh, well . . . I understand."

He was still absorbing this news, but at least he seemed to be taking it pretty well. I thought it must be easier to be rejected in favor of someone, rather than rejected just because you're you. . . . But then I thought of Laughing Girl, and wasn't so sure.

"You have a boyfriend in London, Miranda?" Leila asked, confirming my suspicion that she was eavesdropping on our conversation.

"Um . . . yeah," I said.

Leila frowned. "So, what? You're going to date him long-distance?"

"Mm-hmm," I said, nodding. I realized I was going to have to invent some details to make this more believable. I decided to keep my lie as truthful as possible. "He's going to try to come visit me here. And I might spend the summer in London."

"Wow," Leila said. "So what happened to that guy you were at the Snowflake with?"

*Argh.* Why couldn't Leila mind her own business? I didn't want to talk about Dex right now! Especially not with Nicholas hanging on every word.

"You went to the Snowflake with someone else?" Nicholas asked, looking hurt.

"No, not really. After you canceled, my stepsister arranged for one of her friends to meet me there," I explained.

"Really? I thought you and that guy seemed really close. Really, really close." Leila smirked. "And I could have sworn you were going out with him. Finn said something about . . ."

I had to stop this before she went any further. My face was already flaming red.

"Look, Leila," I said, turning in my seat to look at her. "I *really* don't want to talk about it. Okay?"

I'd spoken more sharply than I meant to. Leila raised her eyebrows in surprise. "Okay, okay," she said coolly. "Didn't meant to pry."

"Shall we get started?" Mr. Gordon asked, from the front of the classroom. "Sanjiv, why don't you take over?"

"Thanks, Mr. Gordon." Sanjiv, our team captain, was sitting in the front row, and he now turned so that he was facing us. When he swallowed, his very prominent Adam's apple bobbed in his throat. "As you all know, our first competition of the year is coming up next weekend against St. Pius. And you know what that means: Austin Strong."

I didn't bother to stifle my sigh of irritation. Austin Strong, the headliner of the St. Pius Mu Alpha Theta team, was nearly as good at math as I was. Nearly . . . but not quite. He hadn't beaten me yet. Yes, St. Pius had won the state finals for the past three years in a row. . . . But that was only because they had yet to face the Geek High team in a state final championship. We'd beaten them at every single one of the regular-season competitions.

"Don't worry about St. Pius," I said. "They've never beaten us before. There's no reason to think they will now."

"I don't want to get overconfident," Sanjiv cautioned. "I think we should fit in extra practice sessions. I drew up a new study schedule." He brandished a stack of papers and handed them to Kyle. "Take one and pass it back."

Kyle passed out the schedules. When I got mine, I stared down at it in disbelief.

"Sanjiv! This is ridiculous. We can't practice every afternoon," I exclaimed.

"He's got practice scheduled on Saturdays, too," Leila said.

She looked up, her eyes narrowed behind her cat's-eye glasses. "Come on, Sanjiv. This is total overkill."

"I gave you Sundays off," Sanjiv pointed out.

"How reasonable of you," I muttered.

"When are we supposed to do our homework?" Kyle asked, sounding as disgruntled as I felt. "I have a quiz in history next week, and a paper due in English, and I already have a pile of chem homework."

Sanjiv held up his hands, palms facing out, as though to ward us off. "Look, I know it's a lot of time. But winning takes commitment and sacrifice. If we want to be champions, we have to earn it. This is just as important as schoolwork. The Geek High MATh team hasn't won the state championship for the past three years."

"Yeah, well school is important, too," Kyle said flatly.

"I agree. I'm applying to colleges in the fall. I can't afford to let my GPA slip now," Leila said.

"Maybe we could come up with a compromise," I suggested. "Like dropping the five-hour practice you have scheduled for Saturday. And rather than practicing every day after school, we'll practice on Tuesdays and Thursdays."

Sanjiv looked stunned. "But that's a cut of . . . of . . ." He trailed off, trying to calculate the percentage in his head.

"Eighty percent," I said.

"Showoff," Kyle muttered.

"We can't afford an eighty-percent cut in our practice hours," Sanjiv argued.

"Look at it this way," Leila said. "It's either cut back the practices . . . or lose the team altogether."

"How do you figure that?" Sanjiv asked.

"Because I'll have to quit," Leila said. "I've got SAT's coming up. And college visits." She waved Sanjiv's schedule. "I can't devote this sort of time to Mu Alpha Theta."

"Same here," Kyle said.

"Seriously, Sanjiv, it's too much," I agreed.

We all looked at Nicholas. He shrugged. "I don't mind," he said. "I don't have anything better to do."

"That's three to two," Kyle said. "We win."

"Okay," Sanjiv said, defeated. "So we'll drop Saturdays."

"And only two practices after school," Leila countered.

"Four," Sanjiv offered.

I sighed. "Let's settle on three. Mondays, Tuesdays, and Thursdays."

Everyone nodded, although Kyle did so reluctantly. I doubted he'd drop the team, though. He didn't have many extracurriculars; a MATh state championship trophy could make or break his college applications.

"Okay," I said. "That's decided. Let's get started on the practice drills for today, or else we'll never get out of here."

Sanjiv looked wounded—he was very sensitive about any perceived threats to his leadership of the team—but the others murmured their assent.

"Good," I said, before Sanjiv could protest. "Mr. Gordon, what did you say we were working on today? Algebraic equations?"

"That's right," Mr. Gordon said. "Who's ready for the first question?"

# Chapter 13

After I finished up my latest e-mail to Henry—the subject of which was the Top Three Favorite Movies (Henry's were *Spiderman 2* and the first and third of the *Lord of the Rings* trilogy; mine were *Say Anything*, *Sixteen Candles*, and *Pretty in Pink*)—I curled up on the low platform bed with *Tender Is the Night*. I'd liked the book at first, but it had fizzled out in the middle and was now limping to its conclusion. It was taking all of my willpower to keep reading on instead of just skimming through the last few chapters. I sighed and rubbed my eyes to stay awake, deciding that if I got through one more chapter, I'd reward myself by carving out an hour to work on my latest short story. Suddenly, the door swung open with a bang, and Hannah wandered in.

"Hey," Hannah said, sitting down on the edge of the bed. "What are you doing?"

I looked up from my book. "I'm teaching myself how to move objects with my mind."

Hannah wrinkled her lovely nose. "Really?" she asked.

"No, not really. I'm reading a book," I said, waving the paperback at her.

"Is it any good?" Hannah asked.

I shrugged. "It's okay. It's about this guy who marries a woman who's mentally ill."

"Oh," Hannah said, quickly losing interest, as she did whenever the topic of academics came up. "What are you wearing tonight?"

Now it was my turn to be confused. "What? Where?"

Hannah rolled her eyes heavenward. "My party. Did you forget?"

I hadn't forgotten. Even if I'd wanted to—which I did, sort of—it would have been impossible. For the past two weeks, Hannah and Peyton had talked of little else. As far as they were concerned, Hannah's sweet-sixteen birthday bash would be the social event of the year among the Orange Cove teen set. Peyton had hammered out most of the details while Hannah was visiting her dad and step-mom in Manhattan.

"You are coming, aren't you?" Hannah persisted.

I nodded without enthusiasm. Hannah's friends were all selfish, materialistic airheads. I wasn't exactly thrilled at having to spend an evening with them.

"Good," Hannah said. "Now. What are you wearing?"

"I hadn't really thought about it. Are we supposed to dress up?" I asked.

Hannah looked at me, her face blank with horror. "Ye-ah," she said, drawing the word into two scathing syllables. "How could you not know that?"

"Sorry," I said, shrugging. Which was a lie—honestly, I couldn't care less—but I didn't want to get in an argument over it, either. "I guess, I'll wear . . . um, maybe a skirt and sweater?"

"No," Hannah said firmly. She stood and marched over to the closet, swung open the doors, and began rifling through my clothes, whipping the hangers aside. Aghast, she turned to stare at me. "Are these really the only clothes you own?"

"Basically. There are some T-shirts and things in the dresser drawer," I said helpfully, gesturing toward the low white modern dresser that sat under the windows.

"But . . . it's just jeans and khakis," Hannah said desperately, turning back to the closet. She shook her head in horror. "How can you live like this?"

"Somehow I manage," I said dryly.

"Wait, what's this?" Hannah asked, pouncing on the garment bag at the back of the closet. She unzipped it and pulled out the pretty rose beaded silk slip dress I'd worn to Henry's house on New Year's Eve. Hannah gasped. "Oh, this is gorgeous! You have to wear this!"

"Okay," I said. It seemed a little over the top for a birthday party, but then, what did I know? There were preschoolers out there who had better fashion sense than I did.

"Do you want me to do your hair for you again?" Hannah offered.

"Why?" I asked, suddenly suspicious.

"I just thought you might want to look nice tonight. Really nice," Hannah said, twisting a lock of golden blond hair around her finger, the way she always did when she was nervous.

"And again, I ask: Why?" I said.

Hannah sighed. "I didn't tell you before because I didn't want you to get all freaked out about it. . . . The thing is . . . Dex is going to be there," she said.

My mouth fell open and my stomach suddenly felt like it had dropped out of my body. Hannah had invited *Dex*? Dex, who'd kissed me, pretended to like me, and then never bothered to call or write me afterward? Which would mean . . . oh, no. *Oh, no no no no no*. Which would mean I'd have to see him. It was what I'd been most dreading since I got back from London.

"Why do you hate me?" I asked, when I'd finally regained the capacity for speech.

"I don't hate you," Hannah said, crossing her arms and frowning at me. "I'm doing this for you."

"For me?" I repeated.

"To help you," she explained.

"To help me?"

"Why do you keep repeating everything I say?" Hannah asked.

"Because, Hannah, I don't *want* to see Dex. He pretended to like me and then he blew me off. Seeing him now would be *humiliating*."

*How can she not understand this?* I wondered wildly. *How?*

"I don't think so," Hannah said. She crossed the room and sat back on the bed. "You said that he dumped you for some other girl, right?"

This was a fun conversation.

"Yes," I said. I blew out an exasperated puff of air.

"Well. I asked around at school, and no one's heard anything about this chick he's supposedly dating," Hannah said.

"So?"

"So I don't think he's seeing anyone. If he was, word would have gotten around," Hannah said.

"Maybe he hasn't told anyone."

"I doubt that. Why would he keep it a secret?"

"I don't know. Maybe he doesn't relish the idea of everyone gossiping about him. Or maybe . . . *maybe*"—my brain spun off into a whirl of speculation—"it's the ex-girlfriend of one of his friends, and he doesn't want his friend to know. Or maybe her parents are super-religious and don't allow her to date, so they have to keep it a secret."

Hannah snorted. "I seriously doubt that."

"Look, I really, *really* don't want to talk about this," I said.

I was seriously not enjoying these speculations about Dex and his new girlfriend. My stomach had a pinched, sour feeling, and my lungs felt like they'd shriveled up so I couldn't take in a deep breath. It wasn't helping that Hannah was looking skeptical, as though the idea of anyone carrying on a relationship at Orange Cove High without her knowledge was unimaginable.

"Okay, whatever," Hannah said, raising her eyebrows. "But I still think you should wear that dress. It's killer."

I stared at her in disbelief. "Wear the dress? Wait . . . you don't think I'm still going to this party, do you?"

"Of course you're going! You have to! It's my birthday party!" Hannah exclaimed.

"Hannah, I can't! Not if Dex is going to be there!"

"But why?" Hannah looked truly confused.

I shook my head in disbelief. "Because, it would be *embarrassing*," I hissed. "What if he's there with *her*?"

Hannah shrugged this off. "He's not bringing her. He would have told me."

"But since you don't know who she is, you could already have invited her," I pointed out.

Hannah hadn't thought of this, and she paused, chewing her lower lip. "Maybe . . . but I doubt it. Besides, even if she is there, that's even more reason for you to show up looking drop-dead gorgeous. That's every girl's fantasy—to see her ex-boyfriend when she looks amazing."

"It is?" I asked.

"Yes," she said. "Well, that and marrying the Prince of England."

"Which one?" I asked.

Hannah rolled her eyes at my stupidity. "William, of course. He's the one who's going to be king, after all."

I used to think that William was the cuter of the two princes. Then I fell for Dex and gained a new appreciation for redheads. Which didn't change the fact that this was perhaps the dumbest conversation I'd ever had. Including the time I once spent two hours listening to Charlie and Finn debate whether Snickers were superior to Milky Way bars.

"Anyway," Hannah continued, "what you have to do is show up at the party looking hotter than hot, and Dex will see you, and . . . *voilà*!" She waved one hand in a flourish.

"*Voilà*?" I repeated. "*Voilà* what?"

"And, *voilà*, he'll feel like crap for not calling you. Or e-mailing you. Whatever. Anyway, he'll totally regret it. Isn't that the whole point?"

"The whole point is to make Dex feel like crap?" I repeated.

Hannah smiled knowingly. "Yes. It is," she said.

As much as I liked the idea of Dex taking one look at me and being overcome with pangs of regret and longing, I could spot two major problems with this plan.

"First of all, I'm not you," I said bluntly.

"What do you mean?"

I sighed. "Hannah, I don't know if you've noticed, but you're gorgeous. I'm not."

With her petite, perfect features and long, shiny blond hair, Hannah could be a teen model. I, on the other hand, was tall and gawky and possessed frizzy hair and a too-big nose.

Hannah looked me over, considering. "You'd be a lot cuter if you made more of an effort," she said. "You know, with your hair and makeup."

"Yeah, well," I said, dismissing this with a shrug. I didn't want Hannah to launch into makeover mode. "And second, I don't want Dex to feel like crap."

"You don't?" Hannah asked, her eyes wide.

"No," I said. "I like Dex. It makes me sad that he doesn't like me. . . . But that doesn't mean I want him to be unhappy."

Hannah shook her head in disbelief. At first I thought she was impressed at how mature I was being. This illusion was quickly shattered when she spoke.

"No way," she said. "I know you're, like, supposed to be a genius or something, and that you go to an 'alternative' school and all." She made bunny ears with her fingers when she said *alternative*. "But not even you could be this weird."

"Gee, thanks," I said.

"Trust me, Miranda, I know about relationships. Everyone wants their ex to pine away for them. Everyone. It's a universal truth. It's like . . . like . . ." She struggled for an appropriate simile. "Like *gravity*."

Hannah was so sure of herself, so sure that she was right, I couldn't help but wonder . . . could she be? *Would* it make me happy if when Dex saw me he was overcome with misery and regret?

I was more than a little disturbed to realize that I didn't hate the idea.

"Told you so," Hannah said smugly, as she accurately read my expression of shock and self-disgust. "Now, come on. I'll help you get ready."

*

I couldn't remember being more nervous in my life than I was when we arrived at the Canyon. Sitting in the backseat of Peyton's huge SUV, I smoothed down the beaded slip dress, hoping I looked okay. Hannah—who had blow-dried my naturally frizzy hair into sleek waves and lacquered my face with more makeup than a beauty pageant queen—had insisted I looked "adorable." I wasn't so sure . . . and I certainly wasn't comfortable. The high-heeled sandals I'd borrowed from Hannah—her feet were two sizes smaller than mine, but she still insisted I cram myself into them—were already hurting my feet, and my lips felt tacky with lip gloss. Without thinking, I pursed them together.

"Don't do that," Hannah instructed me. "You'll rub off the lip gloss."

"It feels weird," I complained.

"You'll get used to it," Hannah said with a shrug.

"Here we are," Dad said, pulling into a parking spot just in front of the restaurant.

The Canyon was at the far end of a red brick L-shaped strip mall that also housed an orthodontist, an interior decorator, and a bakery. There was a covered walkway in front of the stores, as well as a row of palm trees planted in tall cobalt blue pots. Leafy green vines scaled up the outer columns of the walkway.

I'd expected Hannah to be nervous, too, but she seemed completely cool and collected as she unlatched her seat belt and slid gracefully out of the SUV. She looked even more beautiful than usual, in a strapless kelly green Lilly Pulitzer sundress. Her golden blond hair was piled on top of her head in a complicated updo, and her face shimmered with expertly applied makeup. Around her slender neck she wore the gold Tiffany bean necklace her dad and stepmom had given her for Christmas last year.

"Let's get this party started," Hannah said. She turned to look at me, still sitting in the SUV. "Are you stuck to the seat or something, Miranda?"

I was so nervous, I seemed to have frozen in place. I wondered distantly if I could just sit out the party here. It wasn't like anyone would miss me—I hardly knew most of Hannah's friends, and those that I did know I didn't exactly love. But Hannah gave an impatient toss of her head and gestured to me.

"I'm coming," I said.

Reluctantly, I opened my door and slid out. Dad and Peyton were already out, standing with Hannah. The three of them looked like the sort of beautiful, perfect family that photography studios use in their advertisements—Hannah, lovely and lithesome, Peyton and Dad beaming proudly down at her. I felt completely extraneous, a feeling that deepened as they headed toward the restaurant without a backward glance to see if I was following.

I hesitated for a moment—if I was going to bail out on this

party, now was the time to do so. It was a tempting idea. There was a Starbucks just down the street. I could hide there, tossing back mocha lattes, and not have to worry about bumping into Dex and his new girlfriend. But . . . I couldn't. Hannah would be disappointed, my dad would be upset, Peyton would . . . well, forget that, Peyton would probably be overjoyed if I missed the party. She probably counted any night she didn't have to spend in my presence to be a good one.

I puffed out my cheeks and sighed, and then hurried after them. I caught up with them just as they were walking into the restaurant. Hannah went in first, and I could hear her friends applauding her arrival. Peyton, hanging on my dad's arm and beaming at the guests, followed just behind Hannah. I brought up the rear, huffing with the effort of having jogged across the parking lot in the too-small heels.

The Canyon was decorated in a sleek industrial style, from the dark wenge bar to the steel tables covered with crisp white linens. Spare aluminum pendant lamps lit the room, and stark black-and-white photographs of the desert hung on the walls.

Hannah had timed her arrival perfectly to make a high-impact entrance. It looked like most of her guests were already in attendance, sipping fruity drinks and munching on appetizers being circulated by an attractive waitstaff outfitted in white T-shirts and black jeans. There were a ton of people there. I didn't know most of them, although there were a few familiar faces. I assumed they'd been in attendance at Hannah's impromptu kegger in November.

Tiffany and Brit—twins with high cheekbones and long braids—raced forward to greet Hannah, squealing with excitement. Hannah's former best friend, Avery, a thin-faced girl with short, dark hair and narrow gold-flecked hazel eyes, was also there, but she hung back. She and Hannah had a falling-out a few months back when Hannah learned that Avery had stolen a sweater out of Peyton's closet.

I was actually a little surprised to see that Avery was even at the party, and wondered if this meant that she and Hannah had made up. I hoped not—Avery was not my favorite person. Back when Avery and Hannah were still close, and spent every day after school hanging out at the beach house together along with the twins, Avery constantly pestered me to do her homework for her.

The twins swept Hannah away into the crowd of her friends, while Dad and Peyton moved off to circulate among the adults they'd invited. I saw Hannah's boyfriend, Emmett, was there waiting for her. He greeted her with a bunch of sixteen red roses and a kiss that caused all of the girls to swoon and sigh. A few months ago, back when I was still infatuated with Emmett, this sight would have made my heart implode with jealousy, but now I barely registered it. I didn't like Emmett anymore, at least not in that way. Now there was someone I was much, much more interested in seeing. . . .

With my heart beating wildly, I glanced around, trying to appear casual as I looked for Dex.

*Just find him, say hello while staying cool and detached,* I told myself. *Yes, it will suck. Yes, it will be awkward. But you'll get it over with, and you can move on with the rest of your life.*

Spurred on by this silent pep talk, I redoubled my efforts, turning around in a slow circle. Dex was usually easy to spot, with his tall, lanky frame and flame-red hair. . . . But I didn't see him anywhere.

I felt a rush of disappointment tinged with relief. Girlfriend or not, I had really wanted to see Dex. . . . And find out how he would react when he saw me. I knew it didn't make any sense, that he didn't like me the way I liked him. I guess it was the same as worrying at a canker sore. . . . Even though it hurts, you can't leave it alone.

*At least I don't have to see him with Laughing Girl,* I thought.

The party was not fun. Or, I should say, it wasn't fun for me. First of all, the too-small shoes were killing my feet. And since I didn't know many of Hannah's friends, I was pretty much the odd girl out, standing to the side watching everyone else talk and laugh and flirt. Unsurprisingly, while the parents stayed to one side of the room—sitting at the tables near the windows—the kids gravitated to the other side, mostly standing and milling around near the bar area, where the band was set up and playing. The twins' boyfriends—two interchangeable meatheads named Geoff and Roy—tried to order mixed drinks from the bartender, claiming they were getting them for their parents, but they were shot down, which was causing waves of hilarity among Hannah's friends. The parents were either unaware of what was going on or were choosing to ignore it.

After we'd been there for about an hour, the waitstaff set up a buffet—enchiladas, fajitas, taquitos, bean salad, fresh tortillas. The guys swarmed the table as though they hadn't eaten in a month, while the girls—all of them thin and gorgeous—hung back, making noises about how many calories everything had. It reminded me of what Sadie had said about how girls my age suffered from low self-esteem, and I decided that although she might be right, my low self-esteem wouldn't keep me from eating. I was starving, and the food looked too good to pass up.

I sat down at one of the tables off to the side by myself, relieved to be off my aching feet, and dug into my plate of enchiladas and bean salad. Just as I'd taken a bite of the oozy, cheesy enchilada, I heard someone say, "Hi, Miranda."

I looked up, mouth full, and nearly choked on a cheese string when I saw who was standing there.

*Dex.*

He looked . . . well, he looked *amazing*. The same pale blue eyes, the same long, straight nose, the same pale, freckled skin. He'd gotten a haircut since the last time I'd seen him, and was wearing his coppery red curls close to his scalp. He looked unusually serious, though. Normally when I saw him, he was smiling his sexy crooked grin that made my knees go wobbly. But now his eyes were cool and his lips quirked down in a frown.

I chewed and swallowed my bite—which took forever, the cheese, sauce, and tortilla seemingly multiplying in my mouth—and when I'd finally gulped it down, I managed to say, "Hi. You're here."

"I know," Dex said. He motioned toward the empty chair opposite me. "Do you mind if I sit?"

I shook my head and tried to focus on breathing normally, a task made harder by the fact that my pulse was pounding like a jackhammer. He was *here*. And it appeared that he was here alone, unless his new girlfriend was hanging out with the group of girls over by the bar. I looked in that direction, to see if I could pick out the Laughing Girl, but I didn't see anyone who was watching us. And most of Hannah's friends were smiling and giggling. In fact, most of them were interchangeable—they were all thin and pretty, and all wore hip clothes and too much makeup. They were the chosen girls of Orange Cove High, and they knew it, reveling in their status at the top of the social heap.

Dex sat but didn't say anything. Instead, he stared down at his hands resting on the table. I tried to think of something to say, something flirtatious and cutting that would make him regret the way he'd blown me off. But nothing came to mind. Because what I really wanted to know was *why*. Why had he pretended to like me if he didn't? Why had he gotten my hopes up? But, of course, I couldn't ask him that, not unless I wanted to come off as even more pathetic than I already felt.

"I didn't think you were coming," I finally said. Which was true; I had given up on the idea of seeing him.

"I wasn't sure I was going to," Dex said. Still not meeting my eyes, he lifted his lips in a humorless half smile. "I didn't know what I was going to say to you."

I felt a flash of anger then, hot and stabbing.

"You don't have to worry about me," I said acerbically. "I'm not going to start screaming at you or anything. Give me a little credit."

Dex looked up then, his eyebrows furrowed in surprise.

"Scream at *me*?" he asked. "Why would you . . ."

"Hey, Dex," a flirty female voice said, cutting him off before he could finish what he was saying.

Dex and I both looked up to see Avery, Hannah's onetime best friend, standing there. I knew that she used to have a huge crush on Dex. . . . And from the way she was looking at him, in much the same way I'd seen her stare at a pair of shoes she was coveting, I had the distinct feeling that her crush was still going strong.

*Could Avery be Dex's new girlfriend?* I wondered. After all, Charlie didn't know Avery, and so wouldn't have recognized her if Charlie had seen her out with Dex. But surely not. Hannah would have heard if Dex and Avery were dating. And I'd gotten the definite feeling last semester that Dex didn't care for Avery at all.

"I called you earlier. Did your mom give you the message?" Avery now asked.

She seemed to be pretending that I wasn't sitting there. I didn't really mind; every time Avery did talk to me, she just tried to coerce me into being her own personal homework slave.

"Yeah, she did," Dex said shortly. He didn't apologize for not returning her call, or explain why.

"Oh . . . well." Avery looked discomposed for the first time. "I just wanted to see if you needed a ride here."

"No," Dex said. "I got a ride with Andrew."

"Do you want to go get something to eat?" Avery asked, bobbing her head in the direction of the buffet. She shifted slightly, setting her shoulders back so that her large chest—scantily clad in a clingy black tank top—stuck out. I couldn't help rolling my eyes at this blatant play for Dex's attention.

But Dex just shook his head. "No, thanks. Actually, Miranda and I are right in the middle of something."

For the first time, Avery's hazel eyes flickered toward me. "Oh. Right. Hi, Miranda," she said without enthusiasm.

I smiled thinly at her. "Hi, Avery," I said.

"Find me later, okay, Dex?" she said. And then before he could respond, she swiveled around and strode off, her miniskirt-clad hips swaying provocatively from side to side. I wondered if I looked half as good in my slip dress.

"Brrr," I said, with a dramatic shiver. "If looks could freeze, I'd be an icicle right about now."

But Dex didn't crack a smile at this lame joke. Instead, his pale eyes held mine, his expression serious . . . and just a little bit angry. I remembered suddenly what we'd been talking about, and my own smile faded away.

"What did you mean by that when you said you weren't going to scream at me?" he asked.

I shrugged and looked down at my plate of enchiladas. I'd lost my appetite. "Just what I meant. I'm not angry. I understand . . ." My voice trailed off. That was a lie. I didn't understand why he'd blown me off. Not really. Sure, I wasn't as pretty and popular as the girls at the party, flitting around as they tossed their shiny hair over shoulders bared in flirty little dresses. But Dex had already known that about me. . . . Before he'd shown up at the Snowflake, before he'd told me he liked me. I took in a deep breath, exhaled slowly, and said, "Well, actually, that's not true. I don't understand. But I get it. Really."

"Miranda, what are you talking about?" Dex asked, now looking more bewildered than mad. Although the anger was still there, shadowing his eyes and causing a pink stain to rise on his cheeks.

But I didn't care if he was angry, because I was starting to get seriously ticked off. As if it wasn't bad enough that he'd made me think he liked me, gotten my hopes up, and then blown me off to be with some other girl, now he was acting like I was out of line for being annoyed by it!

"What do you think? I'm talking about how you blew me off!" I snapped.

"Wait . . . *I* blew *you* off?" Dex's face was thunderous. "Are you *kidding* me?"

"No, I'm not kidding!" I crossed my arms and glared at him. "What else would you call it? You haven't bothered to get in touch with me in a month!"

"I tried!"

"No, you didn't!"

"Yes," Dex said, making a masterful effort not to shout at me, "I did. You gave me the wrong e-mail address."

"No, I didn't," I said.

"Yes, you did," Dex said again. He reached into his pocket, pulled out a canvas navy blue wallet. He opened it up and extracted a familiar-looking scrap of yellow paper. Dex handed it to me.

I stared down at the paper, and saw the familiar loopy handwriting in which I'd printed out my e-mail address: mirandabloom@ gmail.com.

"Right, mirandajbloom@gmail.com," I said.

And then something occurred to me. . . . Something that caused me to feel like cold water was trickling down my spine. Because as I squinted down at the e-mail address I'd written out for Dex, I noticed that something was missing. The letter J. My middle initial. J for Jane.

"Oops," I said.

"Oops?" Dex repeated. I glanced up at him, and for a moment, I thought I could see some of the old humor glinting in his eyes. But then he was looking stern again, and I thought maybe I'd imagined it.

"I . . . I wrote my e-mail address down wrong," I said, and felt my cheeks flame red with embarrassment. "I left out my middle initial."

"I tried to e-mail you. Each time, it bounced back at me as undeliverable. And I couldn't call, because I didn't have your mom's phone number in London."

"So . . . you *did* try to e-mail me?" I said, and suddenly felt a bubble of hope swell in my chest.

Dex nodded. "About a dozen times."

"I'm really sorry," I said, feeling a rush of mingled relief and happiness. But then I remembered: Laughing Girl. And my elation disappeared as abruptly as it had arrived. "But . . ." I started and then stopped, staring down at the table again. I really, really didn't want to talk about his new girlfriend with him.

"But what?" Dex asked.

I finally looked up at him. "Look . . . what's the point of discussing this? I heard you're dating someone else," I said, trying to keep my voice as calm and free of emotion as possible. Unfortunately, I wasn't very successful; I could feel my throat catch, sending a definite waver into my voice.

"What? Who am I supposed to be dating?" he asked, looking puzzled.

"You don't know?"

Dex let out a short laugh. "No, I don't. Who told you I was seeing someone, anyway? Hannah?"

"No. My friend Charlie saw you out at the movies with someone," I said.

Dex continued to look puzzled, his blondish-red eyebrows furrowed down again. Then comprehension suddenly cleared his face.

"Oh! You mean Cat!" he said. And then, to my astonishment, he grinned. "That's who she saw me with. Cat."

"I guess," I said, trying—and failing—not to sound sullen. *Cat.* What kind of a name was Cat, anyway? "You should know."

"Miranda . . . Cat is my *sister*," Dex said, and then he laughed.

My mouth dropped open. "Your *sister*?"

"Yeah. My big sister. She was home from college on break, and we were hanging out a lot. That must have been who your friend saw me with."

"But . . . I didn't know you had a sister," I said.

"As a matter of fact, I have two," Dex said. "Both older. Cat's twenty. She goes to the University of Florida. And Elise is twenty-four. She lives in Boston."

"Oh," I said, feeling more foolish than I ever had in my life.

"Yeah. *Oh*," Dex said, and this time he grinned at me, although it seemed almost reluctant. "Is that why you never called me back?"

"Call you back?" Now it was my turn to be confused. "Wait . . . you *called* me? When?"

"I called you a few times. I left messages with some woman who answered the phone at the beach house. I think it might have been your stepmother," Dex said. "But when you didn't call me back . . . well, you know. I thought you were blowing me off."

"No!" I exclaimed. "I didn't know you called! She didn't give me the messages!"

I threw a furious look in the direction of my evil stepmother. Peyton didn't notice. She was too busy laughing her fake laugh at something a tall man with silver hair was saying.

Dex chuckled again, this time softly. "Well. I guess that explains a lot," he said.

But it was taking me longer to digest this information. "So, wait . . . it was all just a misunderstanding?" I asked.

"Yeah. I guess it was," Dex said. And this time when he smiled at me, I smiled back at him.

The band suddenly broke into a cool, rocker version of "Happy Birthday," while two of the waiters wheeled out to the middle of the dance floor a huge sheet cake with white icing and the number sixteen formed by pink roses. The sixteen tall pink candles stuck on top of the cake were lit. Conversation broke off as everyone began to sing. Hannah, clutching Peyton's hand, made her way to the cake, laughing and blushing prettily.

I sang along, too, although I was all too conscious of Dex sitting across the table from me. Did this mean he still liked me? I thought so . . . but at the same time, I didn't want to get my hopes up again. After a full month had gone by without our speaking, it seemed like too much to wish for that things would pick up where we'd left off.

And there was something else, too: Henry. If Dex hadn't been blowing me off while I was in London, and if he really had been out with his sister, and not some other girl . . . well, then, did that mean I'd cheated on him when I kissed Henry?

*"Happy birthday, dear Hannah. Happy birthday to you,"* the crowd finished, and then everyone broke out in applause. Some of the girls let out loud *woo-hoo*s.

"Thank you, everyone. And thank you all for coming tonight," Hannah said. She looked at Peyton. "Can I blow out the candles?"

"Absolutely," Peyton said, beaming at her daughter.

Hannah leaned forward and puckered her lips. She looked so pretty in the candlelight, her perfect pale skin glowing and face softened by an excited smile. Then she blew out the candles in one go, and everyone cheered again.

# Chapter 14

"So he didn't ask you out?" Charlie exclaimed the following Monday at lunch.

She and I were sitting alone at our usual table. Finn wasn't sitting with us. Ever since his fight with Charlie, he'd been eating lunch with Tate Metcalf and Jonathan Barker on the other side of the dining room. Charlie hadn't mentioned the fight, or Finn's absence, and I was too preoccupied with my own problems to address it right now.

"No," I said. "Right after the cake came out, my dad insisted I join them for family photographs—which ticked Peyton off, since she likes to pretend that I'm not actually related to them in any way, shape, or form—and right after we were done, Dex's ride was leaving, and he had to go. He said good-bye to me, but that was it. We left it at good-bye."

"That sounds like it should be a line in a movie," Charlie said with a dramatic sigh. "*We left it at good-bye*. It sounds so romantic."

"Yeah, well," I said, taking a bite of my turkey sandwich, "it was a little less romantic in practice. My dad was hovering nearby, worried that I was upset when Peyton tried to insist that Avery be in the family photo instead of me. Meanwhile, Dex's friend was standing behind him, tossing his keys in the air and saying, 'Dude, come on, we gotta go.' It wasn't exactly Romeo and Juliet time."

"That's just as well. You know things did end badly for Romeo and Juliet," Charlie said.

"I guess," I said. I had been hoping that Dex would call me the next day, Sunday, but as far as I knew, he hadn't. Of course, it was possible that he had called while I was out walking Willow—I'd quizzed Peyton mercilessly, and made her promise to write down all of my phone messages in the future, which she finally agreed to just to get rid of me—but I had no idea if she'd keep her word. I certainly didn't trust her. I just couldn't figure out if she was purposely screwing with my life for her own amusement by not giving me Dex's previous messages.

"So, anyway, I didn't tell you what Mitch and I did this weekend," Charlie said.

I swallowed back a sigh. Considering her recent behavior, it was actually pretty amazing that Charlie had held off on yet another one of her long, gushing Mitch stories for this long. They were all pretty much interchangeable—*he's such a great kisser, blah, blah, blah, do you think fifteen is too young to meet the greatest love of your life, blah, blah, blah*—so I was able to zone out and focus back on my problems at hand, which included:

1. Where I stood with Dex;
2. Whether I could make it through the rest of the year cohabitating with Peyton (how could the Demon not have told me Dex called? How???)

and finally, last and very much least,

3. The Mu Alpha Theta competition coming up on Saturday against Austin Strong and the rest of the St. Pius team.

I wasn't worried about winning the Mu Alpha Theta competition. What I was concerned about was how out-of-control Sanjiv was getting as the date of the first competition grew closer. De-

spite our agreement to have only three practices a week, Sanjiv had
scheduled us for five sessions this week, insisting that St. Pius was
a special situation, and we needed the extra prep work.

"And look! He gave me these earrings for our six-week anniversary," Charlie finished, turning her head from side to side to show
off a truly hideous pair of dangling heart-shaped earrings. They
were made out of fake gold, the kind that turns your ears green.

"Oh, they're . . ." Ugly. Tacky. The last earrings I would ever
have thought Charlie would be caught dead in. "Nice," I finished.

Luckily, Charlie was too dreamy-eyed to notice my unenthusi-
astic response.

"I know," she said with a sigh. "I'm so lucky."

I stuffed my sandwich in my mouth to stop myself from making
the snarky comment I so wanted to say. It wouldn't help, for one
thing. And for another, Charlie had just spent all that time listening
to me talk about Dex. What kind of a friend would I be if I wasn't
equally supportive of her?

I swallowed the bite of turkey sandwich, gulped down a sip of
water, and smiled gamely.

"Yes," I said. "You're very lucky."

I distantly heard someone saying my name, and glanced around
to see who was talking to me. Then, catching sight of Felicity's and
Morgan's gleefully malevolent faces, I realized that no one was talking to me. They were talking *about* me.

Normally, I tried not to let Felicity get to me. She's too petty
and unpleasant to bother with. But between all of the stress I'd been
under lately and the constant irritation of listening to Charlie nattering on about Mitch, I suddenly found it hard to rise above it all.

"What's your problem, Felicity?" I snapped.

"Don't even bother," Charlie murmured. "She's not worth
your time."

"Problem?" Felicity put on an expression of mock innocence.
"I don't have a problem."

Despite the advice she had just given me, Charlie couldn't help snorting loudly at this.

"Morgan and I were just wondering what it's like to be someone's pity date, that's all," Felicity said. "That must be really hard, huh, Miranda?"

I opened my mouth, about to furiously reply, but Charlie cut me off.

"Don't," she said sharply. "It just encourages her. The best thing you can do is pretend she doesn't exist. Just picture a black hole where she's sitting."

I shot Felicity and Morgan one last venomous look, but decided Charlie was right. It was better to just not engage them.

"Have you finished *Tender Is the Night*?" I asked Charlie, pointedly ignoring the Felimonster and her toady.

It worked. When they saw I wasn't rising to the bait, they turned away, clearly disappointed that their taunts hadn't affected me.

The problem was . . . they had *affected* me. Maybe Dex and I had just had a misunderstanding, and that was what had kept us from getting together. But if that was true . . . why hadn't Dex asked me out at Hannah's party? I could only think of one reason why he wouldn't: His feelings for me must have cooled.

And that didn't make me feel much better than if I had just been a pity date. Because either way, I still hadn't ended up with the cute guy in the end.

◆

To: mirandajbloom@gmail.com
From: hewent@britmail.net
Subject: lost in translation
Miranda,

Sorry to hear that your two friends are fighting. You're right, I wouldn't be too chuffed to hear one of my mates nattering on about a girl like that.

So, since you asked, "swot" means to study. And "gormless" means stupid. I'll try to provide British-American translations for you in future e-mails! Just be glad I'm not a Cockney . . . you'd never understand a word I was saying, would you?

**My Top Three Favorite British Slang Words**

1. Brilliant
2. Wanker
3. Goolies

I saw your mum the other day. She said you might come visit over the summer?

Henry

•

"Are you nervous about tomorrow?" Dad asked, as he passed a container of mu shu chicken to me.

I shrugged and shook my head. "No, not really."

"What's tomorrow?" Hannah asked.

"I have a math competition," I said shortly.

I saw Hannah's nose wrinkle. I already knew what she thought of academic teams.

"You should come with us, Hannah. Your mom and I are going to go root Miranda on," Dad said jovially.

Peyton looked up sharply from her uneaten dinner. (Peyton never eats. Never. She just pushes her food around on the plate with her fork. I think this freakish ability to survive without nourishment is just one more sign that Peyton is a minion of Satan. Or at least one of the lesser demons.)

"I'm not going," Peyton said.

Dad frowned at her. "Why not?"

"Because I have a million things to do tomorrow." She began to tick off her schedule on her fingers. "I'm having a facial and pedicure in the morning. Then I'm meeting Jill Stansky for lunch. And then I have an appointment with my personal shopper at Saks. Afterwards we're having dinner with the Wassersteins. I can't possibly fit in anything else." She shook her head decisively and tapped her talonlike fingernails on the table.

Frankly, I was glad she wasn't planning to attend the competition. Even though I didn't really care about whether or not we won, I still didn't want the Demon there. She was like a walking, breathing bad-luck talisman.

"That's okay," I said and I turned to Hannah. "You don't have to come, either. It's not that big a deal."

"Yes, it is," my dad said. His voice was calm, but there was a hint of steel in it that hadn't been there before. I glanced over at him and saw that he was glaring at Peyton. "It's important to Miranda, and therefore it's important to me. I want you to come, Peyton."

Peyton narrowed her eyes and stared right back at my father. "I already told you, I can't."

"Dad, really. It's okay," I said.

Dad ignored me. "This is what being a family is," he said. "We support one another."

"Miranda just said she doesn't care if I'm there or not," Peyton said.

"But I said I *do* care," Dad retorted.

Hannah and I exchanged nervous looks. Dad and Peyton had been getting into these little tiffs more and more often. I knew I shouldn't care—after all, wouldn't my life be improved if Dad and Peyton split up?—but instead, it just reminded me of how awful it was back before Dad and Sadie had gotten a divorce. They'd fought constantly, filling the house with a bristling hostility that made my stomach hurt. I didn't want to live through that again.

"Dad," I tried again. "It's not a big deal. Let it go."

Peyton raised her thin eyebrows and favored me with a cold smile. "Thank you, Miranda. That's very adult of you."

"Thanks," I muttered.

My dad stood abruptly and picked up his plate.

"Sit down and finish your dinner, Richard," Peyton instructed him.

Dad just glared at her. "I've lost my appetite," he said. He bussed his plate to the sink, and then turned and strode out of the kitchen.

Hannah turned to look at me again. Her lovely blue eyes were round with shock. Peyton didn't say a word, and, except for a slight thinning of her lips, she looked otherwise unfazed, and she went back to pushing her food around on her plate with a fork.

No one said a word for the rest of the meal.

# Chapter 15

I wasn't sure if it was a good thing that Geek High was hosting the first Mu Alpha Theta competition of the year. On the plus side, we didn't have to travel for three bumpy hours on the school's one bus, purchased secondhand and painted a blindingly bright white. On the other hand, it meant that our team knew most of the spectators sitting in the small auditorium. And while this might not sound like a negative, it was a problem when your team captain suffered from severe performance anxiety, which always became more acute in the presence of his father.

"I can't go out there. I just can't," Sanjiv said. His skin had turned ashen, and his eyes looked large and rimmed with white behind his glasses. He swallowed convulsively, which caused his Adam's apple to bob up and down in his long throat.

"You'll do fine," I said firmly.

"We've never been better prepared," Leila chipped in.

The team was congregating in Mr. Gordon's room for what was supposed to be Sanjiv's pep talk. Instead, Sanjiv was slumped in a chair, his head between his knees, hyperventilating into a brown paper bag. The rest of us stood clustered around him, exchanging uneasy looks.

"Maybe we should ask his dad to leave," I whispered to Leila.

"I tried that last year. Remember? He just shooed me away so he could set up his camera equipment," Leila said.

"Camera equipment?" Kyle asked.

"My dad tapes all of the home meets. He wants me to send them to colleges with my applications," Sanjiv said, sounding as though he might start throwing up at any moment.

"That sounds like a fool-proof plan for making sure you don't get in anywhere," Kyle muttered.

I elbowed him in the side. Hard.

"Ow!" Kyle exclaimed. He shot me a dirty look, but thankfully fell silent.

"Sanjiv, come on. It won't be that bad. Think of it this way—win or lose, it'll be over in an hour. One hour! You can stand anything for an hour," I said.

"He couldn't stand certain forms of torture for that long," Nicholas said. "Like electrocution. Although I suppose that would depend on the amperage."

"Have you ever heard of torture by goat's tongue?" Kyle asked enthusiastically.

"No. What's that?" Nicholas asked.

"It's when they soak your feet in saltwater and then let a goat lick the salt off," Kyle said.

"That doesn't sound so bad," Leila said.

"Yeah? Well what if I told you that the goat doesn't stop licking . . . even after it's licked all your skin off," Kyle said, grinning malevolently. "It just keeps on licking and licking and licking until it reaches the bone."

"Ewwww," Leila and I said in unison.

"Is that for real?" Nicholas asked, looking appalled.

"Look, this isn't helping," I said, rolling my eyes in Sanjiv's direction. He was rocking in his chair and making soft moaning sounds.

"I don't think he's going to be up to giving us the pep talk," Leila said, pointing out the obvious.

"So who's going to pep us up?" Kyle asked.

"You do it, Miranda," Leila said.

"Why me?" I asked.

"Because you're the only one who's not nervous," Leila said.

"I'm not nervous," Kyle said.

"Really?" Leila didn't look as if she believed him. She shrugged. "Even so, I just don't see you as the pep-talk type. You're too negative."

"Why don't you do it?" I asked Leila.

She shook her head decisively. "I don't feel very peppy. I feel like we're about to go out there and get slaughtered by Austin Strong and the Chinese math prodigy."

Austin Strong had bragged on his MySpace page that the St. Pius team now included a foreign exchange student from China who was a math whiz.

"How can you say that? We can take these guys. They're no match for us. I'm going up against Austin, and I've never lost. And any one of us can beat the Chinese guy. Math prodigy or not, this is his first Mu Alpha Theta competition, right? I'm sure he's more nervous than we are. Just stay focused, listen carefully to the questions, and only answer when you're ready. That's the key to winning. We don't need some stupid pep talk to tell us that."

"Don't look now, Miranda," Leila said, somewhat smugly, "but you just gave your first pep talk."

I looked at my other teammates: Kyle looked surly, as usual. Nicholas was gazing at me with awed wonder, as though I'd just invented fried cheese sticks. And Sanjiv had finally lifted his head and looked like he might be able to stand without losing his lunch.

Mr. Gordon poked his head in the room. "Okay, team, we're on!" he said. He gave us a big thumbs-up.

The Mu Alpha Theta competitions work like this: Two teams of five members each sit at tables on either side of a podium. Each team member is given a number; the players in the number one spot sit closest to the moderator, the players in the number two spot sit next to the number one players, and so forth. The moderator stands at the podium, and once the competition has begun, poses a math question to two players at a time. The number one players face off against one another, and then the number two players, and so on. Once the moderator finishes asking the question, the player who hits his buzzer first gets to answer. If he answers correctly, his team wins a certain number of points. If a competitor answers incorrectly, his opponent has a full minute to come up with the answer. The first round of questions is the easiest, so a winning answer earns only five points. During the second round, correct answers win ten points. And during the third and most difficult round, the winning answer scores fifteen points. If the teams are tied at the end of the third round, a tiebreaker round is held to decide the winner. To discourage cheating, the only materials the players may have at the table are pencils and scratch paper.

Sanjiv had dedicated a truly ridiculous amount of time strategizing which Geek High player should be in each spot. Some teams put their strongest player in the number one spot to build confidence for the team. Others liked to have the strongest player go last, hoping to snatch up a last-minute victory. We'd had many more conversations than I would ever have wished to have had on the subject. Many, many, many more conversations.

In the end, Sanjiv decided that I should be paired against Austin Strong. And so, as our team filed into the auditorium, to the applause of the audience, I sat down in seat number four. Leila was number one, Kyle number two, Nicholas number three, and the still pale, still shaky Sanjiv was in the number five spot. I glanced at the St. Pius team sitting across from us. Austin was looking typically smug and self-satisfied. He had thin blond hair, skin so pink it looked like he suffered from a constant case of sunburn, and a shiny, high forehead. He caught my look and smirked back at me.

*Ugh,* I thought, rolling my eyes and turning away. *What a jerk.*

I looked out at the audience, seated in Geek High's small auditorium on red velvet fold-down theater seats. Most of the audience members were parents, like Sanjiv's dad, who was, as usual, armed with his camcorder. My dad was there, too—he grinned at me and gave me a thumbs-up—but Peyton was not. I saw Finn; he was sitting in the front row next to Tate Metcalf. I didn't see Charlie, which was odd, since she always came to the home meets. And then suddenly, I saw a flash of red hair near the back of the auditorium. . . . And felt a thrill of horror.

*Dex was here!*

But before I could dwell on this truly horrifying reality—Dex was going to see me in full math-geek mode! No! *No no no no no!*—the moderator came on stage. He was a slight man with thick, shaggy dark hair and lips so thin, they looked nonexistent. He took his place behind the podium. The moderator tapped on the microphone to make sure it was working, causing a squawk of feedback that made everyone cringe.

"Good afternoon," the moderator said. "Thank you for joining us today for this Mu Alpha Theta math competition. My name is Reggie Bauder, and I'm a professor of mathematics at the Orange Cove Community College. It's my pleasure to be moderating the competition."

There was a scattering of polite applause, which caused Sanjiv to go rigid in his seat. My heart was beating rapidly too, and I could feel my face flushing the hot red it always turns when I'm embarrassed. This had nothing to do with game nerves, though, and everything to do with Dex's presence. While the moderator ran over the rules, I willed myself to not stare out at Dex, and tried to focus instead on taking deep, calming breaths. The only thing worse than Dex seeing me in full math-geek mode would be if I flubbed the competition in a fit of nerves and ended up looking like a loser math geek. It was a lose-lose situation.

"Is everyone ready?" Mr. Bauder asked, looking first at the St. Pius team and then over at us. He smiled reassuringly. "The first question, worth five points, is for the competitors in the number one spots. Why don't you start off by telling us your names?"

"Leila Chang," Leila said, leaning forward toward her microphone. Her voice sounded a bit higher than normal, and I noticed that she was rubbing her hands together nervously.

"Ashley Dubinay," the St. Pius girl sitting opposite from Leila said. She had sallow skin, lank dark hair and a nose that twitched like a rabbit's. Her hand was already hovering just above the buzzer, ready to pounce on it.

"Alright, Leila, Ashley." Mr. Bauder nodded to each girl in turn. "Here's your first question: The ratio of Peter's age to Paul's age is three to five. Paul is thirty years old. How many years old is Peter?"

*Eighteen,* I thought automatically.

Leila hit her buzzer first. "Eighteen years old," she replied.

"That is correct," Mr. Bauder said, favoring Leila with another smile. The crowd applauded politely. Ashley looked crushed.

"Question number two is for players in the number two chairs. Your names are?"

"Jan Pepper."

"Kyle Carpenter."

In a weird coincidence, Jan looked like she could be Kyle's long-lost twin sister. She had the same squat build, the same low hairline, the same sour expression.

"Here's the second question: In 2004, Leap Day occurred on a Sunday. On what day of the week will Leap Day fall on in the year 2020?" Professor Bauder asked.

*Saturday,* I thought. It was one of those questions that sounded harder than it really was. All you had to know is that Leap Day occurs every four years, or every 1,461 days. Which means that the day of the week Leap Day falls on advances five days for every four-year cycle. Easy peasy.

But Kyle and Jan both hesitated. Janice began scribbling on her scratch paper, and Kyle, shooting her a nervous look, followed suit. A moment later, Kyle hit his buzzer.

"Friday," he said.

"No, I'm sorry, that is incorrect," Professor Bauder said. "Miss Pepper, you have sixty seconds in which to come up with the correct answer."

Professor Bauder clicked on a stopwatch to time her, but Jan had already finished her calculations.

"Saturday," Jan said.

"That is correct. Going into question three, the teams are tied at five points apiece."

Nicholas won his question against the third St. Pius female player—a thin black girl with hugely oversized glasses that gave her a bug-eyed look—and then it was my turn.

"I'm Austin Strong," Austin said, when prompted to introduce himself. One of Austin's more annoying traits is that he talks through his teeth with his jaw clamped shut.

"Miranda Bloom," I said.

"Here's your question: What's the numerical value of pi to the fifteenth decimal point?"

*How easy can you get?* I thought. Austin and I both hit our buzzers. Happily, my light lit up first.

"3.141592653589793," I said.

"That is correct," Professor Bauder said.

Again, the audience applauded. I shot a look at Austin—he was fuming—and then dared a glance out at the crowd. My dad was pumping his arm in victory, and Finn cheered loudly. I couldn't see

Dex's expression—he was still all the way in the back, his face in shadows—but I saw that he was clapping. Enthusiastically.

Unfortunately, Sanjiv didn't fare so well with his question. He was facing a boy named Qin Gang, who I assumed was the Chinese exchange student ringer Austin had been bragging about on his MySpace page. Sanjiv was so nervous, I could hear his teeth chattering. Qin Gang, on the other hand, seemed perfectly calm, his round face almost stony in its lack of emotion. He listened to Professor's Bauder's question and then hit his buzzer.

"Seventy-two," he answered correctly, in heavily accented English.

I glanced over at Sanjiv, who had been wildly trying to write down the question, word for word, and had only just begun his calculations. Now, as Professor Bauder confirmed that Qin Gang was correct, Sanjiv made an odd, strangled sound in his throat.

"Don't worry," I whispered encouragingly. "We're still ahead fifteen to ten."

But Sanjiv just hung his head and started to breathe so shallowly, I was worried he was hyperventilating.

Things went downhill in the second round. I don't know if it was Sanjiv's nervousness spreading through the team, but I was the only one on the Geek High side to answer my question correctly. The good news was that this made Austin Strong look like he'd just eaten a turd. The bad news was that we were now behind, fifty to thirty.

There was a brief break in between the second and third rounds, and I used ours to try and pump everyone's spirits back up.

"Look, we can still win this," I said.

"No way," Kyle said. "We're sunk."

"Maybe we should just concede now," Leila concurred gloomily.

"Concede?" I repeated. "We're not going to concede! We're

going to win this thing! All we have to do is answer four out of the next five questions correctly, and it's in the bag."

Kyle snorted at this, Leila sighed, and Nicholas looked wistfully at the exit, as though he were considering an escape. Only Sanjiv remained silent, his head bowed.

"I should have gotten that last one," he muttered to himself. "I knew the answer, I really did. But I thought I'd better work it out on paper first to be sure."

"You see? That's just it! You *knew* the answer. . . . You just need more confidence in yourself," I said bracingly.

"Yeah, dude. You need to chill," Kyle said. "Because you're seriously freaking out the rest of us."

"Kyle . . ." I began irritably, but before I could point out all the ways in which he wasn't being helpful, a voice interrupted me.

"Hey, Miranda."

I spun around. Dex was standing there. He looked a little uneasy, and had his hands thrust into his jean pockets. He was wearing a gray tee with a picture of a Rubik's Cube screen printed on the chest.

"Dex!" I said. "Hi . . . um, I mean . . . hi!"

He grinned impishly at my incoherence. I smiled back at him, and the awkwardness that had been there between us before, at Hannah's party, seemed to fall away.

"What are you doing here?" I asked, stepping away from my teammates. Our huddle was breaking up, anyway. Sanjiv's father had come over to talk to his son, and the others wandered off to use the bathroom or get a drink.

"I came to watch you kick some serious math ass," Dex said. "You're really rocking it, huh?"

I shook my head. "Actually, no, we're losing."

I glanced back to where Sanjiv and his dad were standing at the edge of the stage. Mr. Gupta was talking animatedly, gesturing wildly. Sanjiv just stood there, listening silently and looking miserable. I felt a rush of sympathy for him, and was glad my dad hadn't tried to come over and coach me during the intermission. How mortifying.

"Yeah, but you're doing well. You haven't missed a single question yet," Dex said encouragingly.

I smiled, glad that he'd noticed. "Yeah, well. It's a team event, though. What matters is the final score," I explained.

"So there's no MVP award?" Dex asked.

"Not that anyone's told me about," I said.

"That's too bad. You'd have had a lock on it."

"I don't know. That Chinese guy is pretty good," I said.

"Yeah, he's not bad. But you're better," Dex said.

When he grinned down at me, my stomach did a flip-flop, and I could feel a hot flush spread over my cheeks and down my neck.

"Hey, Miranda, I think we're supposed to sit down," Leila called out.

I glanced back at her, and she smiled and looked knowingly at Dex, her eyebrows raised. Which just made me blush more. But this distraction meant that I hadn't noticed Nicholas sidling up next to Dex and me.

"Hi, I'm Nicholas," Nicholas said in a much deeper voice than normal. He was also standing oddly, with his shoulders set back and his thin chest pushed out. It made him look a little like a rooster. A very short, scrawny rooster. He thrust his hand out at Dex.

"Oh, hey. I'm Dex," Dex said. He hesitated for a moment—I could see his point, since who under the age of thirty shakes hands?—and then took Nicholas's hand. Dex winced, and a look of surprise crossed his face, and I realized that Nicholas had a death grip on him.

It started to dawn on me that Nicholas was putting on this macho act to impress me. Or maybe to scare off Dex. Either way, it wasn't working. I was getting irritated, and I could see Dex looked bemused.

"Nice to meet you, Dex," Nicholas said in the same oddly deep baritone he'd suddenly developed. "That's funny. Your accent isn't very strong."

"What accent?" Dex asked.

"Aren't you English?" Nicholas asked.

"No," Dex said. He was still smiling, although his brow was now wrinkled in confusion. "Why did you think I'm English?"

"Because Miranda said that she was dating a guy she met in London," Nicholas said.

I could have died right there on the spot. I stared, horrified, at Nicholas, as his words hung there between us. When I finally worked up the nerve to look up at Dex, I saw that he was no longer smiling. The worst part was, he didn't even look angry. Just . . . hurt. Really, really hurt.

"Right, Miranda?" Nicholas asked, turning to me. I could tell he wasn't really trying to screw things up between Dex and me. . . . More that he didn't understand, and was trying to sort out the answer to the puzzle. "You said that you met a guy while you were in London, and you were dating long-distance."

"Nicholas," I hissed, turning on him. "Will you please go away?"

Now Nicholas looked hurt. In fact, he had the same hangdog expression that Willow gives me when I forget to give her her after-dinner treat. He turned and hurried away without saying another word. I felt like the world's biggest heel. It wasn't Nicholas's fault. Well, other than his obvious lack of social graces. After all, he had been telling the truth; I *had* told him I had a boyfriend in London.

What was worse, Dex seemed to know that Nicholas hadn't been making it up.

"I can explain," I said automatically. "It's not what it sounds like."

Which is, of course, what everyone who cheats on their boyfriend says, and so made me look even guiltier. I decided to point out the obvious.

"I didn't know what was going on with us when I was in London," I said defensively. "I thought you were dating someone else here. It was just a mix-up."

"And you have a boyfriend there now?" Dex asked quietly.

"No," I said, shaking my head. "No, he's definitely not my boyfriend. He's just a . . . friend. Who happens to be a . . . guy."

*Gah.* This was going from bad to worse to the pit of hell.

Dex shook his head slowly. "Okay, whatever, Miranda. I think I'm just going to take off." He turned to leave.

"No, wait!" I said. "Don't go!"

Professor Bauder chose that moment to tap on his microphone, yet again causing an earsplitting feedback to fill the small auditorium. "Players must now return to their seats. Round three will be starting in one minute. Any player not in his or her seat at that time will forfeit their turn."

"Miranda, come on," Kyle called out, his voice filled with anxiety.

I glanced back at my team; they were all sitting in their seats. And with the noticeable exception of Nicholas—who was staring down at the table in front of him, looking like he was trying very hard not to cry—they were all staring at me imploringly.

I looked back at Dex, who hadn't stopped when I called after him. Instead, he was making his way quickly and resolutely down the steps of the stage and up the aisle, heading toward the rear exit of the auditorium.

"Miranda," Leila called again.

I sighed, returned to the table, and took my seat in between Sanjiv and Nicholas. My head was spinning with everything that had just happened, and my skin was so flushed, it felt like it was burning up. I pressed my hands to my cheeks, hoping to cool them, while thoughts clattered in my mind. What had just happened? Did Dex really think that Henry was my boyfriend?

"We are now ready to begin round number three," Professor Bauder announced. "St. Pius is leading by a score of fifty to thirty. However, since the correct answers to questions in round three are worth fifteen points apiece, the Notting Hill school team still has a chance to catch up." Professor Bauder smiled kindly at our table, but I was still so horrified by what had just happened, I could only stare blankly back at him.

"Are you ready for the first question?" Professor Bauder asked. Leila and her St. Pius counterpart both nodded.

The moderator read the question aloud, but I was barely paying attention. *Should I go after Dex? No, I can't, not right now, not in the middle of the competition. Should I call him after? But what if I called him and he didn't want to talk to me? Or what if I left a message, and then he didn't call back? Would it mean he didn't get the message . . . or that he got it, and just didn't want to talk to me?*

Applause sounded, shocking me briefly out of my reverie. I glanced over and saw Leila beaming, and the girl in the number one seat for St. Pius glowering. Apparently, Leila had won the question, a conclusion that was confirmed when Professor Bauder announced that the score was now fifty to forty-five. We were only five points behind.

But I still couldn't focus, not when Kyle answered his question correctly—putting us ten points in the lead—or when Nicholas, his voice an unhappy bleat, won his question.

"Notting Hill is now in the lead, seventy-five to fifty," Professor Bauder said. "And now for question number four."

*Number four? Oh, no, that's me,* I realized with a start.

I tried to force all thoughts of Dex and Henry and Nicholas's bad timing out of my head, clearing room to hear the question. But try as I might, my brain felt like it was on the fritz. The disastrous conversation I'd just had with Dex kept playing over and over, as though it was on a loop in my mind, and my ears were filled with a distracting buzzing sound. I glanced over at Austin Strong; he smirked back at me. I scowled at him.

Suddenly Professor Bauder was reading the question: "A player pays five dollars to bet on a game of dice. In the game, a single die is rolled. If the number on the die is odd, the player loses. If the number on the die is even, the die is rolled again. On this second roll, the number must be the same as the previous roll. If so, the player wins. If not, the player loses. How much should the player win if the probability of winning times the amount won is what the player should pay?"

I blinked. *What? What was the question?* I'd lost him after the die was rolled the second time. It was actually surreal in a way. For the first time in my entire life, the correct mathematical answer didn't just float into my head all on its own. Instead, it stayed out of reach, slipping away as I grappled for it. I could feel everyone's eyes on me, waiting for the number to come popping out of my mouth. But . . . it didn't. I just sat there, completely clueless.

And then, to my utter horror, Austin Strong hit his buzzer.

"Yes, Mr. Strong," Professor Bauder said, nodding at Austin.

Austin leaned forward. "The answer is sixty dollars," he said into his microphone.

"That is correct," Professor Bauder replied.

My jaw dropped open as Austin Strong sat back in his chair, his face glowing with pleasure as the audience applauded politely for him. After all, he hadn't just gotten the question correct. . . . He'd finally beaten *me*, his arch nemesis, the one competitor he'd never scored a point off of.

For the first time ever, I had lost a question in a Mu Alpha Theta competition.

"This is going to be a close one. Notting Hill is still in the lead with seventy-five, but St. Pius now has a score of sixty-five. The team that answers the next question correctly will win," Professor Bauder announced.

I heard Sanjiv make a strangled noise in his throat, and when I turned to see if he was okay, his face was chalky with fear. His eyes were open wide and unblinking, and he kept shaking his head a little, as though to scare off a pesky fly.

"It'll be okay, Sanjiv," I whispered. "Take a deep breath."

"So here's the final question of the day: What is the square root of 5,184?"

The buzzing left my head suddenly, and the answer came to me so quickly, I was actually relieved. Seventy-two. It wasn't all that hard of a calculation, not if you really understood how square roots worked, but Sanjiv had always struggled with them. I saw him scratching away at his scrap paper, trying to work out the equation.

He hadn't gotten very far when his competitor, Qin Gang, pressed his buzzer.

"Yes," Professor Bauder said, nodding at him.

"Seventy-two," Qin Gang said.

It seemed as though everyone in the room was holding his or her breath.

"That is correct! Which means that St. Pius wins!" Professor Bauder announced.

The small section of the audience that was there rooting for St. Pius cheered energetically. A jubilant Austin Strong slapped hands with Qin Gang, whose round moonlike face remained impassive. I glanced up and down our table; the Geek High team wore matching looks of defeat, except for Sanjiv, who—clearly in a state of denial—was still working out the square root equation. I gently took the pencil out of his hand.

"It's over," I said, putting the pencil back down on the table. "They won."

Sanjiv's shoulders sagged and his head drooped like a wilting flower. I could tell he was fighting back tears. I knew the feeling; I was fighting back tears myself.

Not only had we lost the competition . . . but it looked like I'd ruined things with Dex.

"Come on," I said dully, giving Sanjiv a nudge. "We have to shake hands with St. Pius. Let's just get it over with."

# Chapter 16

To: mirandajbloom@gmail.com
From: hewent@britmail.net
Subject: [RE] Soul Crushing Defeat
Miranda,

You lost a maths competition?!? How is that possible? Did the question you missed involve tracking map coordinates?

Kidding . . . just kidding. Seriously, I'm sure you'll smash them next time. And the victory will be all the sweeter.

Maybe this will make you feel better:

## My Top Three All-Time Most Humiliating Defeats in History

1. Napoleon's loss to the Duke of Wellington at Waterloo
2. The Dardanelles Campaign (what you Yanks called the Battle of Gallipoli) during the First World War
3. The 1950 World Cup, in which the English National Men's Football Team was defeated by the United States.

Yours,

Henry

P.S. I'm too much of a gentleman to tell you what goolies are. I suggest you consult a British slang Web site.

"I thought you didn't care about Mu Alpha Theta," Charlie said as we waited for geology class to start on Monday morning.

"I don't. I mean, I don't *really*. But still. Of course I'd rather win than lose," I said, feeling a bit stung by her obvious lack of interest. Charlie had barely looked up from her laptop, from which she was busily IM'ing Mitch while I told her about the MATh meet. I noticed that she'd colored her hair a conventional shade of strawberry blond, and—remembering what Charlie had said about Mitch liking redheads—guessed that she'd done it for his benefit. This irritated me beyond all sense.

I hadn't even bothered to call her on Sunday—there was no point, as Charlie now reserved her weekends to spend exclusively with Mitch—so this was the first chance I'd had to catch her up on our disastrous match against St. Pius. And, more importantly, my disastrous run-in with Dex. Charlie even managed to look up from her laptop as I told her about it.

"So call him and explain," she said.

"I can't," I said.

"Why not?"

"Because there's nothing to explain. He's angry because I told him I went out with Henry when I was in London," I said, feeling another twinge of unhappiness as I remembered Dex's reaction. "I can't step into a time machine, go back to Saturday, and deny everything."

Although, if I had a time machine at my disposal, I'd go even further back, to the night of the Snowflake, and make sure this time that Dex had my correct e-mail address, *and* my cell phone number, *and* Sadie's number in London. Then none of this would have happened, and Dex would probably, most likely, now be my actual, genuine boyfriend.

"Yeah, telling him about that guy wasn't your best move," Charlie said. She shook her head at my stupidity, which ruffled my already frayed nerves.

"I didn't want to lie to him!" I said. I crossed my arms and slumped back in my chair. "I *was* seeing Henry while I was in London."

"But it wasn't serious," Charlie said. "It's not like you're dating him now."

"Well . . . we do e-mail. Does that count?"

"No. You live on different continents. It's not like you're going to prom with him," Charlie said.

"Geek High doesn't have a prom," I reminded her.

Charlie exhaled the world-weary sigh of one who is in a serious relationship, and so no longer has any patience for the romantic blunderings of the unattached. "It was a figure of speech, Miranda. You should just call Dex, and ask *him* out."

The very idea of doing something so audacious made my stomach turn over. "I'm not going to do that!" I exclaimed.

"Why not?"

"Because it would be mortifying. I'm pretty sure he doesn't like me anymore, if he ever did. If I asked him out, he'd just say no, and I would be humiliated," I said.

"Well, I think you're being ridiculous," Charlie said, in a way that made me want to shake her until her teeth rattled. It was times like this that I missed the old Charlie. That Charlie might have been cynical and unromantic, but she would never have been so condescending.

Finn came in, his messenger bag slung over one shoulder. I saw him cast a nervous glance at the snakes in their glass cages that lined the back of the classroom.

"Hey, M," he said, sliding into the chair next to me. He pointedly ignored Charlie. "Tough break on the St. Pius match. I thought you had it in the bag."

"You went?" Charlie asked him.

Finn nodded curtly at her. "We always go to Miranda's competitions," he said pointedly.

The thing was, they always had, at least to the home MATh

matches. This was the first time Charlie had skipped one. I could tell from the uneasy expression that flitted over her face that she was thinking the same thing.

"I didn't think you'd care if I went," Charlie said, half apologetically, half defensively. "It didn't seem like the competition was all that important to you."

Finn snorted and looked disgusted.

"It's okay," I said quickly.

Charlie shot Finn a dirty look, but then said, her voice small, "I'm sorry, Miranda."

"Really, it's fine," I said. "Forget it. Just one less person to witness our humiliation."

I nodded discreetly in Sanjiv's direction. He was sitting in much the same position I'd last seen him in after our loss on Saturday. His shoulders were slumped forward, and his head drooped down, as though it were too heavy for his thin neck to hold up straight.

"Anyway," I said, glad to change the subject, "are we still on for Saturday night? It's my birthday, and you know what that means: bowling night!"

There was an awkward silence. Both Finn and Charlie looked fixedly in different directions.

I sighed. "Come on, guys. I know you haven't been getting along lately, but we've always spent our birthdays together. It's a tradition."

Still nothing. I decided it was time to pull out the big guns: guilt.

"I don't know if you've noticed, but things haven't been going all that well for me lately. This is the one thing I've had to look forward to," I said.

It worked. Finn shifted in his seat, but then in a soft voice said, "I'll be there." And Charlie nodded and quickly said, "Me, too. Wouldn't miss it."

"Yea!" I cheered, feeling slightly better. Even if I'd once and for all tanked any chance I might ever have had with Dex, and even if the Geek High Mu Alpha Theta team had lost to that pompous jerk Austin Strong, and even if I had to live with the Demon, who had just that morning thrown my writing journal into the garbage (luckily, I'd discovered it in time and was able to retrieve it out from under the used coffee grinds) . . . at least I was going to spend my birthday with my two best friends.

The door to the classroom swung open and Mr. Douglass came lumbering in. He was holding a stack of papers in his hand, and as we fell silent, he held them up and announced, "Pop quiz on the Oceanic crust. Anyone who fails will be staying after school tomorrow to clean out the snake cages."

The class groaned, and Finn gave a visible shudder.

"I think we should consider bagging the rest of the season," Kyle Carpenter announced at our Mu Alpha Theta practice after school.

"Quitting?" I repeated, astonished. "Why would we do that?"

"Well, what's the point? The team already has a losing record. That means there's no chance we'll make state finals, and if we don't make—and win—state finals, then being on this team isn't going to look all that great on our college apps," Kyle said. "It'll just be another ordinary extracurricular. I read that it's better to have a volunteer credential than that. If we disband the team now, I'll have time to volunteer at the retirement home."

"*You* want to volunteer with senior citizens?" Leila asked, her voice round with surprise.

Kyle shrugged. "No. But I've heard that the Ivies look favorably on volunteer experience with old people and kids. And old people who spend all of their time either sleeping or drooling will be less annoying than dealing with a bunch of screaming brats who crap in their pants."

"Lovely," Leila said, looking disgusted with him.

"You're such a humanitarian, Kyle," I said.

I glanced around at the others to see what they thought of the idea Kyle had floated about disbanding our MATh team. Leila and Sanjiv didn't look convinced . . . but they also weren't arguing that we had to keep going. Nicholas just stared down at his practice notebook, refusing to meet my eyes. I'd said hello to him when I first came in, hoping we could just gloss over the unpleasantness of our run-in at the competition. Apparently, he wasn't in a forgiving mood.

In any event, I had bigger problems to worry about. Like Kyle's announcement that we should disband the team. Part of me was able to instantly recognize this for the opportunity it was: If the team disbanded, it would mean that I would be totally off the hook. My agreement with Headmaster Hughes had been that I would compete on the MATh team. . . . But if the team wasn't there, my obligation would end.

But another part of my brain—a louder, more stubborn side— was outraged at how my teammates were ready to throw in the towel.

"We can't quit!" I said, before I'd even thought it through. "I can't believe any of you would even consider the idea!"

"Well . . . maybe Kyle's right. There's no point in fighting for a lost cause," Leila said uncertainly.

"A lost cause? We lost one competition! Big deal! What if the Founding Fathers had given up after the Boston Massacre?" I blazed.

"I don't know if that's really the best analogy," Leila whispered. She shot a worried look at Sanjiv, who had managed to slump even lower in his chair.

"Okay, forget the massacre part," I said quickly. "The point is, we can do this. We have a competition Saturday, and one the weekend after that. We can still make state finals. Sure, we'll have to win all of our matches between now and then, but we can do that," I said. "We just have to work harder! Practice more, and work on our drills. We can totally win!"

"And if we don't?" Kyle asked.

"Then we go down fighting," I said.

I could sense a shift in the air. Leila was nodding, and Nicholas had finally looked up, an expression of determination set on his thin face. Even Kyle looked like he might be won over.

But it was Sanjiv who finally spoke for the group.

"Yeah," he said, squaring his thin shoulders and straightening his glasses. "Yeah. We can do this. Come on, guys. Let's get to work."

◆

"I really didn't think that through," I muttered to myself an hour later, as I left the practice clutching the new schedule Sanjiv had passed out. He'd scheduled practices every day this week and next. But I couldn't very well argue with him over it, not after my speech about how we couldn't give up. What had I been thinking? Now I was stuck in math hell. I wondered if I could at least get some material for a short story out of it.

"Miranda, I'm glad I found you," Mrs. Gordon said, stopping me in the hall.

"Hey, Mrs. Gordon."

"I received your registration materials for the Winston writing competition," Mrs. Gordon said brightly. "Come with me. I left them on my desk."

I followed Mrs. Gordon into her classroom, where she handed me a manila envelope.

"Here you go. You'd better give this to your parents, so they can make travel arrangements for you. Someone will have to go with you, obviously, as a chaperone," Mrs. Gordon said.

"You're not going?" I asked.

She shook her head. "No, I'm sorry, I can't. My parents' fiftieth wedding anniversary is that weekend. We're having a big party for them."

"I understand," I said. "Which weekend is it?"

"April twenty-first," she said. "The schedule of events is enclosed. If you want to attend the party on Friday night, you'll have to miss school that day to travel. I'm sure the headmaster won't mind." Mrs. Gordon smiled. "Especially if you win a new trophy for our trophy case."

"Erm, right," I said, and felt a nervous flip-flop in my stomach. It was real. . . . I was going. My short story was going to be judged by three of the most prestigious English literature professors in the country. They would tell me once and for all if I had the talent to be a writer. . . . Or not.

# Chapter 17

One of my favorite movies of all time is *Sixteen Candles*. In the movie, Molly Ringwald wakes up on the morning of her sixteenth birthday to discover that her entire family has forgotten it's her birthday. It's hilarious and subversive, mostly because it's something you think would never really happen.

At least, I used to think it would never really happen. Not to me.

In past years, when I was living with Sadie, she made a huge deal over my birthday. I'd wake up to find Sadie in the kitchen, making me something decadent for breakfast, like chocolate chip pancakes or Belgian waffles slathered with sugared sliced strawberries and mounds of whipped cream. She'd take the day off from work and let me skip school, and we'd spend the day doing something amazing together. One year, we went down to Miami and had lunch in South Beach. Another year, we went to Disney World for the day. And then I always met Finn and Charlie for pizza and bowling.

I knew that expecting the Sadie treatment now that I was living with Dad and Peyton would be a sure way to end up disappointed. So I tried to expect nothing. Well. Not *nothing*. Surely there would be presents and cards and cake, if not a full-blown day of celebration.

As it turned out, I would have been better off sticking with nothing. Because that's exactly what I got.

The morning of my sixteenth birthday, a Saturday, I woke up in a good mood. I jumped out of bed, dressed quickly, and then padded down the hall into the cold marble foyer, turned left, and headed toward the kitchen. Everyone was already up. Dad was sitting at the kitchen table, reading the newspaper and eating cereal. Hannah was perched on the counter, long, bare legs dangling in front of her, sipping coffee and talking to Peyton, who was slicing up a melon.

"Good morning, everyone," I said brightly.

"Good morning, honey," Dad said. He glanced up and smiled warmly at me before returning to his breakfast and newspaper.

"Hey," Hannah said. "Guess what?"

"What?" I asked.

"I'm getting my car today!" Hannah said.

Peyton had bought Hannah a car for her birthday: a silver Lexus SUV with a buttery tan leather interior and a high-tech stereo system that had to be custom ordered, causing a delay in the delivery date. Peyton had spent an afternoon screaming at the Lexus salesman over the phone—she'd wanted the car parked in the driveway with a big red bow on it, for Hannah to wake up to on her birthday. Finally, the salesman drove over a loaner car to use as a placeholder. I got the feeling that they didn't normally do this, but, then, Peyton rarely failed to get her way.

"Cool," I said. I have to admit, a part of me wondered if I'd be getting a car today, too. I didn't yet have my driver's license, but, then, neither did Hannah. She just had a learner's permit.

"I can't wait," Hannah said, swinging her legs happily. "Mom, you're going to take me, right?"

Peyton nodded. "We'll go after my tennis match," she said.

"Cool," Hannah said. "That'll give me time to shower and get ready."

As beautiful as Hannah is, it's not uncommon for her to spend two hours grooming herself to leave the house. It takes me about ten minutes. And that's including my shower.

Still, this wasn't a day to roll my eyes over my stepsister's bathroom habits. Instead, I just smiled at her and waited for someone to say something. Like,

*Happy Birthday, Miranda!*

*Would you like some special birthday pancakes?*

*I think there's something waiting for you in the driveway. . . .*

But nothing. No one said a word about what day it was. Hannah just went back to chattering about how she couldn't wait to get her license—she was taking her driving test later that week—and then Peyton began to complain loudly about how the most recent housekeeper she'd hired was slacking on the job. Then my dad stood up and announced that he was going to go to the gym. And all the while, I just stood there, staring at all of them, wondering if it was all supposed to be some sort of joke.

"Wait!" I said, catching my dad just as he was headed out of the kitchen.

But when he looked back at me and I saw his expression—surprised interest, without the hint of a mischievous twinkle—I realized that it wasn't a joke. They *had* forgotten my birthday. And not just any birthday . . . my sixteenth birthday.

Well, I certainly wasn't going to remind them. I had my pride.

"What is it, honey?" my dad asked.

"Nothing," I said, shaking my head and turning away from him, so he couldn't see the hurt expression on my face. "Just . . . nothing."

•

To: mirandajbloom@gmail.com

From: hewent@britmail.net

Subject: many happy returns of the day

Seriously? Your family forgot your birthday? That's so unbelievably lame.

I didn't even know it was your birthday (although technically I didn't forget, since you never told me). Still, I feel like a bit of a prat for not sending you a card.

**My Top Three Worst Birthdays**

(1)  age fourteen (measles)

(2)  age eight (petting zoo disaster; I ended up in hospital, after being bitten by a goat)

(3)  age one (don't remember this one, but my mum tells me that there was an incident involving the birthday cake and a dirty nappy)

I'll make it up to you when you come back to London. We'll have a belated birthday bonanza.

Cheers, Happy Birthday,

Henry

•

I spent the rest of the morning and most of the afternoon in my room, studying and feeling sorry for myself. I had to read a few chapters of *1984* for Mod Lit, a chapter in my *Art History of the Renaissance* book, and a paper on World War Two for modern history class, all of which was due on Monday. For lunch, I made a peanut butter and jelly sandwich and brought it back up to my room on a tray, so I wouldn't have to eat with the others. . . . Not that they were even around, from what I could tell.

In the afternoon, I took a break from studying, and took Willow for a walk.

*I can't believe everyone forgot,* I thought sadly, as we made our way down the beach. Finn and Charlie hadn't, of course; we still had plans to meet up at the bowling alley. But I hadn't gotten so much as a single card, not even from Sadie. My own mother had forgotten my birthday! How big of a loser did you have to be for your own mother to forget the day you were born?

But when Willow and I got back, my dad was waiting for us on the back deck, looking chagrined.

"Miranda . . . I'm so sorry," he said. "It's your birthday."

I shrugged. I really wasn't ready to forgive and forget just yet.

"It's okay," I said.

"No, it's not. It's . . . well. I don't know what to say," he said. He hugged me to him. I held my body stiff, away from his for a moment, but finally relented and let him fold me into his arms.

"How'd you figure it out?" I asked.

"This arrived while you were out," he said, handing me a FedEx box. It was addressed to me in Sadie's familiar elegant scrawl. Underneath my name, she'd written: HAPPY SWEET SIXTEEN!

A wave of relief washed over me. At least Sadie hadn't forgotten me. I tore open the package. There was a card and two wrapped packages inside. I sank down on one of the wrought iron porch chairs and opened the card first. It was arty, with a painting of a peacock on the front. Inside, it read:

*Have a very happy birthday, Miranda! I wish I could be there to spend it with you. I miss you terribly!*
*Love and kisses, Sadie*

I opened the larger of the two packages. It was an old book wrapped in multiple layers of lavender tissue paper. Once I got the wrapping off, I recognized it immediately.

"*Wind in the Willows!*" I exclaimed, turning the book over in my hands. "This was my favorite book when I was growing up. I even named Willow after it. Wait, there's a note in here."

Sadie had stuck an index card just inside of the book. It was the sort of card she sketched out her plot points on when she was writing a new book. On this one, she'd jotted a note: *It's a first edition!*

"A first edition," I gasped. "Oh, my gosh!"

"May I see?" Dad asked.

I nodded and handed him the book. He paged through it for a moment and then smiled. A little sadly, I thought.

"I used to read this to you when you were little," he said. "You'd ask for it every night."

"I remember," I said.

"You do?" he asked.

I nodded. Bedtime stories with my dad had been a ritual of my childhood. Well past the age when I could read myself, he'd read a chapter or two aloud to me every night before I went to sleep.

"I wonder what's in here," I said, turning my attention to the smaller box. It was wrapped in shiny red paper, with a large white bow around it. I pulled off the ribbon and tore at the paper, revealing a white jewelry box. I opened it up and gasped. Inside was a gold claddagh ring. It had the traditional Claddagh design: two hands holding a crown-topped heart.

"Wow," I said. "It's beautiful!" I tried it on and admired how it looked on my hand. "What do you think?" I asked, showing it to my dad.

"It's beautiful," he said. He sighed, and shook his head ruefully. "I'm glad your mother, at least, came through. What do you say? Would you like to go out shopping? You can pick out whatever you want. Wait, no, you hate shopping. I guess that wouldn't be much of a treat for you."

"I can't anyway," I said. "I'm going to meet Finn and Charlie at the bowling alley. It's our birthday tradition."

"That sounds like fun," Dad said. He looked disappointed, though, and I had to steel myself against the inevitable surge of guilt this gave me. After all, it wasn't my fault he'd forgotten my birthday.

Just then Hannah danced out onto the back deck, flush with excitement over her new SUV.

"There you are, Richard!" she said. "You haven't seen my new car yet!"

My dad's reaction to this was almost comical in its horror, as the stark contrast of how differently Hannah and I had been treated on our birthdays dawned on him. Hannah had gotten a huge party and an expensive new car, whereas no one had even remembered mine.

"Right," he said, swallowing hard and looking from Hannah to me. "Um . . . Hannah, do you know what today is?"

"It's new car day!" Hannah cheered.

"Ha ha," Dad laughed weakly. "It's also Miranda's birthday."

Hannah stared at me. "Are you serious? Why didn't you say anything?" Her tone was almost accusing, as though I'd planned this just to annoy her.

I shrugged. "I didn't know I had to," I said.

"Oh. That sucks that everyone forgot." Hannah frowned for a minute and then her face brightened with an idea. "I know what'll cheer you up! Let's go for a ride in my new car!"

●

I was glad I wasn't staying at the beach house for dinner. The atmosphere there was oppressive. In his guilt over having forgotten my birthday, Dad was being overly solicitous toward me, and, in turn, seething with anger at Peyton. As it turned out, Peyton had written my birthday down in her calendar. She'd sworn she hadn't looked at it today. . . . But I don't think my dad believed her. She lived by her calendar; it was the only place she was able to track all of her various beauty salon and spa appointments, tennis matches and lunches. Hannah was too jubilant over her new car to pay much attention to anyone else. But at every mention of the new car, my dad looked even more uncomfortable.

Here's the thing: As the heiress to a mouthwash fortune, Peyton has a lot of money. My dad does not. I don't know exactly what their money arrangements are, but I could safely presume that my dad's salary as an architect didn't go all that far. The mouthwash money had paid for the beach house and for Peyton's extensive wardrobe and for the lavish lifestyle she insisted on. It had also paid for Hannah's new car, of course. And I got the sense that my dad was suddenly uncomfortable with this. But I didn't know what I could do about it.

"I'm so sorry, Miranda," Dad said for the two hundredth time as he dropped me off at the bowling alley.

"I know. You don't have to keep apologizing," I said.

"Maybe we could have a redo next Saturday," Dad suggested. "We could go out to dinner or have a party. Whatever you want."

"I can't next Saturday. I have a MATh competition. It's in Orlando, so we probably won't get back until late."

"Oh." Dad looked so crestfallen, I actually felt a little sorry for him. "But we have to do something to celebrate. I want to make it up to you."

"Okay," I said. "We'll have dinner or something."

Dad's face cleared. "Good. How about tomorrow? I could make reservations at Swordfish."

"For just the two of us?" I asked hopefully. I didn't want to spend what was supposed to be my birthday dinner getting zinged by Peyton's nasty barbs or having to listen to Hannah natter on endlessly about her car.

Dad opened his mouth to object—I knew how fond he was of his fantasy of the perfect family—but then he seemed to think better of it. "Okay. Just the two of us," he said.

I knew it was a major concession.

•

I was happy to see that Finn and Charlie were already at the bowling alley, waiting for me by the shoe-rental window. I was less happy to see that Mitch was with them. He was, as usual, wearing far too much hair gel, and he was holding hands with Charlie.

"Hi," I said, arching my eyebrows in surprise.

"Hi, Miranda," Charlie sang out. "Happy birthday!"

"Thanks," I said, looking from her to Mitch and then finally at Finn, who looked like he'd just swallowed a bug.

"Hi," Finn said without enthusiasm. "Happy birthday."

"Thanks," I said, my heart sinking. This was not going to be fun. Not at all. It was going to be awkward and difficult and—if Mitch and Charlie started up with the public displays of affection again—really uncomfortable.

"You guys have gotten your bowling shoes already?" I asked.

"Yep. Look, Mitch and I match," Charlie said, pointing down at her feet. She beamed. "Isn't that cute?"

"Um . . . yeah," I said, turning away before she could see the revolted expression on my face.

I traded in my faded Jack Purcell canvas sneakers for bowling shoes, and then the four of us made our way over to one of the empty bowling alleys. There was one league playing. It was made up entirely of women over the age of seventy, all of whom were wearing lime green shirts. Otherwise, we pretty much had the place to ourselves.

"So how has your birthday been so far?" Charlie asked.

"Pretty rotten," I said.

"Why?"

"Everyone forgot," I said. "Well, everyone but Sadie. She sent me this ring."

I showed off my new Claddagh ring, which Charlie admired. Then she frowned. "What do you mean everyone forgot?"

"Dad, Peyton, Hannah. None of them remembered."

Charlie gasped, and even Finn looked shocked.

"They forgot it was your birthday?" Charlie asked.

"Dude, that sucks. It's like that movie," Mitch said. He scratched at a pimple on his chin.

Charlie shook her head, her eyes narrowing with anger. "I can't believe they did that to you. Well, just you wait, we'll make up for it. This will be the best birthday bowling night in the history of birthday bowling nights."

But it wasn't the best birthday bowling night in the history of birthday bowling nights. It was the worst.

Charlie and Finn didn't talk. Not at all. They sat on opposite sides of our booth, Finn sulkily withdrawn and Charlie perched on Mitch's lap, cooing annoyingly down at him. I sat in the middle, insisting that the birthday girl should keep score, although really, I just wanted to be there to keep the peace if Finn and Charlie started bickering again. But the glacial silence between my two best friends made it unnecessary.

At first, I was frustrated. . . . But that quickly morphed into a simmering anger. Couldn't they pretend to get along for a single night for my sake? Wasn't it bad enough that my so-called family had ruined my birthday? Did my friends really have to make it worse?

Plus, I couldn't bowl to save my life. I've never been a great bowler—Finn is the really talented bowler of our group—but I was stinking up the joint worse than usual. Every ball I threw ended up in the gutter. Over and over again.

"Shoot," I muttered under my breath, as the purple-and-black mottled ball I'd selected veered to the left and shot by the pins without knocking a single one down. "I guess you win, Finn. Another game?"

I thought it was a rhetorical suggestion. We always stayed for a second round, and had only bowled one round of ten frames. But to my surprise, Finn stood up.

"I have to get home."

"Why?" I asked.

"Curfew," Finn said.

Which I knew was a lie. First of all, Finn doesn't have a curfew. Second, it was only seven o'clock.

"You're not really leaving now, are you?" I asked.

Finn nodded and shot a grim look at Charlie, who was still perched on Mitch's lap. They were kissing, oblivious to the world around them.

"Happy birthday, M," Finn said. He held up his fist, and, after hesitating, I sighed, and bumped my fist against his.

"Thanks," I said. "And thanks for my present."

Finn had given me a bobble head greyhound figurine and a new writing journal. Charlie had given me a T-shirt that said LITTLE MISS SUNSHINE on the front, and had a picture of a round yellow ball-shaped girl underneath.

"I was going to get you a T-shirt that read I ONLY DATE BRITS, but I thought under the circumstances you'd prefer this one," Charlie had joked when I opened it.

"Later," Finn now said.

He waved and turned to leave. I sat back down with a sigh. Charlie and Mitch continued to kiss.

Things went rapidly downhill after Finn left. At least while he was there, I had someone to talk to. And if Charlie and Mitch were too enamored of one another to remember to take a turn, Finn and I would just bowl for them.

But now I was basically on my own. I got tired of reminding Charlie to bowl, or asking Mitch if he was going to pass, and finally I just gave up on bowling and slumped back in my molded plastic chair.

The more I thought about the day, the angrier I got. Why couldn't Charlie take one night off from her boyfriend to hang out with me? Was that really too much to ask? We'd barely spent any time together outside of school since I'd gotten back from London. And when I did see her, all she wanted to talk about was Mitch. Well, I was sick of hearing about Mitch. And I was sick of watching Charlie coo and giggle at him as though he were an infant, rather than a seventeen-year-old guy with pimples and fuzz on his chin that I think was supposed to be a goatee. Not only was her behavior nauseating, it made me uncomfortable to be around it.

Finally, I'd had enough. I stood and without a word to Charlie stalked off. I paused just long enough to exchange the bowling shoes for my sneakers, and then stomped out of the bowling alley. As soon as I was outside, I pulled my cell phone out of my pocket and called my dad.

"Hi, it's me," I said. "Can you come get me?"

"Sure," Dad said. "Is everything okay? You sound upset."

"Everything's fine," I lied. "Can you come now?"

But it wasn't fine. I was so angry and hurt that I was actually shaking. My heart was pounding in my chest like a fist, and my skin felt tight and prickly. I stood, waiting for my dad to arrive, and wondered how long it would take Charlie to figure out that I'd left.

The answer? About twenty minutes.

"Miranda? What are you doing out here?"

I spun around and saw Charlie standing behind me. It was already dark out, but the sidewalk in front of the bowling alley was well lit, so I could see the confusion on her face.

"I'm leaving," I said through clenched teeth.

"But . . . why?" Charlie asked.

"Why?" I repeated. "*Why?* Because I don't feel like sitting by myself anymore."

"Where's Finn?"

"He left an hour ago," I said. "Did you seriously not notice?"

"No, I didn't . . . I mean, I did, but I thought he was just in the bathroom or something. I didn't realize he'd taken off. I can't believe Finn—he's so selfish to leave like that." Charlie rolled her eyes skyward.

I stared at her. *She* was criticizing *Finn?* At least he'd talked to me while he was at the bowling alley, which was more than I could say for her.

"Come back inside." Charlie rubbed her hands over her bare arms. "It's too cold to stand out here."

"My dad's on his way to pick me up now."

Charlie kept staring at me as though I had lost my mind, the same way she might have had I stripped off all my clothes and started turning cartwheels through the parking lot.

"Are you mad at me?" she finally asked. As though it was completely inconceivable to her that it would anger me to be left sitting by myself in a bowling alley, on my birthday, while she macked with her boyfriend.

"Yes, I'm mad at you!" I said hotly.

"But . . . why?"

"Why? *Why*? Are you kidding me?"

"No. I seriously have no idea. Do you have PMS or something?"

That was it. The final straw.

"No! I do not have PMS!" I shouted at her. "I can't believe you! You can't even spend one evening—*one evening*—alone with your friends! You have to drag your stupid boyfriend along. And then you spend the entire night sitting in his lap, giggling and baby talking to him and generally acting like an idiot!"

As I yelled at her, Charlie's expression shifted from one of confusion to tight-lipped anger. She folded her arms over her chest and glared at me.

"So now you agree with Finn? You think Mitch is stupid?" she snapped.

It was my turn to be bewildered. "What? What are you talking about?" I asked.

"You just said he's stupid! That's what you think, isn't it? I know it's what Finn thinks. That Mitch is dumber than you are, and therefore beneath you," Charlie fumed.

"I don't think that!" Well. That wasn't entirely honest. From what I knew of Mitch, he didn't strike me as a brain trust. But his brain power—or lack thereof—wasn't the point. "This has nothing to do with Mitch. It wouldn't matter if he was a Nobel Laureate. You're the one who's acting stupid. You're not even painting anymore. The Charlie I knew would have never given up her art for some guy. In fact, that's just it . . . I don't even know you anymore."

Charlie let out a humorless laugh. "And that's just it, isn't it?"

"What?"

"This isn't about me. It's about you. You're just jealous that I have a boyfriend and you don't. If Dex hadn't blown you off, how much do you want to bet you would have been with him tonight, and not begging Finn and me to spend time with you?" Charlie said.

My mouth actually dropped open with surprise. "No, I wouldn't have done that," I finally said. "I wouldn't throw my friends over the minute I got a new boyfriend."

"Maybe that's because you've never *had* a boyfriend," Charlie said.

The force of these words hit me like a physical punch. Charlie knew I was sensitive about the fact that I'd never had a boyfriend . . . and she especially knew how terrible I'd felt since Dex had walked off on me at the Mu Alpha Theta competition. Tears started to sting in my eyes.

Just then, my dad pulled up, giving the horn a playful honk to get my attention. I gave Charlie one last hurt look and then spun around on my heel, and headed to the car. I got in and slammed the door behind me.

"Does Charlie need a ride, too?" Dad asked.

"No," I said shortly. I used the heel of my hand to wipe away my tears. "Charlie already has a ride."

My dad cast a sideways glance at me. "Are you okay?"

I nodded. "Yep. I'm fine."

"How was bowling?"

"Bowling pretty much sucked," I said. I inhaled deeply and blew the air out in a long sigh.

"I'm sorry to hear that. But I have something that I think will cheer you up," Dad said hopefully.

"What?"

"You'll see," he said mysteriously. "It's a surprise." ·

I halfheartedly tried to get more information out of him on the short ride home, but Dad wouldn't budge, so I finally gave up. Because, really? I didn't care. My birthday had been such a complete and total bust, all I wanted to do now was go home and go to bed, and try to forget any of it had ever happened.

As we pulled up to the beach house, Dad honked the horn again.

"What are you doing?" I asked suspiciously.

"Nothing," he said, with feigned innocence.

We went inside. I turned to head off to my room to get Willow for her evening walk, but Dad stopped me.

"Come back to the kitchen," he said.

"But I have to get Willow."

"Come on. It's your surprise."

So I followed Dad into the kitchen, which was dark. . . . Except for the glowing light of the sixteen candles on the sheet cake on the table. Peyton, Hannah, and Hannah's boyfriend, Emmett, were all there, and as soon as they saw me, they started to sing "Happy Birthday." My dad joined in.

I couldn't help smiling. I'd thought I wasn't going to get a birthday cake, which had been a truly depressing thought, considering how much I love birthday cake. But Dad had come through. Dad and Hannah, and even Peyton. Maybe she didn't hate me as much as I thought she did.

"Make a wish and blow out your candles," Hannah said, once they'd finished singing.

I didn't know what to wish for. Should I wish for Dex to call and ask me out? Or that Charlie and I would make up? Or that I'd win the Winston writing contest? Or maybe even for the Geek High Mu Alpha Theta team to win at our competition next Saturday?

I couldn't decide. So finally I just wished for something—

*anything*—good to happen to me soon. And then I blew out my candles. Everyone clapped, and Peyton turned on the light, while my dad got out plates and a gallon tub of vanilla ice cream.

It was only then, with the kitchen lights on, that I realized what the cake said. Written in blue frosting, across a pure white background, were the words HAPPY RETIREMENT, BOB.

" 'Happy Retirement, Bob'?" I read aloud. I looked up, grinning. It was a joke, obviously.

But Hannah exchanged a guilty look with Emmett . . . and Peyton wasn't meeting my eyes.

"What?" Dad said. He came in closer and read the cake, his eyebrows furrowing. Then he looked up at Peyton.

"It was the only one they had at the bakery," Peyton said defensively. "I guess Bob, or whoever ordered the cake for him, never picked it up."

"You couldn't get them to scrape off the words *retirement* and *Bob*, and write in *birthday* and *Miranda*?" Dad asked.

"Well. They offered to. But they said it would take too long, and I didn't want to wait," Peyton said.

"You didn't want to wait," Dad repeated blankly. "How long did they say it would take?"

Peyton shrugged. "At *least* ten minutes," she said.

"You couldn't wait ten minutes so that Miranda would have a cake that actually had *Happy Birthday* on it?" Dad asked. This time it didn't sound like a real question . . . more like an accusation.

"It doesn't matter, Dad," I said. "The cake will still taste good."

"See? Miranda doesn't care," Peyton said.

"Yes, she does. And I care, too. I'm starting to realize that the only person around here who doesn't care is you, Peyton," Dad said.

"Should I go?" I heard Emmett murmur to Hannah.

"No, stay. Let's have some cake," Hannah said. She handed me the knife. "Here, Miranda, you cut."

Dad and Peyton stopped arguing—actually, they stopped talking altogether—long enough for me to cut and serve the cake, and for all of us, except for Peyton, to eat.

Later, after Emmett had left and Hannah and I had gone to bed, I could hear Dad and Peyton fighting behind the closed door of their bedroom. Dad's voice was low and grumbling with anger, while Peyton's was high and shrill. While part of me was glad that my dad was finally sticking up for me . . . another part of me wished they would just call a truce so the whole mess would go away.

# Chapter 18

In a way, I got my birthday wish: something good did happen over the next few weeks. Actually, a few good things happened.

First, Dad and I had a really nice dinner out together. He took me to Swordfish, my favorite restaurant, and we sat at a table by the windows, overlooking the intracoastal waterway. It was actually really nice spending time alone with my dad. We were able to talk and joke more freely, without the conversation being hijacked onto topics like the new handbags of the season or laser hair removal. My dad gave me a pretty necklace, a delicate gold chain with a gold flower pendant hanging on it. In the middle of the flower was a blue topaz stone.

"I love it!" I said, smiling broadly at my dad.

"Really? I'm glad." His expression grew somber for a moment. "I . . . I'm just sorry it's not a new car."

I waved him off. "It's fine, Dad. I don't need a new car."

"Maybe this summer we could look for a used car for you," he suggested.

"That would be great," I said. I held the necklace out to him. "Will you help me fasten this?"

The other good thing that happened was that the Geek High Mu Alpha Theta team made a comeback of sorts. Since Sanjiv needed to work on his competition skills—learning to wean himself off of pen and paper calculation, especially—I ended up taking charge of the practices. I hadn't thought I would want the job, but it was actually sort of fun. . . . Especially as I saw the team improve steadily. Also, I found a relaxation DVD for Sanjiv that taught meditation and deep breathing exercises, and instructed him to practice with it every night. Between that and the fact that the majority of our upcoming MATh meets were away, so his dad wouldn't be watching him, Sanjiv stopped panicking in the middle of the competitions. He was still our weakest player, a fact that rankled him to no end, but the rest of the team was getting stronger, and so Sanjiv's occasional blunders didn't cost us any more victories. In fact, we won our next four competitions.

Nicolas still wasn't talking to me, but I thought that everything considered, that wasn't the worst thing. His moody silences and refusal to meet my eyes made practice a bit uncomfortable, but I didn't know what to do to fix things between us.

My birthday wish didn't extend to all parts of my life, though. Dex never did call. Despite what I'd told Charlie, I did think about calling him and trying to explain about London and Henry. But I couldn't work up the nerve to do it.

Even worse, Charlie and I weren't speaking. It was making school really awkward. We had most of our classes together, but we didn't sit next to each other anymore. I usually sat with Finn, who also wasn't talking to Charlie, and Charlie either sat on her own or with one of our other classmates. I had to endure lunches with Finn and Tate, as they discussed whatever computer game they were currently hooked on. I'd steal glances at Charlie across the lunch room, where she now usually sat with Tabitha Stone. Tabitha would be droning on earnestly about whatever book she was currently reading, while Charlie would look so bored, I kept expecting her to face-plant right into her turkey sandwich.

Part of me wanted to apologize to Charlie, just so we could make up. But then again, I didn't think our fight was my fault. Charlie had been putting her relationship with Mitch in front of her friend-ships. But being right didn't keep me from feeling lonely.

•

"I just don't know what Charlie expects. Does she really think that she can treat us like we don't exist and we'll still be her friends?" I grumbled.

I was sitting on the floor of Finn's bedroom. He'd painted the walls dark blue, and in the afternoon light, they looked almost black. There were a few video game promotional posters tacked to his wall, all of them from games Finn had designed. There was a built-in desk and hutch running along one wall, and it was filled with monitors, CPU units, and gaming systems. The room was incredibly messy, and there was the faint whiff of something rotting wafting up from the waste paper basket. I'd had to shove aside a pile of laundry and a stack of spare computer parts in order to clear enough floor space to sit.

While I talked, Finn was tip-tapping away on his computer key-board. Ever since Charlie and I had our falling-out, I'd been hang-ing out at Finn's house a lot more. But as much as I liked Finn, this wasn't a great substitute for afternoons at Grounded with Charlie. For one thing, Finn was incapable of carrying on a serious conver-sation. This wasn't a problem when you were debating the gastro-nomical merits of Cheez Whiz, or whether '80s hair bands would ever make a comeback, but it wasn't so helpful when you wanted to discuss your best friend's defection to the land of the lovestruck. For another, as soon as Finn started messing around with his com-puter, he completely ignored me.

Finn grunted in response. I knew he wasn't really listening to me. He was too busy with whatever computer game he was in the middle of designing.

"Finn," I said, unable to keep the irritation out of my voice. When he didn't respond, I tried again. Louder. *"Finn!"*

Finn started and looked up. "What?" he asked.

"You haven't been listening to a word I've said!"

"Yes, I have."

"What did I say then?"

"Something about Charlie, and her annoying boyfriend, and then there was a lot of general girly angst," Finn said, waving an airy hand. "To be honest, I zoned out at the part where you started talking about your feelings."

I sighed. "I'm just going to head home," I said.

Finn rubbed his eyes and yawned. "Look, M, I totally agree with you. Like I told you in the beginning, the Charlie we once knew and loved has been abducted by aliens and replaced with Pod Charlie. There's not much we can do but wait it out until the real Charlie returns."

"Do you think that will happen?" I asked hopefully.

Finn shrugged. "I don't know. Maybe a fifty-fifty chance?"

"That's it?"

"I was going to say sixty-forty against it, but I thought that would bum you out even more," Finn said.

"Gee, thanks," I said dryly.

"I do what I can to please," Finn said. He shrugged then, and his expression suddenly turned serious—a rarity for Finn. "I know, it sucks that Charlie's acting like this . . . but like I said, what can we do?"

"We could kidnap her and commence a deprogramming pro-tocol," I said darkly.

"You know, that's not a bad idea," Finn said, pointing a finger at me. "We could videotape her with Mitch and then tie her to a chair and force her to watch it, so she can see how annoying she is. Brilliant! I truly am a genius!"

"Yeah, well, I see a few problems with your plan, genius."

"What?"

"First of all, I think Charlie would notice if we started following her around with a camcorder," I said.

"Please," Finn scoffed. "Like she'd catch me. I'm so sneaky, I could be a ninja. That's what I am—I'm ninja-sneaky."

"Second, I think tying her to a chair might actually qualify as a felony," I continued.

"Perhaps. But it would be a lesser felony. I mean, we wouldn't be facing serious jail for that," Finn said.

"And third, presumably, Charlie knows how she's acting with Mitch, and it doesn't bother her. In fact, to the contrary, she seems to really like acting like that," I said.

Finn looked horrified. "She couldn't possibly."

I shrugged. "I think she does. That's the whole problem."

"Okay. So maybe the kidnapping plan has a few flaws. I'll work on it, and get back to you," Finn said. He laced his fingers together and popped his knuckles. "With all of this brain power," he said, tapping a finger against the side of his head, "it's only a matter of time until I solve the whole problem. Have no fear."

"I'm just so not relieved by that," I said. I stood, stretching. "I'll talk to you tomorrow."

"Ciao," Finn said, turning back to his computer. I could hear his fingers tapping against the keyboard again at lightning speed before I was even out the door.

•

When I got back to the beach house, I was greeted by an ecstatic Willow. My beautiful brindle greyhound wriggled all over with pleasure at seeing me, and she shoved her nose in my hand by way of greeting. I petted her sleek head.

"Hi, girl," I said. "Do you want to go for a walk?"

Willow began to leap about in ecstasy, as though she were a ten-pound lapdog rather than a sixty-five-pound waist-high hound.

"I take that as a yes," I said, laughing at her.

I headed to my room to drop off my school bag and grab Willow's lead. A few minutes later, she and I were walking down the beach, as we had every day since we moved into the beach house at the end of August.

I didn't enjoy the walks as much as I once did, though. One time, when we'd been out walking, I saw Dex. He'd been out on the water para-surfing, but even at a distance I'd recognized his coppery red hair shining in the sun. Even though I had only seen him that one time—and we hadn't even talked—now I couldn't help looking for him every time I was out on the beach. There were almost always surfers out riding the waves in the afternoon, and occasionally even a para-surfer. But I hadn't seen Dex since. I suspected that this was just one more sign he was avoiding me, that rather than risk bumping into me on a beach near my dad's house, he'd instead been para-surfing at one of the other dozens of beaches Orange Cove is famous for.

Today, though, as Willow and I passed onto the public beach, I didn't see any surfers. The tide was low, and the wind blowing off the water was weak. It was also chilly enough out that I was wearing a light cotton sweater over my T-shirt. There were a few brave souls in the water—older women in bathing caps and skirted suits; one or two young families with chubby toddlers playing at the shoreline— but I suspected most of them were Northerners down for a winter holiday. It probably felt warm out to them in comparison to the frozen tundra they'd fled.

"Miranda, wait up."

Surprised to hear my name, I whirled around. . . . And suddenly found myself face-to-face with . . .

*Dex!*

I couldn't believe he was actually here! My heart gave a great lurch and then began to beat so quickly, I actually felt a little faint.

"Hi," I said quickly.

"Hey," Dex said.

And then we just stood there and stared at each other. It was awful. I mean, it was amazing to see him, of course. He was wearing a teal polo shirt that gave his pale eyes an almost greenish tint, and long chino shorts. His hair was a little longer than it had been the last time I saw him, and curled back from his pale, freckled face in short waves. But I had no idea what to say to him, what I could possibly tell him to fix everything that had gone wrong between us.

So instead, I took the inane small-talk route.

"So . . . what's up?" I said. "What are you doing here? You're not surfing today?"

"Oh, no, I'm . . . um . . . just going for a walk. Trying to clear my head," Dex said, stumbling a bit over his words. He looked as uncomfortable as I felt.

"Right. Me, too," I said, gesturing at Willow. She was listening to our conversation, her large ears pricked up and her tongue lolling out of one side of her mouth.

Dex nodded. "Look, I . . . well. I think I owe you an apology," he said awkwardly. "You know. For the way I acted at your MATh competition."

I just managed to keep my mouth from dropping open in shock. *He* was apologizing to *me*?

"I shouldn't have stormed off like that. It really isn't any of my business who you go out with. I mean, it's not like we were . . ." He stopped suddenly without finishing the thought. But I knew what he had been about to say. *It's not like we were a couple.*

I looked down, staring fixedly at my bare feet. I didn't want to see how his hair glowed in the sun, or the humorous glint in his pale blue eyes, or the way his lips twitched up in an easy smile as if the whole world was one big joke that he was in on. No, I didn't want to see any of that . . . not if he was going to stand there and confirm what I already knew: He wasn't romantically interested in me.

"No, don't apologize," I said. I was glad to hear my voice sounded cool and steady, even if that's not how I felt. "It really wasn't a big deal. And . . ." I paused. *It's now or never*, I told myself. I drew in a deep breath. "I . . . I'm not, um, dating anyone. I don't have a boyfriend."

"Oh," Dex said.

*Oh.* It was about the worst response possible. I'd told Dex I was available. . . . And he'd just said "Oh."

*Why? Why did I have to say anything?* I wondered miserably. I should have just kept my big mouth shut. It would have been so much better if Dex believed I was seeing someone else than to know I was unattached, handing him yet another opportunity to reject me.

There was an awkward silence, during which I wished I could just evaporate into a cloud of misery and humiliation.

"So . . . did you win?" Dex asked.

"No," I said. "We didn't. But we've won all of our competitions since then."

"That's good," Dex said.

"Yeah. We may still be able to make the state finals. We'll have to wait and see," I said.

There was another silence. If possible, it was even more awkward than the last one.

"Um. How about you?" I asked.

"Well. Sadly enough, I'm not on my school's MATh team," Dex said. I looked up quickly, and I could see a familiar spark of humor in his eyes. "I'm not even all that sure that O.C. High has a MATh team."

"They do," I said. "But they never have enough members to qualify for competitions."

"You learn something new every day," Dex said.

"I'm sure they'd love to have you on the team. You'd up their cool quotient by about two hundred percent," I said.

"Two hundred percent? I thought there wasn't any such thing."

"Of course there is."

"Well, you are the math genius," Dex said. There was a smile in his voice.

"Maybe I'm overrated," I said.

"I don't think so," Dex said.

My heart skittered, and I glanced at him quickly. Were we still talking about my math skills or had Dex meant something else? But he'd turned his gaze downward and with one long, bare toe was nudging a seashell buried in the sand.

Unfortunately, a woman walking a golden retriever off her leash came up on us then. The retriever dashed up to Willow and rudely sniffed her bottom. Willow was not at all pleased with this attention, and she sidled up next to me, her long body pushing against my legs, trying to avoid the retriever. The other dog just took this as an invitation to play, and he put down his head, stuck his wagging rear end up in the air, and began to bark. Willow looked horrified.

"Sorry!" The retriever's owner—a short, chubby woman with steel gray hair—hurried after him and pulled at his collar to get him moving. It took several vigorous tugs, and by the time the golden retriever had finally trotted off with his owner, Willow was twitching nervously.

"Willow doesn't like other dogs," I explained to Dex, while I stroked her long head to soothe her. She looked up at me and whimpered unhappily. "She really only likes people. And bacon."

"I think she wants to go home," Dex said, nodding at Willow. She was pulling in the direction of the beach house, whining softly.

"Yeah, she probably does. It's her dinner time."

"Well . . . I guess I'll see you around."

"Yeah. See you around," I said. I smiled at him, waiting to see if he'd say anything else. When he didn't, I turned abruptly and started walking quickly back toward the beach house. I wanted to look back and see if Dex was watching me go, but I forced myself not to.

"Hey, wait . . . Miranda?"

I turned, my heart hammering in my chest again, and watched as Dex jogged to catch up with me, spraying sand as he ran. "I forgot to tell you. You know I'm on the lacrosse team, right?"

I nodded. "You're captain, aren't you?"

He nodded. "Yeah. Anyway . . . the season has started, and we have games almost every weekend. You should come to one sometime."

"Okay," I said, not at all sure what was happening here. Was he asking me to the game because he *wanted* me there . . . or was this more of a general *FYI-if-you-happen-to-like-lacrosse-and-want-to-catch-a-game* situation? I was starting to seriously think that boys should come equipped with instruction manuals.

"Good." Dex smiled uncertainly at me. "Well. Bye again."

"Right. Bye," I said. This time, it was Dex who turned and walked away from me, his back straight and shoulders squared, leaving behind a trail of footprints in the sand.

# Chapter 19

To: mirandajbloom@gmail.com
From: hewent@britmail.net
Subject: revenge!!!

I know you're not a believer in practical jokes, but maybe it's time you start thinking outside the box and declare a prank war on your evil stepmother. Why settle for getting even, when you can aspire so much higher?

**The Top Three Best Pranks to Annoy Evil Stepmothers**
1.  Replace her perfume with something really foul-smelling.
2.  Hide things that she's looking for in weird places—her keys in the fish tank, glasses in the freezer.
3.  Sign her up for a lonely hearts ad, and make sure to include her home and mobile numbers.

Cheers,
Henry

"This is it," I said. "If we win this meet, we make states."

The Geek High Mu Alpha Theta team was gathered in an empty classroom for our pre-game pep rally. It was an away meet, at Dolphin

Prep in Ft. Lauderdale, so we had to endure a slow, two-and-a-half-hour bumpy bus ride. Sanjiv had thrown up three times en route, and was still looking so green I suspected that he might puke again soon. Hopefully before the competition began, and not during it.

Since Sanjiv was always incapacitated this way right before a match, I'd taken over delivering the pep talks. The irony of this wasn't lost on me. I was the only member of the Geek High Mu Alpha Theta team there against her will, and yet somehow the burden of getting everyone pumped up for the meet had fallen on me. But if I was being totally honest, I'd have to admit that I was proud of my team. After all, they'd overcome the tough loss against St. Pius and Sanjiv's habitual stage fright to stage a comeback, winning all of our subsequent competitions.

"I thought we had to win by at least twenty points to make states," Kyle said.

"Yes, Kyle, thank you for pointing that out," I said, not able to bite back my sarcasm.

The top eight teams in the state went to the Mu Alpha Theta final tournament. The ranking wasn't based on wins and losses, but on a team's cumulative score. Theoretically, a team could win every competition, but if their scoring was low, not make finals. So even though our current record was a not-too-shabby five wins and one loss, the truth was, a few of those wins had been close scrapes.

So we definitely had a stab at making finals. . . . But Kyle was right: We'd have to win today's meet by twenty points to do it. Which was going to be tough against Dolphin Prep, one of the more formidable schools we competed with.

"Sanjiv, are you okay?" Leila asked.

I turned to look at Sanjiv. He was bent over with his head between his knees, and his breath was coming in shallow gasps.

"Dude. Are you going to puke again?" Kyle asked, sounding disgusted.

Sanjiv groaned.

"Kyle. Seriously, you're not helping," I said.

"I just don't know how he could have anything left in his stomach to puke up," Kyle said, far too loudly. "He even threw up the orange juice Mr. Gordon gave him on the bus to settle his stomach."

"I think it was apple juice," Nicholas said.

"I thought apple juice was supposed to make you feel more nauseated," Kyle said.

"My mom gives me ginger ale to settle my stomach when I'm sick," Nicholas said.

"Apple juice tastes rank anyway," Kyle said. "Especially when it comes back up."

At this Sanjiv blanched, muttered something that sounded like "apple juice," and ran for the boy's bathroom. Leila, Kyle, Nicholas, and I exchanged nervous looks.

"Is he going to be okay?" Nicholas asked. "I've never seen him this bad."

"He'll be fine," I said. "We'll all be fine. Really. It'll be a piece of cake."

◆

"What was that you said about this meet being a piece of cake?" Kyle asked an hour later.

"Okay, so maybe I spoke too soon," I said.

Kyle shook his head, discouraged. "Maybe we should just concede and spare the continued humiliation."

After two disastrous rounds, things were not looking good for the Geek High MATh team. The score was forty-five to thirty, with Dolphin High in a masterful lead. It wasn't that their team was stronger than ours—I really didn't think they were—but our team was having a terrible day. I was the only member to have won both my questions. Leila got hers right in the first round, and Nicholas got his in the second round, but other than that, we'd lost every single question. Kyle had hit the buzzer first with both of his questions, but had gotten them both wrong, giving his Dolphin High opponent a full leisurely minute to work out the correct answer. And Sanjiv was just floundering, unable to do anything but open and close his mouth like a fish when it was his turn. I thought he might be having a full-fledged panic attack.

"Look, we can still win this," I said.

"Yeah. Dream on," Kyle muttered.

"No, really," I said, squelching the impulse to kick him in the shin. Kyle's constant pessimism was enough to get the Dalai Lama down. "We can do this. We just have to win by twenty points. That's it. Twenty little points."

"But we're already down fifteen," Leila pointed out.

"So all we need to do is win four out of five questions in round three," I said.

A group groan went up at this.

"That's nothing," I continued. "Four measly questions. We can do it. We've done it before. I know we have it in us to win this competition and get into the finals. Isn't that what we want? What we've been working for?"

I looked around at them. Nicholas was the first one to meet my eyes, something he had been mostly avoiding up until now. But his gaze was level, and a smile stretched across his thin, homely face. He nodded resolutely, and I smiled back at him.

"Leila?" I said, turning to look at her.

Leila looked less confident, but she nodded, and her chin rose a few millimeters. I knew she wouldn't give up; Leila was a scrapper.

"Kyle, Sanjiv?" I said.

Kyle hesitated, and finally gave a slight nod paired with a shrug. It wasn't a vote of confidence, I knew, but he was in. I turned to face Sanjiv, who still hadn't spoken. In fact, he hadn't said a single word since the competition had begun.

"I don't think I can go back out there," he said in a strangled whisper.

"Yes, you can," I said firmly. "You're just letting your nerves get the best of you."

He laughed bitterly at this.

"No, really. It's mind over matter. Just keep thinking that: mind over matter," I said.

He nodded and stared down at the ground.

The moderator cleared his throat, and then leaned forward and spoke into the microphone. "It's time for round three to commence. Teams, please take your seats."

"Come on," I said, and pumped one arm into the air. "Let's go get 'em!"

Leila was up first. She answered her question correctly while her Dolphin Prep opponent was still scribbling on his scratch paper. The score was tied. Then Kyle got his first correct answer of the day, putting us in the lead. Next up was Nicholas. He hit his buzzer a fraction of a second before a pretty girl with dark caramel skin and long, thick, blue-black hair, and correctly answered the quadratic equation.

"Yes," I whispered excitedly to Sanjiv. "We're up by thirty points!"

Sanjiv was sitting in the number four position today. After our disastrous showing against St. Pius, I had thought it prudent to take the fifth chair, for strategic reasons, and Sanjiv hadn't fought me on it. Right now I was regretting it, though. All we needed was one more correct answer, and not only would we win the competition, we'd win by at least thirty points. . . . Ten points more than we needed to make it to states. If I was number four, all pressure would be off Sanjiv. As it was, his skin had taken on a greenish tint and I could see the sweat beading up on his forehead.

"Question number four," the moderator said. "Jane buys thirteen lollipops and three packs of gum for one dollar. A lollipop costs more than a pack of gum, and both items cost a whole number of cents. What is the total cost of one lollipop and one pack of gum?"

*Ten cents,* I thought immediately. It was a tricky question, which sounded deceptively easy. But I knew Sanjiv could do it. All he had to remember was that if $x$ is the cost of one lollipop and $y$ is the cost of one lollipop and one pack of gum, both in cents, then $3y + 13x = 100$.

Both Sanjiv and his competitor were working out the calculations on scrap paper. Sanjiv suddenly dropped his pencil and hit his buzzer. My heart gave a leap of excitement. Sanjiv was going to do it! He was going to answer the winning question and get Geek High into the state finals!

"Yes, Notting Hill," the moderator said, nodding to Sanjiv.

"The answer," Sanjiv said, his voice wavering, "is twelve cents."

My heart plummeted even before the moderator shook his head, and said, "No, I'm sorry, that is not the correct answer."

Sanjiv's entire body seemed to sink in on itself in misery. I glanced sideways at him and realized with a sickening certainty that there were tears in his eyes. Sanjiv's Dolphin Prep opponent brightened, and, hunching his shoulders, continued to work out the calculation.

After a protracted silence, he finally straightened in his seat and said, "Ten cents."

"That is correct," the moderator said. The audience, made up almost entirely of Dolphin Prep fans, cheered.

"Notting Hill is in the lead, seventy-five points to sixty," the moderator said.

Which meant that if I answered my question correctly, we'd go to states. If not, we'd tie. We could still win the instant-death tie-breaker, but even if we did, we wouldn't win by enough points. The team's future success was now resting on my shoulders. And for the first time that day, I felt a twinge of nervousness. I didn't want to let the others down, not after the pep talk I'd given them. I knew if we lost, Sanjiv would feel even worse than he did now.

"Question number five: What is the square root of 576?" the moderator asked.

I hit my buzzer immediately, happiness already surging through me. If there was one thing my calculator of a brain knew cold, it was square roots. The moderator nodded at me.

I leaned forward to speak into my microphone. "The answer is 24," I said.

"That is correct."

Our team exploded into cheers, joined by Mr. Gordon, who was sitting in the front row of the auditorium. The rest of the audience, made up of Dolphin Prep parents and supporters, joined in the applause, although theirs was somewhat muted. It was understandable, but we didn't care. The Geek High team rose as one and slapped hands and exchanged hugs.

"We're going to states!" Leila said excitedly.

"We're going to states!" the rest of us echoed.

Only Sanjiv, still stinging from his personal defeat, looked less than enthused at the prospect.

We were still in high spirits as we began the long bus ride home. The Geek High bus was short and had been painted white at some point, but like all school buses, it was uncomfortable, hot, and more than a little smelly. The floor was grimy and sticky, and one of the back windows banged open every time the bus hit a pothole.

Since there were only the seven of us on board—the team, Mr. Gordon, and the driver, Mr. Pott—there was room for us each to have our own seat. I was sitting in the front, chatting with Leila, but after a while she started to doze off. I glanced around. Sanjiv was also sitting with his eyes closed, although I had the definite feeling that he wasn't sleeping and just wanted to avoid conversation. Kyle had his iPod on and was nodding his head along to the beat of Fall Out Boy. Nicholas was sitting alone at the back of the bus, awake and staring out the window at the passing scenery on the interstate.

I stood, and moved to the back.

"Mind if I sit here?" I asked, pointing to the empty seat next to Nicholas.

He looked up in surprise but shook his head, so I sat down.

"You did a really good job today," I said.

He shrugged. "I did okay. You were the real star of the team."

I shrugged, too. It always seemed odd to me to take credit for a skill that I really had no true ownership of. It wasn't like I'd studied hard to be a math whiz; it came easily to me.

"So . . . I've been wanting to talk to you," I said hesitantly.

Nicholas glanced at me, his eyes wary, and then he looked away. He didn't say anything. I sighed. He really wasn't going to make this easy for me.

"Actually, what I really wanted to do is to apologize," I continued.

"For lying to me," Nicholas said flatly.

"Right," I said. "For lying to you."

"You didn't have to do that, you know. You could have just told me you didn't want to go out with me. I'm used to rejection," Nicholas said, with an honesty that made my heart go out to him.

"I could have. But I was trying not to hurt your feelings," I said.

Nicholas nodded. "I know."

"And I was taking the easy way out," I continued.

Nicholas's lips twitched up. It wasn't really a smile; more of a confirmation that he'd heard what I had to say. Still, I figured it wasn't a bad sign.

"So, I apologize," I said.

Nicholas nodded slowly. "Apology accepted."

It wasn't until I felt the instant relief that I realized how much our rift had been bothering me. It was like removing an itchy tag from a shirt. "Thanks," I said, and he nodded again.

We were both silent for a moment, and I was just considering moving back to my old seat when Nicholas spoke again.

"So that guy who came to our competition . . . is he your boyfriend?" he asked.

"No," I said ruefully. "He might have been . . . but, no. I screwed things up. I seem to do that a lot."

This got a real smile. "No, you don't. You're really nice, Miranda. You go out of your way to be nice to everyone."

"No more so than everyone else does."

Nicholas stared at me, frowning so that his sparse eyebrows furrowed. "What do you think Felicity Glen would have done if I'd asked her to go to the Snowflake Gala with me?"

I considered this. The Felimonster would have likely laughed in Nicholas's face, and then proceeded to tell everyone in the school how pathetic it was for someone like him to think someone like her would go out with him. I wasn't about to say this to Nicholas, of course, but he read the truth in my face.

"Yeah. She would have run over me, backed up over my dead body, and then run over me again," Nicholas said.

"Well, yeah, she probably would have," I agreed.

We both smiled, and this time I glanced down, looking at my hands. My fingers were long but ended in stubby, bitten nails. I'd never been able to wear nail polish without it chipping away immediately, so I didn't bother. This horrified Hannah, who would no sooner go out unpolished than she would shave her head.

"Do you really think we have a chance of winning states?" Nicholas asked.

"Yeah, I really do," I said, although I couldn't help glancing at Sanjiv. The truth was, that to have any shot of winning the state finals, every last member of the Geek High MATh team would have to perform at top level. There wasn't room for panic attacks or botched answers.

Nicholas followed my gaze. "Yeah, that's what I'm worried about, too," he said softly.

"It'll be okay," I said, determined to be positive. "We'll do fine. Win or lose."

Nicholas snorted.

"Okay," I conceded. "Losing would suck."

"Yeah, it would," Nicholas said. And we both laughed.

# Chapter 20

"We have to make our travel plans for your writing contest," Dad said over breakfast a few days later.

I felt a prickle of nervous excitement. "That's right." I hesitated. "Are you going with me, then?"

Dad looked up from his paper, surprised. "Of course! I'm not sending you off to DC by yourself. Unless . . . your mother's not coming over from London to go to it, is she?"

I snorted at this. You know how—in sappy movies or sitcoms—the divorced parents make a big show of getting along with each other for the sake of the children? Yeah, well, my parents don't do that. Sadie and my dad can barely stand to be in a room together.

"No, I don't think so. Not that she's mentioned," I said.

Dad didn't bother to hide his relief. "Then yes, I'm definitely going. It'll be fun. We haven't taken a trip together in a long time."

"When is it?" Peyton asked. She was sitting at the table, drinking a mug of black coffee, glancing at the style section of the newspaper.

"Next month," I said.

Peyton arched her thin eyebrows. "April? But, Richard, we're booked every weekend in April. We have two dinner parties, a charity ball, and we're supposed to go down to Lotta and Bill's house in the Keys one weekend."

Dad shrugged, unconcerned. "So we'll have to shift something. Miranda, what weekend is the contest?"

I swallowed my bite of buttered toast. "I'm not sure. Mrs. Gordon gave me a packet of information on it, though. It's in my room. I'll go get it."

Dad nodded, and I stood and went back to my room, passing Hannah in the hall on my way. She was still in her nightshirt and her eyes were sleepy, but even though she'd clearly just rolled out of bed, her hair looked as perfect as if she'd just spent an hour blow drying it. Life was so unfair.

"Hey," I said.

"Morning," she said, yawning.

I grabbed my book bag and rummaged through it. The manila envelope containing the contest information that Mrs. Gordon had given me had gotten mushed up on the bottom of the bag. I pulled out the information packet, smoothed the wrinkles, and began to read. And then my jaw dropped open.

I lunged back toward my book bag, seized the calendar where I wrote down homework assignments, and flipped it open to April.

"Oh, no," I said aloud. "No no no no no!"

The Winston Creative Writing Contest finals were being held in Washington, DC, on the twenty-first of April. . . . The very same day the Mu Alpha Theta state competition was set to take place in West Palm Beach.

"I am so totally screwed," I said.

•

"There has to be a way to work it out," Dad said. "What time is the MATh competition? If it's in the morning, maybe we'll have time to catch a flight up to DC afterward, and still make the awards ceremony."

I shook my head. "Not unless I suddenly develop the ability to teleport. The MATh competition is an all-day event. It starts with eight teams in the morning for the quarterfinal round. That takes hours. Then there are the semis, and then the finals, with the last two remaining teams going up against one another sometime in the late afternoon."

"Maybe your team will lose early," Hannah said helpfully, as she nibbled on a Pop-Tart.

I shrugged. "Maybe. But I can't count on that happening."

"You could throw your first match," Hannah suggested.

"I can't do that!" I said, at the same time my dad said, "She can't do that!"

Hannah rolled her eyes. "Geesh. Overreact much? It's not like I was suggesting you kill somebody. Besides, I thought you didn't even want to be on your math academic team thingy," Hannah said.

"I didn't. I mean, I don't," I said. Although really, I wasn't sure that was true anymore. Sure, I hadn't wanted to be on the MATh team at first . . . but the season had been sort of fun. I was proud of my team for how far they'd come. I looked longingly at the information packed on the Winston Creative Writing Contest. "This stinks. I can't miss the writing contest. It's a huge deal. I mean, I know there's no chance I'll actually win. . . ." I trailed off, not wanting to say out loud what I was thinking: If I did happen to win, it would be the sign I'd been waiting for, the one that would tell me I was meant to be a writer.

"Then you should go to the writing finals. That's more important," Hannah said.

"I guess," I said doubtfully. "But if I do that, I'll be letting down my teammates."

"How so?" Hannah looked blank.

"You have to have five people on your team in order to compete in a Mu Alpha Theta competition. And our team only has five members on it. If I don't show, the whole team will be disqualified," I explained.

She shook her head and shrugged. "So?"

Peyton, meanwhile, had flipped open her calendar. "Richard, that is the weekend we're going down to the Keys," she said. She tapped her calendar with the tip of a long, polished fingernail.

My dad looked at her, impatience etched on his features. "So we'll cancel," he said. "Whatever Miranda ends up doing, I'll want to go and watch her."

"We can't cancel!" Peyton exclaimed. "These plans have been set for weeks! What will Lotta and Bill think?"

"They'll think we care more about our daughters than we do about our social obligations," Dad said evenly.

Hannah and I exchanged a quick look. The storm clouds had rolled in again, threatening another big blowup between Dad and Peyton.

"You mean your daughter is more important to you than I am?" Peyton said.

We all went silent at this. Dad was staring coolly at Peyton, Hannah was gaping at me, and I was looking at my dad. It was the most uncomfortable silence I had ever endured in my life.

"Peyton," Dad said slowly, "this is neither the time nor place for this discussion."

"Oh yes, it damn well is!" Peyton said. The color was rising in her pale cheeks. "You can't just back out of plans we've already made. It's unforgivably rude!"

"*We* didn't make the plans. *You* made the plans," Dad said. He glanced over at Hannah and me. "Girls, could you please excuse us? Peyton and I need to talk. *Privately*," he said, emphasizing this last word with a glacial finality.

"Sure," I said, jumping up and gathering my papers and calendar.

"Absolutely," Hannah said, also rising, Pop-Tart still in hand.

Hannah and I hurried out of the kitchen. Once the door was closed behind us, we could hear Peyton and my dad's voices, low but buzzing with anger.

"Have you noticed how much they've been fighting lately?" Hannah asked as we turned down the hallway toward our bedrooms.

I nodded. "Yeah. It would be sort of hard not to."

Hannah snorted. "No kidding. Do you think they're going to split up?"

"I don't know. What do you think?"

Hannah frowned and shrugged. "I don't know. I hope not. I like Richard. He's a lot nicer than any of the other guys my mom dated. Some of them were real creeps." She tossed her hair back over her shoulders and gathered it back in her hands, making a ponytail out of it. "Do you want the first shower, or can I go ahead?"

I stared at Hannah, shocked at the thoughtfulness of this question. Normally, she just announced that not only was she going to take the first shower, but that she'd be in there for at least an hour, forcing me to grab my toothbrush and toothpaste and brush my teeth at the kitchen sink.

"Um . . . no, go ahead," I said. "I already showered."

Hannah rolled her eyes. "Great. You didn't get the floor all wet again, did you? You do know that's what the bath mat is there for, right?"

And then she pirouetted in place and headed into our shared bathroom. This was so much more like the Hannah I knew, I actually grinned in relief.

●

All day at school, my thoughts tumbled around and around, until I almost felt dizzy. I couldn't decide what I was going to do. Even worse, I didn't have Charlie to talk the problem out with. She and I still weren't speaking. During Mod Lit, I glanced across the classroom at her a few times, wondering if I should make the first move to patch things up. But Charlie refused to meet my gaze, and then spent the period tapping away on her IM program—from her dreamy, goofy expression, it wasn't hard to figure out whom she was IM'ing—and I lost the impulse.

I tried to talk my dilemma over with Finn.

"Dude, are you serious?" he asked, when I'd finished setting it out for him. "You're actually undecided about whether you should spend a weekend partying in DC or stuck at some boring math tournament? That's not even a real question."

I knew that making the finals of the Winston Creative Writing Contest was a big deal. There were only ten finalists in the entire country. Just being included in that group was a huge honor. . . . And it would be an even bigger honor if I actually won. The rules of the contest specifically stated that you had to be present at the ceremony in order to win anything. So I had to go, right? After all, I wanted to be a writer. If I actually managed to win the Winston Creative Writing Contest, it could make all the difference in the world when I applied to colleges with good creative writing programs.

*So I should go to DC*, I thought, as I walked to my Latin class. It would be better for me, personally, if I did. And not just better now, but better in the long run, better for college applications and career prospects.

But if I did go to the Winston finals . . . that would mean that the Geek High MATh team would have to drop out of state finals for the fourth year in a row. And the team had worked so hard to make finals. They'd dealt with a devastating loss to the St. Pius team and Sanjiv's constant stage fright, and *still* made it. How could I look my team members in the eye, and tell them I was bailing on them now?

*I can't do that*, I thought miserably. *I can't let them down.*

But then again . . . Hannah was right. I hadn't even *wanted* to be on the MATh team. Headmaster Hughes had blackmailed me into it. In fact, if he hadn't manipulated me into rejoining the MATh team, I wouldn't even be in this position. This was all his fault! Anger flared up inside of me like a flame.

*This is why you don't go around screwing with other people's lives,* I thought furiously, hugging my binder up to my chest. *Because they end up in situations like this.*

Suddenly, I knew what I had to do. I whirled around, surprising the freshman walking down the school corridor behind me. He dodged to one side as I stalked past him down toward the central building, where the administrative offices were housed. I was going to dump this entire mess right where it belonged. . . . In the lap of one Headmaster C. Phillip Hughes.

●

Mrs. Boxer, the headmaster's secretary, wasn't at her desk, so I rapped softly on the headmaster's office door.

"Come in," I heard him call out.

I steeled myself and pushed open the door.

Headmaster Hughes's office was large, but even so, it was so cluttered that I always felt a little claustrophobic when I was in the room. Bookshelves, couches, oriental rugs, and a very large desk competed for floor space. Framed award certificates and pictures of the headmaster with donors lined the walls.

The headmaster was sitting behind his desk, pen in hand, signing some papers. The top of his head was completely bald, although he had thick, furry eyebrows. And when he smiled, his lips drew down, as though he were really frowning.

"Miranda," he said when he saw me. He set his gold pen down on his desk, and frown-smiled at me. "To what do I owe the pleasure?"

"I have something I need to talk to you about," I said. Then, remembering, quickly added, "Sir."

Headmaster Hughes graciously waved me toward one of the wing chairs that faced his desk. "Please have a seat."

I sat, setting my book bag on the floor next to me.

"How are you, Miranda?" the headmaster asked.

"Actually . . . not so good at the moment," I said.

His furry eyebrows quirked up. "Oh, dear," he said mildly. "I am sorry to hear that."

"It's the Mu Alpha Theta finals," I said.

The headmaster frown-smiled warmly. "Yes, I was pleased to see the team qualify for the state finals," he said. "I'm counting on adding the state champion trophy to our collection downstairs. And if you bring home the Winston Writing Contest trophy, too, we may have to start a special Miranda Bloom trophy case."

"That's just it. . . . The MATh finals are the same weekend as the Winston Writing Contest finals in DC," I said.

He grasped the point immediately. "Which means that you won't be able to attend both. You are on the horns of an unhappy dilemma." The headmaster frowned for real this time, and he bridged his hands together.

"So what should I do?" I asked. I didn't—as I had meant to—add that this was all his fault, and if he hadn't forced me to be on the MATh team, I wouldn't be in this position. Because now that I was here, I realized I really did want his advice. Headmaster Hughes might be devious and underhanded, and a blackmailer to boot, but he was also a pretty smart guy. I was sure—well, fairly sure—that he really did have the school's best interest at heart.

"There's only one thing you can do," the headmaster said. He looked faintly surprised, as though the solution were so obvious, only an idiot would have failed to have grasped it.

"What?"

"You have to go to DC and attend the Winston Writing Competition finals. You can't win if you're not present, correct?"

I nodded. "That's what the rules say."

"Then that's what you have to do," Mr. Hughes said.

"But what about the MATh team? If I don't compete, they'll have to drop out of the state finals," I said.

"An unfortunate consequence, I agree. But it can't be helped.

Miranda, the Alfred Q. Winston Creative Writing Contest is the preeminent writing competition for high school students in the country. Being selected as a finalist is a great honor in and of itself. If you should win, it would be one of the most—if not the most—important prize any student has ever earned in the history of the Notting Hill Independent School for Gifted Children," the headmaster said.

I had to admit, I did like the sound of that. The idea that I'd bring glory to the school and leave behind the legacy of a huge silver cup with my name engraved on it.

"Okay," I said slowly. Everyone who had weighed in on my dilemma—my dad, the headmaster, Hannah, Finn—had all told me they thought I should go to the writing contest. If the right choice was that obvious to everyone else, then that must mean it was what I should do. "I guess I'll tell the MATh team at our practice tomorrow afternoon."

Although . . . it wouldn't be a practice. Not if we weren't going to finals.

*They're all going to be so disappointed,* I thought, and my stomach hurt a little as I imagined their reaction.

"Can I help you with anything else?" the headmaster asked.

"No," I said, rising out of my seat. I shouldered my bag. "Thank you, sir."

"Any time." The headmaster frown-smiled at me. "My door is always open, Miranda."

# Chapter 21

To: mirandajbloom@gmail.com
From: hewent@britmail.net
Subject: [re] disaster

**Top three things that are worse than telling your mates you're skiving off the maths tourney:**

1. Eating a plate of live, wriggling grubs.
2. Being doused with gasoline and set on fire.
3. Having what you think is a normal bug bite, but when you scratch it, it bursts open and hundreds of little spiders come crawling out (this actually happened to someone my mate Oliver knows).

Cheers,
Henry

"Why do you keep scratching yourself?" Finn asked.

I shuddered, and yet again scratched at a small mosquito bite on my arm that I was now—thanks to Henry's spider e-mail—totally freaked out about.

"Nothing," I muttered. I opened my locker and threw my books in. "Where are you off to? Grounded?"

Finn gave me a cold look. "You know I'm boycotting that place until they fire Mitchy."

"Finn, they're not going to fire Mitch," I said. "He's the owner's nephew."

"Then they've lost me as a customer," Finn said loftily. "I'm sticking to my principles."

"Your principles are telling you to put economic pressure on Grounded to fire Mitch just because you don't like the fact that he's dating Charlie?" I asked.

"You don't like him dating Charlie, either," Finn reminded me.

"No, I don't mind him dating Charlie. I mind that Charlie acts like a blithering idiot whenever she's around him," I said irritably, slamming my locker door shut. "It's like her IQ drops to that of a not-very-bright shoe."

I heard a gasp and spun around. Charlie was standing behind me, as though she'd been waiting to speak to me. . . . And she'd clearly been there long enough to have overheard what I'd just said about her. Her eyes were wide and she was blinking rapidly, as though to keep from crying.

"Charlie . . ." I said, stepping forward toward her.

But before I could apologize, she spun around and rushed away. I watched her, feeling like the world's biggest jerk.

"Well, isn't that just *great*," I said flatly.

Finn slung an arm around my shoulders. "That's my Miranda," he said. "Winning friends and influencing people." Then he dodged as I attempted to elbow him in his scrawny side.

"Are you walking out?" he asked me, slinging his book bag over one shoulder.

I shook my head sadly. "I wish I was. I have to go Mu Alpha Theta."

"Today's the big day? You're going to tell everyone you're bailing on finals?"

"Yep. Wish me luck."

"Good luck," Finn said. And then, dropping his voice to an ominous whisper, he added, "You're going to need it."

"Gee, thanks," I said, rolling my eyes. I took in a deep breath, sighed, and turned to head off to the MATh meeting.

•

I was the last one to arrive at Mr. Gordon's room. The rest of the MATh team was already there, sitting at desks with their practice books out, looking excited.

"Hey, Miranda!" Leila said, waving to me. "We were just talking about the lineup we should use for states. I think what we did this past weekend worked well, don't you? Me first, then Kyle, Nicholas, Sanjiv, and then you last?"

"I don't know," Kyle said dubiously. He shot a sideways look at Sanjiv, who was noticeably less animated than the rest of the team. "Maybe Sanjiv should switch to third, and Nicholas or I should go fourth."

Sanjiv's shoulders slumped and he sighed audibly.

"Well . . ." Leila said, considering this. "That's a thought."

*Just tell them*, I thought. *Tell them and get it over with.*

I drew in a deep breath, and was just about to say *I have some bad news* when Sanjiv suddenly spoke.

"I'm not going to finals," he said flatly.

There was a stunned silence, and then everyone began to talk at once.

"What do you mean?" Nicholas asked.

"But you have to," Leila said.

"Dude, if you don't go, we're disqualified," Kyle said.

I didn't say anything. I just sat there, trying to take it all in. But suddenly, it dawned on me that this was the answer to all of my problems. If Sanjiv dropped off the team, then I was off the hook. Kyle was right—with only four remaining members, the Geek High

MATh team would be automatically disqualified from state finals. And I wouldn't be the one letting everyone down.

"I'm sorry," Sanjiv said, his voice still oddly hollow. "I know what this means for the rest of you. But I just can't do it. . . . I can't get up there in front of everyone again. . . . It's just . . . too . . . too . . ." He paused and stared down at his hands. His fingers were long and bony, and oddly feminine-looking. "Too humiliating."

No one said anything for a long, awkward moment. Leila and Nicholas both seemed stricken, Kyle was angry, and Sanjiv was just marinating in misery. I looked around at them, at my ragtag team, and thought of how much we'd accomplished that year just by making finals. How if we let it end here, if we let Sanjiv quit now, how very wrong that would be. Sanjiv might spend the rest of his life regretting his decision. It could undermine his self-confidence for years to come.

Before I thought through what I was saying—what it would mean for me personally—I opened my mouth and the words tumbled out.

"Sanjiv, you're *not* dropping off the team. We won't let you. And there's no reason for you to. You're a fine player. You rarely miss a question during practices. The only problem you have is with your self-confidence. You just have to start believing in yourself the way we believe in you," I said.

I looked around at my teammates' faces . . . and immediately hoped that Sanjiv didn't. Because I didn't see a whole lot of confidence there. If anything, Kyle, Leila, and Nicholas all looked dubious, as if they weren't at all sure that Sanjiv wouldn't choke at the state finals, just as he'd choked at our match against Dolphin Prep.

But, amazingly, Sanjiv seemed to be perking up at my vote of confidence in him. His head rose and his shoulders straightened, and I could swear that there was a hopeful gleam in his dark brown eyes that hadn't been there a moment earlier.

"Really?" he asked.

"Really," I said firmly. "You can do this. I know you can. We've come this far, and we're not quitting now."

There was a long, pregnant pause. I could feel everyone's eyes shifting from me to Sanjiv, as we waited for his verdict.

Finally, Sanjiv sighed. "I don't know why I'm agreeing to do this. . . . But okay," he said.

"Yay!" Leila cheered, and Kyle and Nicholas looked relieved and happy.

"Miranda," Sanjiv began. But then he stopped, and looked embarrassed.

"Yes?" I asked.

"Would you . . . I mean, do you think you could . . . I could really use your help on square roots," Sanjiv said.

I knew how much it cost him to ask me for help. It had always bothered Sanjiv that I was better at math than he was. And as much as I wanted to help him, I wasn't sure how I could. Square root calculations came easily to me, the answers popping into my head effortlessly. It wasn't something I could teach him to do. But Sanjiv needed my help. I'd do whatever I could.

"Absolutely," I said. "We'll start working on them today."

"Great, thanks," Sanjiv said. He smiled weakly and looked around at us. "I guess we'd better get started. We're going to need all the practice we can get."

•

The next day, I waited outside the Mod Lit classroom for Mrs. Gordon to arrive before class began.

"Hi, Miranda," Mrs. Gordon said, smiling warmly at me. She was carrying our essays on *1984*, marked and ready to be handed back. Her hair was pulled up in a messy ponytail, and there was a coffee stain on her yellow blouse. "Coming to class?"

"Yes. I just have something I needed to tell you in private," I said. I explained about the MATh team, and how if I didn't go to finals, the whole team would be disqualified, and how I couldn't do that to them, even if it meant that I would miss the Winston Creative Writing Contest finals.

Mrs. Gordon was disappointed, but she smiled and said she understood.

"I know you didn't ask my opinion, but for what it's worth, I think you're doing the right thing," she said.

"You do?" I asked. My disappointment over missing the writing contest felt heavy, pressing on my shoulders and twisting in my stomach. It was as though not only had I received the worst news of my life, I'd had to deliver it to myself. I sighed. "No one else thinks that I am."

I'd told my dad, Hannah, and Finn my decision, and all three had been first startled and then skeptical at the wisdom of it. Even Sadie had sent me an e-mail urging me to rethink my choice.

"I do," Mrs. Gordon said firmly. "You're making the brave choice. The selfless choice. That's the kind of person you are, Miranda, and you should be proud of that. I'm proud of you."

"Thanks," I said. Her words had lifted some of the sadness weighing on me.

"Come on. Let's get to class," Mrs. Gordon said. "Oh, hi, Charlie, you're just in time."

I turned and saw Charlie there, standing just behind me.

"Hi," I said, before I remembered that we weren't speaking.

"Hi," Charlie said.

She glanced away then, as we all turned to walk into the classroom. But I'd gotten the definite feeling that before she'd turned, Charlie had been looking at me thoughtfully. As though she were just recognizing me after being away for a long time.

And I'd noticed something else: Charlie's eyes were rimmed with red, as though she'd been crying. I wanted to ask her what was wrong, but I didn't act fast enough. Charlie moved away and sat down next to Tabitha. She didn't look up at me again, and instead focused her attention on getting out her books and laptop. I sat next to Finn, as usual. But throughout the rest of the period, as we talked about the symbolism in *Native Son*, which we had just started reading that week, I couldn't help glancing over at Charlie. Once or twice, from the way her eyes flicked quickly away, I could have sworn that she'd been looking back at me only a moment earlier.

# Chapter 22

The Mu Alpha Theta State Finals were held in a huge carpeted ballroom on the second floor of a hotel in downtown West Palm Beach. There was a stage at the front of the room, where the moderator's podium and two team tables were set up. On the table, in front of each chair, there was a microphone and a buzzer that lit up a red light when hit.

St. Pius had already faced off against Pine Hill Academy in the first round of the quarterfinals, and Austin Strong's team had easily won, moving forward into the semifinals. The Geek High team was up next, competing against Hibiscus High from Gainesville. We'd never gone up against this particular school before, but word was that their team was good, mostly because they fielded a large bench, and so had the luxury of being able to pick and choose their best players.

Our team was milling around with the rest of the gathered crowd, receiving final well-wishes before our round began. I was standing with my dad, the only spectator there on my behalf. Finn couldn't come—he was on a business trip to California to meet with representatives of a gaming company—and Charlie still wasn't speaking to me. Hannah had surprised me at breakfast by making a halfhearted offer to come with us. I'd thanked her but told her she'd probably be bored out of her mind. At this, Peyton—filing her talonlike nails while she read the real estate section of the newspaper—had snorted in a nasty way. Peyton was still furious at Dad for canceling their trip to the Keys that weekend. She certainly didn't offer to come with us, not that I wanted her there. The Demon could lower the temperature in a room ten degrees just by walking into it.

"Good luck, honey," Dad now said, squeezing my shoulder reassuringly. "Break a leg!"

"Thanks, Dad. And thanks for coming," I said.

"You know I wouldn't miss it," he said.

"I wouldn't either," a familiar voice said.

*Was it . . . ? No . . . it couldn't be. Could it?*

I spun around, and my mouth dropped open.

*"Mom?"*

"Hello, darling," Sadie said, beaming at me. She held her arms open. I gave a cry of delight and charged toward her.

"What are you doing here?" I asked, as she squeezed me against her perfumey crimson silk blouse. "Are you home for good?"

"No, just for the week," Sadie said. "I couldn't miss watching you win the state championship, after all."

"If we win," I said doubtfully.

"I have complete faith in you," Sadie said, hugging me to her again.

"Hello, Sadie," Dad said, sounding stiff.

"Hello, Richard," Sadie said. She looked around. "Where's . . . ?"

Sadie never said Peyton's name. She usually just called her That Woman.

Dad turned red and looked down at the floor. "Peyton couldn't make it," he said.

"Isn't that a surprise," Sadie said tartly.

"Sadie, don't start," Dad said, his voice testy.

I broke in then. "As much as I'm enjoying this trip down

memory lane—Miranda Bloom, the tween years—I have to go. My team's waiting for me," I said. I nodded over at where the other members of the Geek High Mu Alpha Theta team were congregating up on the stage.

My parents stopped glaring at each other long enough to wish me luck, and then I left them to their nostalgic fighting, making my way through the crowd to the stage.

"Is everyone ready?" I asked brightly. The team was grouped together, behind our table.

"Absolutely," Nicholas said.

"Why not?" Kyle said, which was positively optimistic coming from him.

"Do you have a pep talk for us, Miranda?" Leila asked.

I looked at Sanjiv. His face was ashen and he was nervously licking his lips, but there was also an air of resolution about him. For better or worse, he was here to compete.

"Sanjiv is the team captain," I said. "He should give the pep talk."

But Sanjiv shook his head. "No. You're better at pep talks than I am," he said.

"Okay, well," I hesitated, and drew in a deep breath while I thought. "We're certainly ready. I doubt if any Mu Alpha Theta team in the history of Geek High has worked harder than we have to prepare for this day. So whether we win or lose, we can be proud of ourselves." I hesitated to let these words sink in before continuing. "But I gave up the chance to win a really prestigious writing award to be here, and I really, really want to win. So don't let me down out there."

The rest of the team laughed, which broke the tension. And then the moderator switched on his microphone and said, "Will the teams competing in the second quarterfinal round match please take their seats."

"This is it," I said under my breath. "Good luck, everyone."

•

We won the quarterfinals easily. Even Sanjiv got one question right, which seemed to give him a much-needed confidence boost. He was in high spirits at lunch, and seemed primed and ready to go for our semifinal match against Poinciana High, which was scheduled to take place after lunch.

Unfortunately, just as we were sitting down for the semifinals, Sanjiv's dad showed up, waving around his camcorder and cheering loudly whenever it was Sanjiv's turn. The end result was that although we were able to barely scrape by with a win in our semifinal competition, Sanjiv missed all three of his questions.

The good news: We were in the finals. The bad news: We were competing against St. Pius, who had cruised easily through its two earlier rounds to get there.

While Sanjiv bolted to the bathroom—presumably to throw up—I quickly gathered the rest of our teammates in a huddle.

"We have to get rid of Sanjiv's dad," I said.

Kyle nodded knowingly. "Like a poisonous dart in the neck? Or do you want to try and slip something in his drink?"

"No!" I said. I wasn't entirely sure Kyle was joking. "I meant we have to get rid of him in a legal and nonviolent way."

"We could tell him that he got an urgent phone message saying he had to go home right away," Leila suggested.

"Except why would we get a phone call like that? Why wouldn't whoever was supposedly calling him just reach him on his cell phone?" I asked.

Leila looked disgruntled. "It was just an idea," she said testily.

"Why don't we just tell him the truth," Nicholas said.

We all stared at him. "The truth?" Leila asked.

But I nodded slowly. "He's right. We just should tell Mr. Gupta the truth. Come on, I'm not doing this alone."

I marched off the stage, the others trailing behind me. We made our way over to the front row, where Mr. Gupta had managed to wrangle a seat despite his late arrival. He was busily making adjustments to his tripod, and so he didn't notice the four of us standing in front of him.

"Mr. Gupta, may we talk to you for a minute?" I asked.

He glanced up, blinking and Adam's apple bobbing, looking in that moment exactly like his son.

"Hello, team," he said. He looked around. "Where is Sanjiv?"

"He's puking his guts out at the moment," Kyle said baldly.

Mr. Gupta looked startled, so I hastened to reassure him.

"He's going to be fine," I said. "But you really have to go. When you're in the audience, it makes Sanjiv too nervous to perform well."

"This is nonsense," Mr. Gupta said. His accent was heavy, and it gave his words a pecular importance.

"It's true," Leila chimed in. "He always does better when you're not watching him."

"Is this true?" Mr. Gupta asked. He looked at us, and we all nodded.

"It's pretty obvious," Nicholas said. "When you're in the audience, he's never able to answer any of the questions."

"And this is going to be a tough competition for us," I said, gesturing back at the stage, where the St. Pius team was congregating. "We need Sanjiv at his best if we're going to win."

"Well . . . all right, then," Mr. Gupta said, looking crestfallen. "I just wanted to watch Sanjiv win."

"I have an idea," I said. "Here, give me your camcorder. I'll give it to my dad, and he can tape the competition for you. That way, you'll still be able to see the whole competition. . . . Just not live."

"Well . . . all right," Mr. Gupta said hesitantly. He didn't seem especially eager to hand over his camcorder. I had to give it a little tug to free it from his grasp.

"Thank you, Mr. Gupta," I said, turning before he could change his mind. I hurried off to give the camcorder to my dad, who was sitting uneasily next to Sadie.

"Shouldn't you be up on stage?" Sadie asked, frowning.

"Yeah, I should," I said. Then I launched into the explanation about Sanjiv's nervousness, and how Mr. Gupta had agreed to leave, and finished up by showing my dad how to work the camcorder.

"So I just hold it up like this, and push this button here?" Dad asked. "That's all there is to it?"

"That's it," I said. I glanced up at the stage, where the rest of the Geek High team, including Sanjiv, had regrouped. They were all taking their seats. "Oops, I'd better get up there."

"Good luck!" Sadie and my dad chorused together.

I started to hurry back through the crowd when I heard someone calling my name.

"Miranda!"

I turned, my eyes scanning the crowd. It took several long beats before I saw who was calling me: It was *Charlie*. She stepped forward, looking nervous but smiling. Her hair was purple today, the color of a grape lollipop, and she was wearing a pink T-shirt with FRANKIE SAYS RELAX on the front in big black letters.

"Charlie? What are you doing here?" I asked.

"I came to watch you win," Charlie said.

"Oh. Thanks," I said.

"And also to tell you . . . well, I'm sorry," Charlie said. "For how I've been acting lately. And for your birthday. For everything."

"I'm sorry, too," I said quickly. "I should have been more supportive."

"No! You were right, I was acting like an idiot!"

I shook my head. "You weren't being an idiot. You're in love. I should have understood."

Charlie winced, and her eyes darkened. "I'm not in love," she said flatly. "Mitch and I broke up."

I gasped. "You did? Why? When?"

"A week ago . . . and, I don't want to get into the details right now," Charlie said. She suddenly looked shy and hopeful. "But I'd really like to talk to you about it. You know, later, when you have time."

"I'd like that, too," I said. Then I had an idea. "What are you doing later on?"

Charlie shook her head. "Nothing. Why?"

"Do you want to go to a lacrosse game with me?"

"A lacrosse game? Since when do you watch lacrosse?" Charlie asked. "It hasn't been that long since we've talked, has it?"

I laughed. "No. It'll be my first game."

The moderator's voice blared out from the speakers set up around the perimeter of the room: "The final round of the Mu Alpha Theta state championship will begin in two minutes. All competitors should now be on stage and in their seats."

"Go," Charlie said. She reached forward and squeezed my hand. "Good luck."

"Thanks," I said. And then, on impulse, I gave her a quick hug. "Thanks for being here. It really means a lot to me."

◆

We sat in the same seat positions we had all day: Leila was first, then Kyle, Sanjiv, Nicholas, and, finally, me. I leaned forward, craning my neck to look at the St. Pius table. Austin Strong also sat in the fifth seat, opposite me. He met my gaze for a moment, and for a change, he didn't smirk. He just nodded gravely, almost nervously, and I nodded back. I noticed Qin Gang had moved to sit in the third seat, opposite Sanjiv.

The moderator, a tall man with a ruddy face and short, snowy white hair, began to speak, his voice magnified to fill the room. "Good afternoon, ladies and gentlemen. Welcome to the finals of the Mu Alpha Theta state championship. The two teams you see before you—St. Pius to my left, and Notting Hill Independent

School to my right—have faced tough competition to make it here. In fact, St. Pius has an unblemished record, having won every match they've competed in this season." The audience clapped politely. A few of the rowdier St. Pius parents threw in some whistles and hoots. The moderator waited for a moment until the crowd settled down before continuing. "Round one will now commence."

As the moderator posed the first question, which Leila answered correctly, earning our team the first five points, I suddenly realized how nervous I was. My palms were sweaty, my mouth was dry, and there was an uncomfortable fluttering sensation in my stomach. It wasn't until that moment that I realized how much I wanted our team to win. And not just to show up Austin Strong and his smug teammates, or to see Sanjiv overcome his nerves. I wanted to win just for the sake of winning. I wanted to bring home the big trophy on display at the back of the room for Geek High's trophy case.

Unfortunately, we weren't off to a strong start. Although Leila and I both answered our first-round questions correctly, Nicholas, Kyle, and Sanjiv all lost theirs, putting the score at ten for Geek High, fifteen for St. Pius. We didn't fare much better in the second round. This time, only Nicholas and I won our questions, which brought the score to thirty to forty-five, with St. Pius in the lead.

"We're only fifteen points behind," I told the others during the break before the final round. "That's nothing. We can still win. We've done it before."

"She's right," Sanjiv said unexpectedly. We all looked at him. Normally at this point in the competition, he looked miserable—shoulders slumped, chin down, an air of misery clinging to him. But now he looked determined. "Fifteen points is one round-three question. We can still win."

"*If* we can win three questions," Kyle said dubiously. "I haven't gotten the chance to answer one yet. That girl I'm up against is a quick draw on her buzzer. She keeps managing to hit it just as the moderator finishes the question."

"Look, Kyle, rather than complaining, why don't you just try harder?" Sanjiv snapped. Which was so unlike him, we all stared at him. "What?" Sanjiv said, rather aggressively.

"You just seem a little . . ." Leila grappled for the right word. "Intense," she finished.

"I'm just sick of it. I'm sick of being a loser," Sanjiv said.

"You're not a loser," I said.

"Yes, I am. And I'm not going to put up with it anymore. It stops right here, right now. From this moment on, I'm going to play like a champion," Sanjiv said. He looked around at us, his expression fierce. "We're all going to play like champions. We know we can win this thing. So let's go do it."

With that, Sanjiv turned smartly and marched back to the table to take his seat.

"Wow. He's on fire," Kyle said.

I just grinned. It was Sanjiv's first pep talk of the season, and it had been a doozy.

As our team sat back down, everyone did seem energized. The Geek High team members were all sitting on the edges of their seats, looking focused. When the moderator started the third round, I was suddenly hopeful. We *could* do this. We *could* win.

The first question went to St. Pius. It wasn't Leila's fault—the girl she was up against hit the buzzer too quickly out of nerves, and then made a lucky correct guess when called upon. Kyle was up next, and this time, he was primed and ready to go. He managed to hit his buzzer a microsecond before his St. Pius competitor.

"Question to Notting Hill," the moderator said.

Kyle was silent for what seemed like a very long time, but really could only have been a few seconds.

*Oh, no,* I thought, chewing my lip nervously. *He doesn't know the answer.*

"Geek High, you must answer, or the question goes to St. Pius."

There was an excited murmur in the audience. If St. Pius won this question, they'd have forty-five points. We'd have to win all the remaining questions just to tie.

*Come on*, I silently urged Kyle. *Come on. Get it right. Please just get it right.*

"Twenty-two," Kyle said unexpectedly.

The moderator paused for a long moment. "That is correct," he said.

A relieved cheer went up from our spectators in the audience; we were now only fifteen points behind again . . . which meant we still had a fighting chance of winning this thing.

It was now Sanjiv's turn. I said a silent prayer up to the gods of math that it wouldn't be a question about square roots, Sanjiv's biggest weakness.

"This question is for players number three. What is the square root of 1,369?" the moderator asked.

My stomach felt like it was dropping out of my body. *Even if he gets this wrong, we can still tie and win in the tiebreaker*, I told myself. *Nicholas and I would both have to get our questions right, but it would at least be possible.*

I leaned over to look at Qin Gang, who was quickly computing the square root on a piece of scrap paper. He straightened suddenly and slapped the buzzer. My heart sank.

"The question goes to Notting Hill," the moderator said.

Surprised, I glanced back at our table. I had been so busy watching Qin Gang's progress, I hadn't noticed Sanjiv putting down his pencil and hitting his buzzer before Qin Gang had hit his. Now I held my breath. Sanjiv inhaled deeply and leaned forward into his microphone.

"Thirty-seven," he said.

"Correct!" the moderator said.

The audience cheered again, and Sanjiv beamed. I let out my breath, shaking my head. We were tied. It was now up to Nicholas and me. If we got both of our questions right, we'd win. If we won one and lost one, we'd tie. If we lost both . . . then St. Pius would take the state championship.

I was suddenly so nervous, I couldn't focus on what the moderator was saying, so I had no idea when Nicholas suddenly hit his buzzer and said, "The answer is x equals seventeen," whether or not he'd gotten it right.

"That is correct. The score is now seventy-five to sixty, with Notting Hill in the lead," the moderator said.

This was it. It all came down to me. I glanced over at Austin Strong. He was sitting up straight in his seat, leaning forward a little, hand poised over his buzzer. I quickly did the same thing.

"And here's the final question of regular tournament play," the moderator said. "Water flows into a tank at a rate of one gallon per second. Water leaves the tank at a rate of one gallon per second for each one hundred gallons in the tank. The tank is initially empty. How long will it take for the tank to fill with fifty gallons of water?"

It was a partial differential equation. I picked up my pencil and quickly jotted down the calculation.

*Sixty-nine-point-three seconds*, I thought excitedly, and went to hit the buzzer. But instead of calling on me, the moderator said, "St. Pius, to tie."

I gasped. Austin Strong had beaten me to the buzzer! We'd come so close to a victory—so very close—and now, if Austin answered this question correctly, we'd be stuck in a sudden-death tie-breaker. And who knew what would happen then?

"St. Pius," the moderator said again.

Austin opened his mouth and then closed it. . . . And with a swell of hope, I suddenly realized . . . *he didn't know the answer!* He'd only hit the buzzer in a last-ditch effort to try and beat me!

"I need your answer, St. Pius," the moderator said again.

"Seventy-two seconds," Austin said.

"That is incorrect. Notting Hill, you have one minute to give the correct answer."

But I didn't need a minute. I was ready. A lifetime of math prowess—a skill I'd never fully appreciated until now—had prepared me for this moment.

I leaned forward and spoke directly into the microphone. "The answer is sixty-nine-point-three seconds," I said, my heart pounding wildly.

The auditorium was eerily quiet. No one coughed or shuffled their feet. Everyone was still and silent, waiting to hear what the outcome would be.

"Ladies and gentlemen, we have a new Mu Alpha Theta state champion: The Notting Hill Independent School of Orange Cove!" the moderator announced.

"Yes!" Leila cheered, thrusting one triumphant fist up in the air.

"We did it!" Kyle yelled.

Suddenly, we were all jumping up out of our seats and crushing together into a big group hug.

"I can't believe we won and my dad wasn't here to see it," Sanjiv said from the middle of the huddle.

"He will," I said, laughing. "Unless my dad dropped the camcorder in the excitement!"

# Chapter 23

Dad took Charlie, Sadie, and me out for a victory dinner of cheeseburgers and chocolate shakes at the Orange Cove Grill. As an added bonus, Dad and Sadie managed to get through the whole meal without bickering. After dinner, I asked Sadie if she'd mind if I went out on her first night home.

"No, you go ahead, darling. I'm still on London time. I'm going to fall into bed as soon as I get home," Sadie assured me.

Dad dropped Sadie off first—"My bougainvillea bush is so overgrown," she cried out when he pulled into her driveway—and then took Charlie and me to Orange Cove High.

"Call me when you're ready to be picked up," Dad said.

"Okay. Thanks, Dad," I said, as I climbed out of his SUV.

"Congratulations again!" he said. I closed the door and waved good-bye to him.

"You still haven't told me exactly why we're going to an Orange Cove High lacrosse game," Charlie said, as we followed the crowd toward the outdoor fields at the back of the school. I didn't see anyone I knew among the Orange Cove High students and their parents, all wearing orange shirts or carrying orange pom-poms. Even so, I suddenly felt caught up in the spirit of the event.

*This is what it must be like going to a normal high school,* I thought. *Attending team sporting events and feeling school pride.*

Then again, after a day like today, I wasn't exactly a stranger to school pride.

"It's good to take an interest in new things, don't you think?" I said.

Charlie snorted. "Okay, so don't tell me," she said.

The thing was, I wasn't sure what to tell her. We'd just made up from our fight over her neglecting our friendship so she could spend all of her time with her boyfriend, and now I was dragging her to Dex's lacrosse game.

We sat down on the wooden bleachers, squeezing in between a pair of camcorder-wielding dads and a group of giggling freshman girls, all of whom were wearing matching orange headbands. There was a good-sized crowd; clearly lacrosse was a popular spectator sport at the high school. It was just dusk, still light enough to see, but they'd already turned on the huge overhead lights that towered over the field, and the massive scoreboard at one end was lit up. The crowd suddenly let out a wild cheer as the two lacrosse teams came running out on the field and began their warm-ups on opposite ends of the field, flipping their sticks to pass the tiny balls back and forth in a series of complicated maneuvers. Even though he was wearing a helmet, I spotted Dex immediately and my heart gave an excited lurch.

I wasn't the only one who noticed.

"Look, isn't that Dex McConnell?" one of the freshman girls squealed.

"He's *so* yummy," one of her friends groaned. "I'd give anything to go out with him."

Charlie overheard their conversation, too. "Oh ho," she said, a sly smile spreading on her face as she turned to look at me. I blushed. "I think I just figured out your sudden interest in the sport."

"He invited me to watch one of his games," I explained. "Do you mind?"

Charlie shook her head. "Of course not," she said. "Going to a high school athletic event is an interesting anthropological experience. Not one I think I'd care to repeat all that often, but still educational. Maybe it'll even inspire a painting."

"You're painting again?" I asked.

"Mm-hmm," Charlie said. "I'm trying to get enough works together to do that gallery show down in Miami." She made a face. "I've been sort of slacking off lately."

"You'll catch up," I said supportively.

"Well, I'll have plenty of time to now," Charlie said. She let out a short, humorless bark of laughter. "Now that Mitch and I have broken up."

"About that . . . are you okay?" I turned to look at her. Charlie's face was pale, but her expression was serene.

She gave a tiny shrug. "Yeah, I'm okay. It happened a week ago. I've had some time to get used to it."

"What happened?" I asked.

Charlie drew in a deep breath and let it out in a long sigh. "Actually, it started back on your birthday. I knew that you were upset with me, and for good reason—it was like I could actually look down from above and see how I was so wrapped up in Mitch that I was ignoring you. I didn't like myself for that. But I also couldn't seem to stop. It was almost like an . . . well, this sounds stupid, but it was like an irresistible compulsion," she said.

I nodded but didn't say anything.

"So there was that, this feeling that I was out of control and just getting swept along. Then Mitch started pushing me, to, well . . ." Her voice trailed off, and she actually blushed, which I don't think I'd ever seen Charlie do before.

"To what?" I asked softly.

She looked at me, her eyes dark and fathomless. "You know . . ." she said in a lowered voice. Then she glanced around to see if anyone had heard what she'd said. But the game had just started, and the crowd was cheering and loudly stamping their feet on the bleachers. No one was paying any attention to us.

"So . . ." I hesitated, not sure I wanted to ask, but feeling like I had to for the sake of our friendship. "Did you?"

Charlie shook her head. "No." She shrugged again. "I wasn't ready. And he wouldn't let it drop, so last week I told him that if he wouldn't back off, then I didn't want to see him anymore. And that was pretty much that. Well. Except for the part where he's been calling me ten times a day asking me to get back together with him, and e-mailing me play lists of sappy music." She rolled her eyes, but I could tell that this was an act. She was clearly still really torn up about it.

"Are you going to get back together with him?" I asked.

"I don't know," Charlie said simply. "I guess I miss him. But I don't miss the intensity of it all. I want to do the right thing. . . . I just don't know what that is."

"You'll figure it out," I said, nudging her with my shoulder. "We'll figure it out together."

Charlie smiled. "Thanks, Miranda. That means a lot to me."

"Now . . . what about Finn?"

"What about him?" Charlie asked innocently. I looked at her, and she sighed. "Yeah, I know. It's time he and I made up, too. I'll go see him tomorrow, okay?"

"Good," I said, feeling happier than I had in a long time.

Charlie suddenly nodded her chin toward the game. "Look! I think Dex just made a goal! Or a point, or whatever."

"Really?" I craned my head, trying to see. "Oh, no, I missed it!" I clapped along with the crowds. "This is really kind of exciting, huh?"

Charlie laughed and clapped too. "Yeah, I guess it sort of is," she said.

Orange Cove High won the game by a score of eleven to ten. Dex scored the winning shot, a thrilling maneuver where he jumped up from behind the goal and flipped the ball in with a kind of hook shot, much to the delight of the crowd, who cheered him like a newly coronated king. Somehow, Charlie and I had really gotten into the game, and so at this final goal, we joined the rest of the crowd by leaping to our feet, hugging each other, and then applauding wildly.

"Why am I so happy?" Charlie yelled into my ear. "I don't even like this stupid game. I don't like any sports games."

"I don't know," I yelled back. "But Dex was pretty amazing, wasn't he?"

Fans were flooding onto the field, still cheering and slapping the players on the back in congratulations.

"Are you going to go talk to Dex?" Charlie asked.

I suddenly felt shy. "I don't know," I said, watching him down on the field being hugged by a tall dark-haired man and a pretty woman with curly red hair. "I think he's with his parents."

"So? You have to talk to him. That's why we're here, isn't it?" Charlie asked, nudging me.

"Don't push," I said.

"Will if I want to," Charlie said, and she nudged me again. "Come on, Miranda, he invited you to come. He'll be happy to see you."

"What if he isn't? I don't think he invited me because he liked me," I said. "I think he was just being polite."

"You are so naive," Charlie said with an exasperated sigh.

"What's that supposed to mean?"

"Guys do not ask girls that they don't like to come watch them in sporting events."

"They might if they're friends," I said.

"But you and Dex are not friends," Charlie said.

"We're *friendly*. We ran into one another on the beach. That's when he asked me to come to his game."

Charlie snorted in disbelief.

"What?" I asked.

"*Miranda*. You did not accidentally bump into him on the beach. He was *waiting* there for you. He knew that's when you always walk Willow."

"You really think so?"

"Yes. I really think so. What would you be risking?"

"Total humiliation. Public rejection."

"You're being ridiculous. Stop procrastinating, and go talk to him," Charlie said.

I took in a deep breath and squared my shoulders. "Okay. Here goes nothing," I said.

My heart was fluttering and my stomach was squirming with nerves as I left Charlie behind at the bleachers and made my way down toward the field. The crowd had thinned out by now, so I didn't have to push my way through to get to Dex. In fact, it took a disturbingly short amount of time to reach the edge of the field where Dex was standing, still chatting with his parents. I walked up behind him, hesitating for a moment. They looked like a nice family. His parents had kind faces, and seemed really proud of Dex. His mom kept reaching out to touch his arm or brush a lock of hair off his face. His dad saw me standing there, waiting, and he smiled at me. Dex glanced back to see who his dad was looking at. Our eyes met, and I felt my heart give a violent lurch.

"Miranda, hey," Dex said, his pale blue eyes holding my gaze. His face was flushed and he was still sweating. "You came."

"You were *amazing*," I said honestly.

"Thanks," he said. "Wait! How did your math competition go today?"

"You knew about that?" I asked.

He nodded. "Hannah told me. I wanted to come watch, but coach scheduled a practice this afternoon."

"It went really well. We won," I said.

His eyes brightened, and his smile grew even wider. "Wow, that's great. Congratulations."

"Thanks," I said, trying not to blush and failing miserably. I glanced at his parents. They were both tall and athletic-looking. His dad had a cleft chin and thick dark hair, and his mother had bright green eyes and a wide smile. I could instantly see that Dex had gotten his pale blue eyes from his father, but had inherited his mother's pale skin and red hair.

"Mom, Dad, this is Miranda," Dex said.

"Hello, Miranda. It's nice to meet you," Mrs. McConnell said.

"Hello," Mr. McConnell said.

"Hi," I said, giving a little wave.

"Do you have a ride, or do you want us to wait?" Mr. McConnell asked Dex.

"I have a ride. I'll catch up with you back at home," Dex said.

His parents said good-bye and left. Dex and I just stood there for a moment, not saying anything.

"Hey, do you want to . . ." Dex finally began, at the same moment that I'd said, "So, my friend, Charlie, is waiting . . ."

Then we both stopped suddenly, and waited for the other to speak.

"Go ahead," Dex said.

"No, you," I said, really, really hoping that he would, because I'd gotten the definite feeling that he was about to ask me out.

"Ladies first," Dex insisted.

"I was just saying that my friend Charlie is waiting for me up by the bleachers," I said, pointing back to where Charlie was sitting, her purple hair vivid under the lights. She waved at us, and Dex waved back at her.

"I have to get going anyway," Dex said. "The coach likes to do a postgame review in the locker room. Plus, I really need a shower."

He wasn't asking me out after all. I looked down and kicked at a divot in the grass. I hoped my disappointment wasn't too obvious.

"Okay. Well . . . congratulations again," I said.

"Wait! What are you doing tomorrow?" Dex asked.

I looked up. "Tomorrow? Nothing!" I said quickly.

"Do you want to get together? We could maybe go for a walk, or catch a movie, or whatever you want," he said.

"Yes. I'd like that," I said. Which was maybe the understatement of the year. A bubble of happiness was swelling inside my chest, and I wouldn't have been at all surprised if I floated up off the ground.

"Great! I'll come pick you up at the beach house at five," he said.

"Okay," I said. "Oh, wait! No!"

Dex looked startled.

"I mean, no, not at the beach house. I'll be at my house. My real house. With my mom. She's home for a visit. I'm staying with her while she's here."

"Okay. I'll pick you up at your mom's house then," Dex said, smiling his crooked grin at me. "Bye, Miranda."

"Bye," I said happily. We exchanged one last meaningful look, and then he turned and followed his teammates back toward the school. Suddenly, he stopped and wheeled around.

"Wait," he said, calling back to me. "Where does your mom live?"

I laughed and caught up with him. "Don't worry. I have an excellent sense of direction," I said.

# Chapter 24

To: mirandajbloom@gmail.com
From: hewent@britmail.net
Subject: cheers
Hi Miranda,

   Thanks for your e-mail, and for letting me know about Dex. We can definitely continue being pen pals. And who knows? Maybe we'll meet up again if you come to London to visit your mum.

Best wishes,
Henry

"I can't believe you're leaving already. It seems like you just got here," I complained.

I was sitting cross-legged on Sadie's four-poster bed, watching her pack. She was still wearing her dark hair in a short, sleek bob, and she looked like she'd lost a little weight. I was especially glad to see that she seemed to have finally gotten over her Stevie Nicks phase and was no longer wearing long, flowy hippie dresses. Instead she now seemed to favor smart pantsuits and red lipstick. It was a good look on her.

"I know, this week has just flown by," Sadie said. She folded a sweater and laid it in her suitcase. She glanced up at me, her eyes twinkling with mischief. "Of course, you've spent it with your head in the clouds."

"I have not," I protested. Then, thinking again of the time I'd spent with Dex, I grinned. "Okay, maybe a little."

I was starting to understand why Charlie had gone into such a lovestruck stupor when she started dating Mitch. I just felt so good, so unbelievably happy whenever I thought of Dex. Of course, I also remembered how annoying Charlie had been, so I made a point of tempering my giddiness when I was around my friends and family. Maybe I hadn't been doing as good a job of that as I'd thought.

"So, I was thinking," Sadie said. She looked suddenly serious. "Why don't you think about coming and living with me in London next year?"

The one sour note of the week had been learning that Sadie was planning to extend her stay in London. Her original plan had been to stay for one year; now she wasn't sure when she would be returning home.

"What about school?" I asked.

"You can go to school there," Sadie said. "I think it would be a fabulous experience for you."

She was right. Living in London would be amazing. But how could I leave now that Dex and I were finally together? Then again, I didn't want to be the sort of girl who would turn down a once-in-a-lifetime experience for a guy. No matter how much I liked him.

"You wouldn't have to continue living with your father and . . . that woman," Sadie said, her nostrils flaring at the thought of Peyton.

I had to admit, that made her offer even more tempting. The tension between Dad and Peyton had been so thick lately, even Willow had sensed it. She'd been slinking around with her tail between her legs. It had taken a full week back home—my mom's house, that is—for her to unwind.

"It's a big decision," I finally said. "May I think about it?"

"Absolutely," Sadie said, closing her suitcase, and zipping it shut. "Take all the time you need, darling."

•

"When I find out who's behind this, I'm going to make them pay!" Felicity snarled. She looked around our Modern Lit classroom and seemed to crackle with fury.

Class hadn't started, and Mrs. Gordon hadn't yet arrived, but the rest of the class was there and seated at their desks. I was sitting between Finn and Charlie, although, for once, I didn't have to take on the role of peacekeeper. Finn and Charlie had managed to put their differences aside, although certain topics—Mitch, Grounded, and the *Sims* among them—were off-limits by tacit agreement.

"What's up, Felicity?" Charlie asked. "Did your boyfriend finally figure out that you can only be killed by being stabbed in the heart with a wooden stake?"

"Ha, ha," Felicity sneered. "You think you're so funny, you purple-haired freak."

"Actually, yes," Charlie said serenely. "Yes, I do."

Finn and I snickered. Felicity looked at me, her moss green eyes narrowed malevolently.

"Don't think I don't know what's going on, Miranda," she said.

"That's good," I said. "Because I have no idea what you're talking about."

"Right. Like you didn't write it!"

"Write what?" I asked, genuinely perplexed.

"That geekhigh.com blog," Felicity spat. "The one that you convinced the headmaster you have nothing to do with."

Actually, I didn't write the blog; it was Finn's. And last time I'd checked, the blog had been on hiatus. I opened my laptop, clicked on a browser and typed in geekhigh.com. Charlie leaned forward to read over my shoulder.

*RIBBIT, RIBBIT*
*Which Geek High singing sensation was knocked out of the*
American Idol *competition in the first round? GEEKHIGH.*
*COM has learned that this inaptly named diva flubbed a Mariah*
*Carey cover so badly, one of the judges said she sounded like a*
*gargling frog. Developing . . .*

"Did you really audition for *American Idol*, Felicity?" I asked, looking up at her over the top of my computer.

"Shut it," Felicity snarled. "And for your information, I was getting over laryngitis that day."

"I wonder if they'll show her audition on the air," Charlie said. "Please, let them do it." She looked up at the ceiling in mock prayer. "God, if you're a fair and just God, please let them air Felicity's gargling-frog audition. If you do that, I'll never ask for anything ever again. Thank you for your attention to this matter. Amen."

"Amen," I echoed.

While part of me knew that it was mean to laugh at Felicity's misfortune . . . it was really, really hard not to take some pleasure in it.

What goes around comes around, as Sadie always says. And it looked like Felicity's nastiness had finally come around and nailed her.

•

"How's life back at your dad's house?" Dex asked the next day. We were walking down the beach, hand in hand, Willow trailing behind us. The tide was coming in, and the water was dark and rumbling like thunder as it washed up on the shore.

"It's a little weird," I said. "I think my dad and stepmom are still fighting, but they don't fight the way my parents used to before they split up. Dad and Peyton don't yell or throw things. It's more like the whole house has gone icy cold. No one's talking much."

"That sucks," Dex said. He squeezed my hand. "It's too bad your mom couldn't stay for the summer, so you could get a break from living with them."

"Yeah, it is," I said.

I hadn't yet told Dex about Sadie's offer for me to live with her in London. I knew he'd encourage me to go, that he wouldn't want me to miss out on the experience because of him. But I still hadn't decided what I wanted to do.

Just that morning, I'd gotten an e-mail from the editor of the *Ampersand*, our school's literary journal, inviting me to join the staff next year. It was a huge honor to be asked, since there was always a lot of competition for the few open spots each year. I'd planned to apply for one of the open positions in the fall, but the incoming editor-in-chief, Ramona Jones, had told me in her e-mail that I'd been selected early because of having made the finals of the Winston Creative Writing Contest. Ramona said that if I had that sort of talent, the *Ampersand* would love to have me on staff. So even though I hadn't been able to make it to the finals of the writing contest, and would never know if I might have won had I gone, something good—something amazing, in fact—had still come of it.

And now I was torn. On the one hand, there was London, a city I'd already fallen in love with and couldn't wait to visit again, and Sadie, and not having to live with Peyton anymore. On the other hand, there was Dex, my friends, the *Ampersand*, and Geek High. I had no idea what I should do. But the one thing I knew for sure was that I had to make the decision myself.

So out loud, I said, "It's going to be a long, hot summer. I don't think I can handle spending all my time at the beach house, not if Dad and Peyton are still fighting. Maybe I should get a job or an internship or something."

Dex stopped and gently tugged on my hand, so that I turned to face him. Willow grunted, but was quickly distracted by sniffing a bunch of seaweed that had washed ashore.

"I think it's going to be a great summer," Dex said softly.

The sand was hot under my bare feet, but staring into Dex's pale eyes, I barely noticed it. Then he bent down to kiss me, his warm lips pressing softly against mine. After a few delicious minutes, Dex leaned back and looked down at me, his eyes squinting a bit from the bright sunlight.

"You do?" I asked. My voice sounded a little shaky. It was the effect Dex's kisses always had on me. Everything went shaky—my voice, my knees, my toes.

Dex lifted a hand and brushed a stray lock of my hair back, tucking it behind my ear. I shivered at his touch. He misread my goose bumps, thinking that the breeze blowing off the ocean was chilling me, and he rubbed my arms with his hands, as though to warm me.

"Yeah," Dex said. "I do. I think it's going to be the best summer ever."

And then he leaned forward and kissed me again.

## About the Author

Photo by Marie Langmore

**Piper Banks** lives in South Florida with her husband, son and smelly pug dog. You can visit her Web site at www.piperbanks. com.